BONEC

Three spine-tingling, hair-raising, goose-bumping stories to chill your bones and scare you silly!

BONECHILLERS

3

TO SCARE YOU SILLY

More BONECHILLERS to scare you silly!

BONECHILLERS

BACK TO SCHOOL

LITTLE PET SHOP OF HORRORS

THE SHOPPING SPREE

B. R. HAYNES

Collins

An imprint of HarperCollinsPublishers

First published as single editions in the USA by
HarperCollins*Publishers* in 1994
First published as single editions in Great Britain in Lions in 1994
This edition first published by Collins in 1996

Collins is an imprint of HarperCollins*Publishers* Ltd,
77-85 Fulham Palace Road, Hammersmith, London W6 8JB

1 3 5 7 9 10 8 6 4 2

ISBN 0 00 675276 4

The author asserts the moral right to be identified
as the author of this work

Printed and bound in Great Britain by
Caledonian International Book Manufacturing Ltd, Glasgow, G64

THE SHOPPING SPREE

For Frankenstein, The Wolf Man, The Mummy, Dracula, and all the rest of my spooky friends

Chapter

"**W**onderland Mall Opens Today!**" I shouted happily.

I read the giant billboard aloud as Mom drove past it and followed the long stream of traffic into the main parking area for the new shopping mall.

"This is where Mournful Swamp used to be when I was your age." Mom looked over at me and chuckled. "It was a da-a-ark and scary place, filled with quicksand and deep ravines and monsters." she said, trying to sound spooky. "I'll never forget when three teenagers disappeared in the swamp. It was back when I was in high school. Everybody assumed they walked into quicksand and were sucked under, but nobody really knows what happened to them. Remember that story?"

1

I nodded. Who cared about that stuff? It was ancient history. Wonderland Mall was the most exciting thing that had happened to the town of Meadowdale in a long, long time. It wouldn't have mattered to me if it had been built on top of a graveyard.

"For years people were too frightened to come near this place," Mom went on. "Everybody said it was haunted. Can you believe they'd actually build a mall out here? Oooh, it gives me the creeps."

I grinned at her and shrugged. "That's progress, I guess. Wow! Would you check that out!"

The new mall had just come into sight. It was humongous, with multicolored banners fluttering in the breeze. Moving spotlights danced over it, creating a spectacular light show. The main part of the mall was three stories high. I had read in the paper that it had six movie screens, a video arcade, a food court, an ice-skating rink, and dozens of stores. I could hardly wait to see for myself.

I took a deep breath and stared up at the colossal mall. I was imagining shopping *big time* with my friends, pigging out at the food court, and maybe even catching a movie.

"Mom, can't we go a little faster?" I pleaded. "I'm already late!"

Mom snorted in exasperation and gestured at

2

the slow-moving traffic ahead of us. "Only if this car sprouts wings and flies. You know this is the big opening day. The whole town is here."

I sighed and slumped against the passenger door. I was supposed to meet some friends by the main entrance to the mall at eight A.M. And it was already eight fifteen. We had to be among the first one hundred shoppers in the front door when the mall opened at nine o'clock to get a chance at a lottery for a free trip to Hawaii. I was dying to go to Hawaii.

Traffic was moving at a crawl as long lines of cars snaked up and down the parking-lot rows, searching for empty spaces. Suddenly I had an idea.

"Why don't you just let me out here?" I blurted. "I can make better time on foot. Thanks, Mom. I'll call you when I'm ready to come home."

I jumped out of the barely moving car before Mom could argue. Then I tossed her a quick smile and a wave over my shoulder and zigzagged through the traffic toward the main entrance to Wonderland Mall. I groaned when I saw the size of the crowd that was already forming at the door.

"Over here! Over here!"

I looked toward the shouts and saw Lisa, Shannon, and Eric at the edge of the crowd. They were waving wildly. "Robin Fagin, where have

3

you been?" Lisa demanded, flipping a strand of dark curly hair over one shoulder. Lisa Karl was really cute, and the first thing everyone noticed about her was her beautiful thick hair and her big smile. "Look at all the people who are already ahead of us."

"I got here as fast as I could," I grumbled. "Besides, I don't see Jamie."

"She isn't here yet," said Eric, gazing up the long driveway leading from the highway to the entrance of the mall. Even though Eric Sandifer was part of our group of friends, being around him made me a little jittery sometimes. I had a secret crush on Eric, and I would die if anyone ever found out. He was tall and slim and athletic, and he had an incredible dimple in his chin when he smiled.

"She said she was coming on the bus," said Shannon Markoff, pushing her wire-frame glasses up on her nose. "Since the mall is the last stop on the bus line, and since it's opening day, I bet it was so crowded she couldn't get on. She probably had to wait for a later bus."

I looked through the crowd again. Jamie England's short-cut white-blond hair and huge blue eyes were hard to miss, even in a crowd like this. But I didn't see her anywhere.

"Come on, guys, we can't wait forever," urged Shannon. She pushed her glasses up on her nose again and looked around anxiously. The crowd had grown even bigger while we stood there talking.

"Video Showcase is giving away T-shirts. I'm going to kill Jamie if I don't get one!" said Shannon. "Just look at how many people are ahead of us."

The instant she got the words out, a large lady wearing a purple raincoat rushed past us, heading for the crowded entrance and shoving Shannon aside as she went by.

"Geez!" said Shannon, frowning after the lady. "This place is a zoo. We'll never get inside in time to get in on the drawing for the trip to Hawaii."

"Hey, everybody! Look over there," said Eric. He was pointing to a side entrance where a sign on the door said Employees Only. "Maybe we could go in there and sneak into the main part of the mall ahead of the crowd."

"Get serious," said Lisa. She tossed her curly head impatiently. "We're not employees."

"Besides, it's probably locked," I said dejectedly.

"There's one way to find out," said Shannon. She marched straight to the door and gave it a tug.

It swung open.

We looked at each other, hesitating.

5

"We could get into big trouble if anybody caught us," Lisa warned.

"Get real, Lisa," Shannon said with a grin. "Who's going to catch us?"

Then she stepped inside.

Chapter

2

"**M**aybe we should have waited for Jamie. She'll never find us now," I said as soon as the door clanged shut behind us. We were in a long empty corridor. My voice sounded unusually loud as it echoed off the walls.

"Shhh," cautioned Lisa. She raised a finger to her lips and frowned at me.

I frowned back at her. "We really aren't supposed to be here, you know. We could get in big trouble."

"Come on, guys," Shannon said. "Don't any of you wimp out. Let's see if we can find the main part of the mall." She pushed her glasses up on her nose and stared down the long silent hallway.

"Yeah," said Eric, "there's nothing to worry about. We're all alone down here."

I followed the others past empty offices on either side of the hall. The lights were off in all the offices.

I sighed with relief. "I guess it's too early in the morning for anyone to be at work yet."

Eric nodded and gave me a sort of half smile that made his dimple appear really fast and then disappear again. "So far, so good."

"Right," I said, staring at his chin.

"Will you two be quiet?" Lisa cautioned again. She frowned over her shoulder at Eric and me.

"Don't be so bossy," I grumbled under my breath. Then I stuck my tongue out at the back of her head.

We crept through the corridors, rounding first one corner and then another, looking for the way into the main part of the mall. We turned into a hallway where all the doors were closed, and every few seconds I threw an anxious glance over my shoulder in case someone came up behind us.

Just as we turned another corner, Shannon stopped dead in her tracks. It caused a chain-reaction collision. Lisa barreled into Shannon. Eric barreled into Lisa. And I barreled into Eric.

Shannon's eyes opened wide, and she pointed to a man coming toward us. He was tall and bulky, with a deeply tanned face and a full head of white hair. He was wearing a dark business suit, and he was busily reading some papers as he hurried

8

along. And he looked mean—real mean.

"Quick, find some place to hide before he sees us!" Shannon said in a loud whisper.

I started backpedaling as fast as I could. I searched frantically for an empty room to duck into. But the doors along the corridor were all locked!

The man still hadn't seen us, but any minute he could finish reading his papers and look up. What if he caught us? What if he called the security guards? What if he had us arrested for trespassing?

In desperation I tried one door after another until one finally opened. "In here!" I called.

The room was pitch-black and stuffy, but at first I was too relieved to care. My legs were rubbery, and my hands were shaking. As I leaned against the door to catch my breath, I could hear my pulse pounding in my ears.

"I wonder where we are." Eric's voice came from somewhere in the darkness.

"I don't know, but I don't like it," Lisa squeaked from another direction.

"Hey, everybody," said Shannon. Her usually chirpy voice was deadly serious. "I hate to tell you this, but I think we have company."

My eyes were beginning to adjust to the darkness. I blinked and looked around. I could make out the forms of my friends now as the blackness softened into deep gray. Lisa and Eric were stand-

9

ing to my left, and Shannon was just behind them.
But who was that fourth person in the middle of
the room? And the fifth and sixth and seventh
near the other wall?

I stuffed a fist into my mouth to stifle a cry. I
could see pretty clearly now. The room was the
size of a classroom. And it was filled with people.
Dozens of them.

Silent, motionless people. Some adults. Some
children. Some sitting. Some standing.

And every one of them was staring straight at
me.

Chapter

3

Suddenly Shannon burst out laughing.

"They're only mannequins," she cried. "A whole roomful of dummies."

I giggled nervously and looked at the figures again. Shannon was right. They were just a bunch of plastic dummies. Some of them had arms missing. Or legs. One female mannequin near me didn't have a head!

"I think we stumbled into a storage room," I said in a breathy whisper. "This place is too weird. Let's get out of here."

"Be careful," Lisa said as we moved toward the door that would take us back into the corridor. "That man could still be out there."

"Hey, wait a minute," said Shannon. "There's another door over here. Let's see where it goes. Maybe it's the one we've been looking for. The

11

one to the main floor of the mall."

Shannon was already heading for the second door. Eric followed. And Lisa skittered after them like a frightened mouse.

I hesitated, pinned to the spot where I was standing by the sightless eyes of the mannequins. I couldn't shake the feeling that they were really watching me. Following my every move.

"Come on, slowpoke," called Shannon. She reached for the door and turned the knob.

I started toward my friends, holding my breath as I tiptoed past the ghostly figures. A large cardboard box sat directly in my path. As I walked around it, I stiffened and stopped cold. A jumble of mannequin heads were in the box. A jumble of heads that were all looking up at me.

"Eeek!" I shrieked and jumped back.

"What's the matter?" Eric asked.

I took a deep breath to slow the pounding of my heart. No matter which way each head was facing in the box, its eyes seemed to be turned on me.

"Oh, nothing," I said as casually as I could. "Just heads. Mannequin heads."

If I told my friends what I'd seen, they'd think I was totally freaking out.

I caught up with them just as they disappeared through the door, and clanked behind them down a flight of metal stairs. A soft light burned below.

"I don't think this is where we want to be," said Eric as we clustered at the bottom of the stairs outside still another door. He looked less confident than he had before.

"Cluck, cluck, cluck," taunted Shannon. "You guys are such chickens. We should at least find out where we are."

Before anyone could protest, she opened the door just enough to slip through, and disappeared. I felt a blast of cold air as the door slammed shut behind her.

"I think we should get out of here," Lisa said loudly. "It's really creepy down here. We shouldn't have come down those stairs in the first place."

"I agree," said Eric. "Let's split."

"But we can't leave Shannon," I protested.

We stood there, glancing back and forth at each other.

"I wonder why she hasn't come back," Eric said after a while. "I mean, since we didn't come after her, you'd think . . ." His voice trailed off.

"Do you think she's okay?" Lisa murmured.

"I don't know," I said, "but we've got to find out."

I took a deep breath and opened the door. Peering into a shadowy room, I sucked in my breath and shrank back.

"Oh, no!" I shrieked.

13

"What is it?" Eric and Lisa demanded in unison.
All I could do was step aside and point.

Shannon's body was sprawled facedown on the cold concrete floor.

14

Chapter

4

hannon wasn't moving, and it didn't look as if she was breathing either.

The three of us moved slowly toward her and crouched around her still figure.

"Shannon, can you hear me?" I whispered, terrified. I gently nudged Shannon's shoulder. "Shannon, answer me! Are you okay?"

"Couldn't be better," Shannon cried, rolling over and cracking up. "I wish you guys could see your faces right now. What a bunch of chickens."

Eric groaned in exasperation.

Lisa rolled her eyes toward the ceiling.

"Very funny," I said. Sometimes Shannon could be a real jerk.

Shannon jumped to her feet. "Come on, let's get going," she called out. "It's almost opening time. We're going to miss the drawing for the free trip to Hawaii."

"Wait a minute," I said, looking around.

I had just become aware of the dimly lit room we were in. Crouched in the shadows were monstrous machines, pulsing and humming and groaning so hard that the floor vibrated beneath our feet. Over our heads pipes stuck out of the machines and snaked across the ceiling, where they disappeared into the walls.

"We must be in the basement," said Lisa. "These are probably the air-conditioning units for the whole mall."

I knelt on one knee and examined the floor. My eerie feeling was back. "Remember that article in the newspaper a couple of weeks ago about how a crack opened up down here in the basement floor?" I asked.

"I saw that," said Lisa. "The paper said it was right over the spot where the ravine used to be when this was Mournful Swamp."

"Yeah," said Shannon. "They were afraid the mall wouldn't be able to open on time."

"But they cemented it up, and everything was okay," Eric said. "It's funny when you think about it, though. So many creepy things happened while this mall was being built. Remember the dump truck that poured a load of rocks on one of the workmen and killed him?"

16

"Yeah," I said. That story was especially weird because nobody was at the controls of the truck. It seemed to have been driving itself. The police investigated, and couldn't find anything. So they wound up calling it an accident.

"And a lot of things disappeared mysteriously," said Lisa. "Big pieces of machinery and stuff like that."

"And what about the guy who fell into that vat of wet cement?" Shannon asked.

"I heard they fished around for a long time but couldn't find his body. A lot of people thought the construction sight was jinxed," I said. Then I added hurriedly, "Come on, let's go. I don't like it down here."

I got slowly to my feet. The cemented crack looked like a giant scar. It ran across the floor exactly where Shannon had been lying. I suddenly wondered what would happen if the crack opened up and sucked me under the mall. The thought made me shiver, so I turned quickly and raced after the others.

Just then lights started blinking on one of the giant machines, and the sound it was making changed.

Ay-in. Ay-in. Ay-in.

I stopped, but the others hadn't seemed to notice. I glanced at the machine. The lights had stopped blinking, but the sound was becoming louder and more distinct.

17

AY-IN. AY-IN. AY-IN.

I frowned. Why didn't anyone else hear it?

AY-IN! AY-IN! AY-IN!

I called out to my friends to listen, but they had already gone through the door. Suddenly it changed again. FA-GIN. FA-GIN. FA-GIN.

Fagin? That was my name! My last name! But a machine couldn't say somebody's name, I reasoned, trying to stay calm.

I reached the door in one gigantic step and bolted out of the room.

Chapter

A few minutes later we finally found the main entrance to the mall. The spooky events in the basement seemed so unreal that I didn't mention them to the others. I didn't want them to think I was going psycho or something.

"Wow! Would you look at this!" Shannon cried as we entered the mammoth center court. I watched her spread her arms wide and circle slowly, as I tried to take it all in.

A teenage rock band blasted music from a stage at one end of the center court. At the other end, a jungle of plants and trees surrounded a miniature waterfall. Beside the waterfall shoppers were sitting on benches watching giant goldfish swim lazily in a pond. Everywhere bright helium-filled balloons leaped upward. People bustled in and out of stores. The faint smell of popcorn and hamburgers hung in the air.

"I don't believe it," whispered Lisa. "It's paradise."

"It's *awesome*," I added, spinning around. "I don't know which way to look first."

A giddy sense of carnival magic was everywhere. Smiling people looked down from the railings on the second and third floors. And escalators jammed with laughing shoppers moved slowly up and down. Above it all, sunshine poured through the skylighted roof and settled on everyone like fairy dust.

"I'm starved. I want to find the food court," said Lisa, bouncing impatiently on her toes. "I think it's over there."

"Hey, there's the arcade over there," Eric said, pointing in the opposite direction. "Anybody want to play some video games?"

I made a face. "Food and video games? Are you guys kidding?" I asked. "I came here for one reason, and one reason only: to *shop*."

"Me, too," said Shannon. "Have you ever seen so many stores in your life? It's unbelievable."

"Welcome to Wonderland Mall!"

A pretty blond girl who didn't look much older than my friends and me was walking toward us, smiling. Her golden hair was long and silky, and she had dazzling blue eyes. She was dressed in a miniskirt and a knockout sweater.

"I know you're going to love the new mall," she said in a perky voice, "and to help you find your way around, here's a map of all the shops and attractions."

She handed each of us a map and mentioned several opening-day sales. Then, turning to leave, she added with a cheery smile, "Have a nice day."

"Gosh, did you check her out?" exclaimed Shannon as the girl moved to another group of shoppers nearby.

Eric nodded and stared after her as if he were in a trance.

"Looks to die for," Lisa murmured, shaking her head.

"Tell me about it," I added, sighing. "She's almost too perfect to be real."

Maps in hand, we headed off to check out the opening-day sales in some of the stores.

"Since it's already nine fifteen, it's too late to get into the lottery for the free trip to Hawaii. Why don't we find Video Showcase and see if they still have any T-shirts to give away?" Shannon suggested. She stopped in the middle of the crowd, almost causing a traffic jam. Pushing her glasses up on her nose, she studied her map. "It's right here," she said, stabbing the map with a finger. "Up on the second level."

Wonderland Mall was getting more crowded by

the moment, and we had to stand in line to get on the escalator. It was packed, and we got separated immediately. I ended up riding up to the second floor with my face practically jammed into the back of a tall thin woman with bushy white hair.

"Now, where is this Video Showcase?" I asked Shannon when we had all gotten off the escalator.

"This way," said Shannon. She plunged into the crowd.

I took off after her, but the crowd was so thick that I lost sight both of Shannon and the others immediately.

I wasn't sure where I was going, so I made my way to the balcony railing, stopping in frustration to consult my map. Video Showcase was only a few stores away.

When I reached the video store, the others were already there, waiting outside.

"What happened to you, slowpoke?" asked Shannon, grinning.

"Nothing," I retorted. Then I dashed for the door and entered the store ahead of the others. The instant I got inside, I stopped. My mouth dropped open in surprise.

"Welcome to Video Showcase!"

A blond teenage girl was greeting us at the door. Her golden hair was long and silky. And she had dazzling blue eyes. And she was dressed in a miniskirt and a great-looking sweater.

She was the same girl who had handed us the maps downstairs in the center court a few minutes before. But that was impossible.

How could she be in two places at once?

Chapter

"How did you get up here so quickly?" I asked the blonde.

"Yeah, we just saw you downstairs," said Shannon.

The blonde laughed. "That must have been someone else," she said. "I've been here in Video Showcase ever since the mall opened. This is where I work."

"Oh, come on," scoffed Lisa. "We saw you downstairs. You were handing out maps of the mall."

"It wasn't me," the blond girl said. "Honest."

"Then you've got a twin," said Eric.

"Look, guys." She was starting to sound irritated. "I didn't hand out maps downstairs. I work here in the Video Showcase, and I've been here since nine o'clock. And I don't have a twin. Okay?"

25

Her face clouded for a second, and then her smile returned. She reached into a cardboard box and pulled out a handful of T-shirts. "Here. Have a free shirt."

We each took a shirt, and then we browsed among the videos and CD's for a couple of minutes before leaving the store.

"That was really weird," said Eric when we were outside. "I could have sworn that she was the same girl we saw downstairs."

I had been thinking about her the whole time we were in the video store. "I bet they really are twins," I said. "It's probably some kind of advertising gimmick that the mall people thought up. Maybe they hired lots of twins and they're going to have a contest to see how many sets people can find."

"Yeah, right, sure, Robin," Shannon said, giving me an oddball look. "Maybe they're going to let us have all the free clothes we want, too."

"It was only an idea," I responded defensively.

We walked along for a while, looking in the store windows and stopping now and then to talk to friends from school.

"Where's Jamie?" asked Kristin Bergner when she and Amy Hamilton walked up to us in front of a frozen-yogurt stand. "I thought she was going to come out with you guys today."

"Yeah, we thought she was coming with us, too." said Lisa. "She said she'd meet us at the front entrance at eight o'clock, but she didn't show."

"Are you sure that you two haven't seen her wandering around the mall looking for us?" I asked. "I'd feel awful if she's here and she thinks we deserted her."

"No," said Kristin, shaking her head. "But if we see her, we'll tell her you're looking for her."

"Thanks," I said, feeling better.

We had only gone a little farther when we heard the sound of running behind us.

"Hey, Eric. Wait up."

I turned around and saw a group of boys from our school hurrying along behind us. They stopped by the pet-shop window, and one of them, Aaron Stemple, was motioning for Eric to come over and talk to them.

Eric gave me an apologetic shrug and sauntered over to them.

Apparently Lisa and Shannon hadn't noticed and were heading on down the walkway. I hesitated. Maybe I should go with them and let Eric catch up. Still, I really liked being with him. I decided to stick around for a couple of minutes and see if he was coming with us or if he would decide to hang out with the other boys.

I glanced over at the guys. They must have told

Eric something really funny, because all of them were laughing their heads off.

I pretended to be interested in something in the window of a camera store. I could see Eric and the boys' reflection in the window. They were still talking and laughing like crazy.

My friends had disappeared in the crowd by now, and I was beginning to think that Eric was going to stay with the guys.

I moved slowly away from the camera shop, still not certain what to do. Eric was so cute, and I didn't have that many chances to be around him outside of school. Still, I didn't want to lose Lisa and Shannon in the crowd either.

Suddenly I remembered Jamie again. I felt awful. She was one of my best friends. What if she really was here, and she thought we were avoiding her?

Maybe I should go looking for her, I thought. But what would I say to her if I found her? *"Gosh, Jamie, there you are. We forgot all about you. Are you having fun in the new mall?"*

Of course not. That would sound dumb.

As I stood there, staring blankly in a swim-shop window, I had the strange feeling that someone was watching me. The swim shop was called Mermaid Magic. Was there someone inside who was staring out at me? A clerk or someone?

I peered through the display. The store was

crowded, and everyone inside appeared to be busy. No one was looking at me. I must have imagined it.

I glanced closer at the scene in the window. Several mannequins wearing gorgeous bikinis were standing around on a fake beach while other mannequins in swimsuits sat in the sand.

Suddenly I knew who was watching me. My mouth went dry. I tried to move away from the window, but I couldn't.

Staring out at me from the swim shop's display was a mannequin.

A mannequin that looked exactly like Jamie!

Chapter

It was incredible. The mannequin had the same white-blond hair as Jamie. And even though it was a wig, it was styled in the same short cut that Jamie wore. The eyes were the same, too. Big and blue. But most incredible of all was the face. It was identical to Jamie's face.

I shuddered. That expressionless plastic face seemed to be following my every movement!

Just then I remembered Eric. I glanced quickly over my shoulder. He was still standing there with the guys. I couldn't let him see me freak out over a mannequin. But I wanted to get out of there—fast.

I turned around again, trying to act cool.

"I'm going to go ahead and find Shannon and Lisa," I called to him. "You can catch up. Okay?"

"Sure. See you around," Eric called back.

I ran off down the hall, dodging people and

looking for a familiar face. That mannequin had really shaken me up, and I was suddenly uncomfortable being alone, even in such a big crowd. Where could Lisa and Shannon have gone so quickly? I had been waiting for Eric for only a couple of minutes.

A sea of heads bobbed in front of me. But none of them looked familiar. My friends had disappeared.

Up ahead I saw a fudge shop and heard a loud gong. I had been in a fudge shop before and knew that the gong meant a new batch of fudge was about to be poured out on a marble countertop. It also meant free samples. That had to be where my friends were. Especially Lisa. She would do anything for free food.

"Shannon! Lisa!" I called out as I pushed my way into the throng of people crowding toward the counter and the free fudge. "Are you in here, guys?"

A skinny man with a scraggly ponytail and an earring dangling from one ear came up to me. "You rang?" he asked, grinning. "My name's Shannon. What can you do for me?" He snapped his fingers and gazed off into space as if he heard music.

"Uh, wrong Shannon," I mumbled, and ducked out of the shop. What a weirdo!

I looked in a couple of other stores, but no Lisa

or Shannon. I was beginning to feel annoyed. Why hadn't they noticed that I wasn't with them anymore? How come they hadn't come back to find me?

I rode the escalator back down to the main level, thinking maybe they had gone to the food court. Lisa was always starving, and she had wanted to go there when we first got to the mall this morning.

I fished around in my jeans pockets for my map, but I couldn't find it. I must have lost it, but I knew that the food court was somewhere on the main level.

I hurried along, not really paying attention to where I was going. I couldn't get the picture of the mannequin that looked like Jamie out of my mind. The thought of those plastic eyes staring at me made me shudder. Still, it had to be a big co-incidence, I reassured myself. She had probably stayed home today and had forgotten to call any of us and tell us. Maybe she had a cold or something.

I suddenly realized that I was in a dark hallway. I hadn't noticed turning into it, and I stopped and peered ahead through the shadows. It was a little spooky, and I started to turn around.

Just then a woman hurried past me in clicky high heels. As soon as she disappeared down the dimly lit hall, I heard a door close.

The rest room! I thought. Maybe that's where

my friends were. It made sense. Shannon and Lisa had probably ducked in to brush their hair and primp in front of the mirror. I might even find Jamie there.

I headed down the hall at a jog. When I reached the door, I started to push it open.

At that instant a pair of hands clamped my shoulders. Someone was grabbing me from behind!

Chapter

I opened my mouth and tried to scream, but nothing came out. Just then laughter rang in my ears and filled the dark corridor.

As quickly as they had grabbed me, the hands dropped from my shoulders, and I slowly turned around to face Lisa and Shannon, giggling hysterically.

"You look like you've seen a *ghost!*" said Shannon between giggles.

I was still too shaky to speak, so I glared at her.

"We've been following you ever since you stopped to wait for Eric," bragged Lisa.

"Yeah, we know a secret. You like Eric Sandifer," said Shannon in a singsong voice.

I felt my face turning red. "I do not!" I lied.

"Then why is your face red?" asked Shannon, giggling again.

35

"So what was the big idea of following me?" I asked, trying to change the subject.

"For fun," said Lisa. "You almost spotted us a couple of times."

"We had to duck into stores," said Shannon.

I turned to Shannon and said, "I suppose this was your idea." She was really getting on my nerves.

"Naturally," said Shannon. She grinned and then bowed like an actress getting a standing ovation. "And it was worth it to see the look on your face."

You should find out how it feels sometime, I thought. *I almost had a heart attack.*

I didn't appreciate Shannon's stupid joke. But mostly I was upset because they knew about my crush on Eric. It was embarrassing for them to know I had a crush on someone who thought of me only as a friend.

"Come on, guys," Shannon said. "We're wasting valuable time that we could be using to shop."

"Or eat," Lisa added emphatically. "Isn't anyone hungry yet? I'm starved."

As if on cue, my stomach growled loudly. We all started laughing. That broke the tension, and we were friends again.

Back out in the main part of the mall we sauntered along arm in arm, heading in the general direction of the food court. We made slow progress, though, because we couldn't resist stopping to check out great-looking clothes in shops along the way.

"Everything's too expensive," I grumbled as we came out of a store called Junior Jungle. It carried only junior sizes and was decorated in a jungle theme with fake monkeys hanging from fake palm trees.

"Tell me about it," said Shannon. "I absolutely have to have a new pair of jeans, and I haven't seen one pair yet that I can afford."

"Why don't you look in Zimmer's?" I suggested. We were walking past the department store, which had jeans of every style and color displayed in its window.

"Great idea," said Shannon. She made a quick left turn into the store. "Anybody want to come with me?"

"I think I'll check the shoe department," said Lisa, hurrying into Zimmer's after her. "I need new tennis shoes. Are you coming, Robin?"

I hung back. I could have used some new tennis shoes, too, but I kept thinking about the mannequin that looked so much like Jamie. I wanted to look at it again—alone.

"No, I need to find the rest room," I lied. "I'll be back in a few minutes."

As I rode the escalator up to the second level and Mermaid Magic, I tried to figure out what I would do if I still thought the dummy looked like

Jamie. I couldn't explain it, even to myself, but I could sense something sinister about that mannequin. I didn't want to tell my friends about it yet. They would think I was nuts.

It probably doesn't look like her at all, I reasoned. I must have been so worried about her not showing up that I only imagined it.

But as I approached the store window, I could see that I had been right the first time. The mannequin really did look just like Jamie.

I tried to look away, but something held me. It was the eyes. I had thought their gaze was blank when I had looked at them before. But now they seemed different. Hard. Angry. Glaring.

Where's Jamie? I wanted to shout at the mannequin. *Why are you here at the mall and she isn't?*

I shuddered. This mannequin couldn't possibly have anything to do with my friend.

But where had it come from? And where was Jamie?

Suddenly my heart stopped.

The mannequin standing next to Jamie was *moving.*

Chapter

9

I gasped and whirled away from the window. The mannequin's arm had been turned upward at the elbow. Now it had dropped to the mannequin's side.

It couldn't have possibly happened.

But I had seen it.

Just chill out, I ordered myself, and purposely walked away from Mermaid Magic without looking back.

So what if I thought I saw a mannequin's hand move? A customer probably bumped against it. Plastic dummies don't move by themselves. And so what if the store had a mannequin that looked like Jamie? And its eyes gave me the creeps? It was only a coincidence. That's all. It's silly to get all freaked out over a couple of mannequins.

Shannon and Lisa were waiting for me outside

the department store when I got back. Neither of them carried any packages.

"What's the matter?" I asked. "Couldn't you find anything you liked?"

"Too expensive," Lisa said.

"How about you, Shannon?" I asked. "You must have been able to find a pair of jeans in there."

"None that I really liked," she said. "Come on, guys. Let's get something to eat."

I shrugged and walked along with the others to the food court. With all the shops and cool things to buy I hated to spend money on food. But I was definitely getting hungry. In fact, my stomach was growling so loudly at one point that a man walking in front of me had actually turned around and looked at me.

"Why don't we see a movie?" suggested Lisa, dragging a french fry through a blob of ketchup a few minutes later. "I've been smelling the popcorn all morning."

"Don't you ever think about anything but food?" I teased.

Lisa pretended to look hurt. Then she grinned slyly and said, "I thought it might help me keep my mind off those diamonds in that jewelry-store window over there. I'm just dying to buy some earrings and maybe a tiara or two."

I looked toward the jewelry-store window,

where a mannequin head modeled a brilliant diamond necklace, matching earrings, and a ruby-and-emerald tiara.

"I see exactly what you mean, dahling," I said, speaking with a bogus English accent. "It's a *terrible* temptation."

Giggling, we dumped our lunch trash into a bin and headed for the lobby of Cinema Six to study the posters of the six movies playing. There were a couple of sappy-looking romances, a cop movie, a horror flick, a cartoon, and a comedy. After a lot of discussion we finally settled on the comedy and bought our tickets.

"We have forty-five minutes until the movie starts," said Shannon. "Let's kill some time by looking in a couple more stores."

"You're kidding, right?" I groaned. "After paying for lunch and a movie ticket, I can't even afford to window-shop!"

The department store at this end of the mall was called Stryker's, and I could see right away that it was a lot less expensive than Zimmer's. My friends and I split up, and I made a beeline for the jewelry department.

I looked at earrings for a while. I didn't see anything that I liked all that much, so I went to find my friends. Walking past the young men's department, I glanced toward the dressing-room area. That's not something I usually do. I mean, I wasn't

41

trying to see guys without clothes on or anything. I guess something just attracted my attention.

I looked again and then stopped in my tracks. One of the dressing-room stall doors was partway open, and a mannequin was standing in front of the mirror. Or was it a mannequin? The body looked like an ordinary mannequin, but the head seemed wrong. There was definitely something weird about the head.

I squinted and looked again. Above the stiff, shiny vinyl body was the head of a teenage boy.

His eyes were open wide, and his mouth was moving!

He was alive!

42

Chapter

I closed my eyes and shook my head in disbelief. When I opened them again, a salesclerk with a long black French braid was standing right outside the dressing room. She was glaring at me, and when she saw me looking back, she quickly closed the stall door.

She knows I saw him! I thought in a panic. *And now she's guarding the door. This is ridiculous,* I scolded myself. *There's no such thing as half mannequin and half person. I must be going berserk.*

I pretended to be looking at some merchandise while I tried to get a grip on myself. I must have been standing there five minutes before I realized that I was in the little boys' department.

So what, I thought with a defiant toss of my

head. *I could be shopping for my little brother—
if I had one.*

Finally the salesclerk with the long black French braid went off to help a customer. I glanced at the dressing-room door. It was still closed.

I had to know what was inside. I crept closer. The young men's department was practically deserted. No one would notice if I quickly opened the door and peeked inside.

Besides, if I got caught, I could always say I was looking for my brother.

All the other stall doors were open in the dressing-room area. At least no one would come popping out of a stall and start asking a lot of embarrassing questions.

I closed my hand around the doorknob and slowly turned it. Then I eased the door open with my foot. I jumped with a start as the mannequin came into view, and then I collapsed with relief when I saw that it was only a mannequin.

A plain old dummy with a plastic body and a plastic head. I stared at it for a moment. I had been crazy to think its mouth was moving.

I turned to walk away when something about the mannequin made me stop. I didn't know what it was, but something wasn't quite right. I had to look closer.

The dummy looked like one of the boys Eric had been talking to a little while ago. The long thin nose. The dark unruly hair. Even the Pittsburgh Steelers sweatshirt was familiar.

The mannequin *did* look like one of Eric's friends.

It looked *exactly* like Aaron Stemple!

Chapter

11

backed slowly away from the dressing room, keeping my eyes fastened on the dummy's face. I had to show someone. *Fast.*

Turning around, I broke into a run, zigzagging through the clothing displays. Shannon and Lisa were somewhere in this store. But where? *Jeans, maybe,* I thought. *Or shoes.*

"Robin!"

I screeched to a stop at the sound of my name and whirled around. It was Eric, and he was jogging toward me through the racks of sport shirts with a big grin on his face.

I was too frightened even to notice whether or not there was a dimple in his chin.

"What's happening?" he asked.

"Come on! You've got to see this!" I cried in a high-pitched voice I hardly recognized as mine. "I think I'm going crazy!"

I grabbed him by the arm and pulled him toward the young men's department.

"You're acting totally bizarre, Robin," he said in a puzzled voice. "What's wrong?"

"It's Aaron. You know. Aaron Stemple," I stammered. "You were just talking to him, right?"

Eric frowned. "Yeah, sure. What about Aaron? Did he get hurt or something?"

"Just hurry!" I insisted.

Half dragging Eric behind me, I marched straight into the dressing-room area and headed toward the stall where I'd seen the mannequin.

"Hey, wait a minute!" cried Eric. "You can't go in there. That's where *guys* change."

"It doesn't matter," I said, still charging full speed ahead.

I grabbed the knob and jerked the door open.

"Hey! Get outta here!"

I had walked in on a good-looking blond teenage boy, trying on clothes. He was clutching a pair of jeans in front of him and staring at me with bugged-out eyes.

Heat raced up my neck and turned my cheeks bright pink as I stared back at him. "I—I—"

"Geez, Robin, I told you that you couldn't come in here," Eric said from behind me. I could tell from the sound of his voice that he was almost as embarrassed as I was. "Come on. Let's get out of here before they call security."

There was nothing in the world that I wanted to do more than turn around and run away from the half-naked boy. But I had to know about Aaron.

"Excuse me," I said, being careful to keep my eyes on the boy's face. "Could you tell me if there was a mannequin in here when you came in?"

"What!" he shrieked.

"Have you completely lost it?" Eric cried.

He grabbed my arm and tried to pull me away, but I wouldn't budge.

"Well? Was there?" I pressed. "Right here in this dressing room. A dummy with dark hair and a Pittsburgh Steelers sweatshirt. I have to know!"

"The only dummy around here is you!" the boy said angrily. "Now get outta here."

"Come on, Robin," said Eric, pulling my arm again.

This time I didn't resist.

When we got outside the dressing-room area, Eric gave me a disgusted look and walked away.

"Listen, Eric, you've got to believe me," I said, hurrying after him. "It looked exactly like Aaron. I swear."

Eric stopped and glared over his shoulder at me. "Look, Robin, I saw Aaron about twenty minutes ago, and he was a perfectly normal kid," he said angrily. "No plastic skin. No glassy eyes. Just a kid. Got that?"

"But do you know where he is now?" I asked quickly.

"Sure. In the arcade, playing video games."

"Do you know *for sure* that he's in there?" I pressed.

"That's where he was heading, okay?" He shook his head in amazement. "When you said you were going crazy, you hit it right on the nose."

"Eric, listen to me," I said. "I don't care what you think about me, just find Aaron. I've got to make sure he's okay."

"Find him yourself," he said, and walked away.

Chapter

I watched him go with a lump in my throat. I had never felt so alone in my life. Eric didn't believe a word I had said. In fact, he was convinced that I had come totally unglued.

Maybe he was right. No sane person could possibly believe that human beings could turn into mannequins.

But I had seen it with my own eyes.

"Hey, Robin. There you are. We've been looking all over for you."

Lisa and Shannon were rushing toward me.

"Where have you been?" Shannon asked. "It's almost time for the movie to start."

I glanced down at my watch, hoping they wouldn't notice how shook up I was.

"I've been looking for you, too," I said. Then I got an idea. "We've still got ten minutes. Come on, there's something I want to show you guys."

"Sure. What is it?" asked Lisa.

"Come with me and find out," I said, trying my best to sound mysterious.

It worked, because they practically fell all over themselves following me up the escalator to the second level.

I was heading for Mermaid Magic. I would lead them up to the window display and wait for their reaction. If they didn't notice the mannequin and say it looked like Jamie, then I would know that I had imagined everything. But if they did see Jamie's face in that plastic one, I would tell them about Aaron. Then we could go to the arcade and look for him together.

The second floor of the mall was less crowded than the main level, and I could see the window display when we were three stores away. I frowned. Who was that person moving around inside?

"Oh, no!" I whispered. "They're changing the display!"

I dashed ahead of my friends, stopping outside the window and doing a double take. A teenage girl was arranging new mannequins on the fake beach. I had seen her before. She was the clerk with the black French braid who worked in Stryker's. The one who had closed the dressing-room door when I thought I had spotted a mannequin with a live boy's head—Aaron's head.

My mind was racing. *What's she doing here? And where's the mannequin that looks like Jamie?*

Just as my friends came up beside me, the clerk picked up a mannequin from the floor behind her and walked toward the back of the store. It was the Jamie-mannequin!

Pushing Lisa and Shannon aside, I raced into Mermaid Magic after her.

"Stop!" I shouted. "Bring that mannequin back!"

The clerk with the French braid didn't even hesitate. She marched straight to a door that was marked Storage and pushed it open.

"Please, miss," I called in desperation. "Please wait a minute. I need to see that mannequin. It's important!"

Still ignoring me, she went inside the storage room and slammed the door in my face.

Lisa was the first to catch up with me, and she touched my shoulder gently and said, "Robin, what are you doing? What's the matter with you?"

"Yeah, how come you're weirding out?" Shannon added.

"I'm not weirding out," I snapped. Then I turned back to the storage-room door and pounded on it with my fist. "Open this door and let me in!" I shouted. "Open it right now!"

"I'm sorry," came an icy voice from the other side of the panel. "Only authorized personnel are allowed in this room."

At that moment something seemed to burst inside me, and I started crying hysterically. "You can't do this!" I sobbed. "I want *Jamie* back! I want *Jamie* back! I want *Jamie* . . . *Jamie* . . . *Jamie* . . ."

Chapter

"Robin! It's okay!" Shannon said, pulling me away from the storage-room door.

"Shh. Don't cry," soothed Lisa. "Everything's going to be all right."

My friends clustered around me. I buried my face in Shannon's shoulder, feeling grateful that they were there. But my mind was still swirling, and I knew I wasn't making much sense.

"It was Jamie . . . she was in the window . . . but she wasn't real . . . she was a mannequin," I babbled uncontrollably. "And then there's Aaron . . . Aaron Stemple . . . his head was alive. . . ."

"Come on, Robin. Let's go back down to the food court and get you something cold to drink," urged Shannon. She put an arm around me and led me toward the door.

I started to go with her and then stopped.

"But the mannequin," I said stubbornly. "You have to see it."

"We'll see it later," Lisa assured me. "Right now we need to go down to the food court."

"You can tell us all about it there," said Shannon. "Here, take this tissue."

I thanked her for the tissue and blew my nose. I knew that my eyes were red and puffy. Who cared? What was important was that the clerk with the black French braid had been carrying Jamie away!

But that wasn't Jamie, I reminded myself. *It was a mannequin. One who* looked *like Jamie,* I thought, my mind reeling in total confusion.

Suddenly I had the creepy feeling that someone was watching me. Had the clerk with the French braid followed me to the food court?

Slowly I raised my eyes and looked around, abruptly coming face-to-face with Kitty Lopez and Diane Davies at a nearby table. They were both in my gym class and were the biggest gossips in school. I felt my face turning red as I realized that they had probably seen me crying. I would die if they came over and asked what was wrong.

The moment my eyes met theirs, they looked away from me and started talking and giggling together. *They're probably talking about me!* I thought angrily.

By the time we had finished our drinks, Kitty and Diane had left the food court, and I had calmed down and told Lisa and Shannon about both of the mannequins. I left out the part about Eric and me walking into the dressing room where the boy was changing clothes.

That was too embarrassing to tell even my best friends about.

"Wow," said Shannon, shaking her head in amazement when I had stopped talking. "What a story."

"You can say that again," said Lisa. "Now let me see if I've got this straight. You want us to believe that there is a mannequin that looks exactly like Jamie, and that it's been standing in the window at Mermaid Magic and staring at you whenever you stopped by. You also want us to believe you saw Aaron Stemple being turned into a mannequin in the young men's department of Stryker's Department Store."

I could see that she thought I was crazy, too. "Well, if that boggles your mind, listen to this," I said sarcastically. "That same salesclerk—the one with the black French braid who was carrying Jamie away—was working in Stryker's guarding the dressing room where Aaron was." I sat back in my chair and looked at them defiantly.

No one said anything for a moment.

57

Finally Lisa sighed deeply and said, "I know you think those things really happened, but you're so upset over Jamie not showing up today that you're not making sense. You're imagining things."

I knew I wasn't getting anywhere, so I decided to play along. "You're probably right," I murmured. "I guess when I saw that mannequin that looked so much like Jamie, I kind of lost it."

We sat there for a little while longer watching the shoppers go by. Finally Shannon jumped up.

"Eeek, we forgot all about the movie," she said. "It's almost half-over."

"Oh, no." I groaned. It was my fault. "I'm sorry, guys. I really am. Come on, let's see if we can turn in our tickets and get our money back."

"We could hang around for the next showing," offered Lisa.

"Naw," said Shannon. "I'm not really interested in seeing a movie anymore."

"Me, either," I said. Then another idea hit me. "After we stop by the ticket booth, we can go to the arcade and see if any cute boys are playing video games."

"What you mean is, see if Eric Sandifer's playing video games," Shannon said slyly.

Lisa giggled. "You can't fool us. We know you have a crush on Eric."

I smiled to myself. *Let them think that if they want to,* I thought. Of course, it was true that I had a crush on Eric, but more important, it was my chance to look for Aaron Stemple.

Chapter

14

When we asked for our money back, the boy in the ticket booth at Cinema Six shrugged and said, "Your tickets are still good. Just go on in."

"We don't want to go on in," argued Lisa. "The movie already started."

"It hasn't been on that long," he said.

"Yes, it has," I fired back. "We've missed the entire beginning."

He heaved a sigh and looked from one of us to the other. He was sort of good-looking, with an athletic build and wavy dark hair. He was wearing a T-shirt that said PROPERTY OF THE NEW YORK YANKEES.

"So?" the guy said. "When it's over, just stay in your seats. When it starts again, you can watch the stuff you missed. Like I said, go ahead. Go on in."

"We don't *want* to do that," said Shannon. "We've changed our minds. You couldn't *pay* us to sit through that movie."

"Hey, you'd really love this flick. A million laughs. I'm serious. Check it out." When we didn't answer, he bent closer to the opening in the booth's window and whispered, "What's the matter? Afraid of the dark?"

Lisa's eyes flared angrily. "Our money, please," she said, holding out her hand. "And hurry up with it."

The boy shrugged and exchanged our tickets for cash. "Boy, was he ever pushy," said Lisa as we moved out into the mall again.

"Yeah," I grumbled. "He really wanted us to go in that theater. Afraid of the dark! Huh! What a bozo."

Shannon shrugged. "Maybe the manager doesn't like it when he refunds people's money."

By now we could see the arcade. It was just ahead on the left. The closer I got to it, the more nervous I became.

"I sure hope Aaron's in there," I muttered, not realizing I had said it out loud.

"Aaron?" Lisa said in surprise. "I thought you liked Eric."

"I do, but—" I broke off, realizing what I had admitted. "Come on, guys. Give me a break. I need to find out if Aaron's okay, or if he's . . . well, you know."

62

"We know. A mannequin," scoffed Shannon, rolling her eyes. "You guys can go to the arcade if you want to, but I'm going into that western-wear store over there. I want to check out their jeans. Lisa, want to come with me?"

Lisa threw me a guilty look and said, "Sure. I could use some new jeans, too."

"Go ahead, think I'm crazy. That's okay. I'll go to the arcade by myself," I said, sighing. "And I'll meet you two right here in ten minutes."

Stepping out of the bright lights of the mall, I needed a minute for my eyes to adjust to the darkness inside the arcade.

The rows of video machines shot out bursts of ear-splitting noises. Eerie lights bathed the faces of the players in ghostly colors.

I started up and down the rows of machines, stopping first at a game called Dueling Gangsters, where twenties-style gangsters jumped out of hiding places and shot machine guns at each other with loud rat-a-tat-tats. A girl was playing that game, so I moved on.

There were groups of cheering boys and girls clustered around the players at every set of controls. Once I thought I saw Aaron at Monsters of the Catacomb, but when I got closer, it wasn't him. Then I spotted a boy in a Steelers sweatshirt playing a martial arts game called Shadow Ninjas, but that wasn't Aaron either.

63

"Want to get in on the action, miss?" a voice asked. "I can set you up on The Haunted Shopping Mall back in the corner." I felt a tap on my shoulder.

I jumped a mile and turned around. "The haunted shop—" I started to say, and froze.

The teenage boy standing there was exactly the same person who had refunded our money at Cinema Six not five minutes before!

The only thing different about him was that now he was wearing a T-shirt with Wonderland Mall Arcade printed across the front.

My mind was spinning again. This was the third salesclerk that had reappeared at different stores all over the mall. What was going on?

"But . . . you . . . ," I stammered.

"It's a great game," he urged, motioning for me to come with him. His eyes glowed red in the reflected lights from the machines. "But it's back in the corner where kids hardly ever notice it. Come on. You can play the first time free." There was something about the way he said the words that made me shiver. It was almost as if he were daring me to play the game.

The one back in the corner.

That kids hardly ever noticed.

Called The Haunted Shopping Mall!

Chapter

15

"**C**an't. I'm in a hurry," I said. "I'm looking for somebody. Maybe you've seen him. He's got dark hair and he's wearing a Steelers sweatshirt."

The boy didn't say anything for a moment. He just stared at me with those blood-red eyes. Finally his gaze flickered and he said, "Oh, yeah. I remember him. He was here, but he left."

"When?" I asked quickly.

The boy shrugged. "I dunno. Five minutes ago. Ten, maybe."

"Thanks," I said. "I have to find him."

I started to leave, but he reached out, stopping me. He bent closer, cupping his hand near my ear as if he were going to tell me a secret.

"Sure you won't play the game?" he asked in a whisper. "It's free. It won't cost you a penny."

Then he looked deep into my eyes again. The red glow seemed to be slowly spreading from his eyes to cover his entire face.

I suddenly felt weak and a little dizzy. I wanted to look away, but I couldn't. It was as if I was paralyzed by his gaze.

I knew my feet were on the ground, but it felt as if I were floating. Floating toward two points of blazing red light. The whole world was turning red as I floated closer.

And closer.

Chapter

16

I felt as if I were drifting into the sun. The heat was incredible. The light was blinding me. I was powerless to fight it. And yet, I didn't even want to fight it. I wanted to drift on . . . and on . . . and on.

Suddenly I was aware of movement in my line of vision. I squinted into the brightness. I could make out a form. A small form. It seemed to be a little girl, and she had darted in between the boy and me and was tugging on his arm.

"Hey, mister," the little girl said. "Got change for a dollar?"

"No change," he growled, and shot her an angry look.

The instant he glanced away from me, the spell was broken. The weakness I'd felt was gone, and strength surged back into me. I was firmly on the ground again. Putting one foot carefully behind the other one, I cautiously backed toward the door.

"Wait!" he shouted. "The free game. Don't you want to play?"

"No, thanks," I muttered, bolting out of the arcade as fast as I could.

Out in the mall again, I was panting so hard I could barely breathe. I had to find Shannon and Lisa and get out of there. As much as I wanted to head straight to the exit, I couldn't leave them. I didn't know what was happening, but something terrible was going on at Wonderland Mall. We were all in danger.

Shannon and Lisa weren't waiting at the spot we'd agreed on, so I headed toward the western-wear store at a run. Maybe they had gotten carried away trying on jeans and were still inside.

I stopped at the entrance of the store and scanned the showroom. I sighed with relief. There was Shannon, talking to a clerk.

I started toward her and stopped. The clerk had her back to me, so her face was hidden. But she had blond hair cascading over her shoulders, and she was wearing a miniskirt and a sweater!

Fear clogged my throat. I tried to call out a warning to Shannon to get away from that clerk as fast as she could. But the only sound I could get out was a croak.

"Oh, there you are, Robin. I thought we were

supposed to meet out in the mall."

It was Lisa, and I gulped in some air and turned around, still trying to speak.

"I didn't see anything I liked in here," she was saying, "so I tried another place a couple of doors down. They had the most adorable . . ."

Suddenly her mouth dropped open and her face went pale. She was staring over my shoulder. She must have seen something happening behind me. Behind me where Shannon and the girl with the blond hair were.

"Oh, no!" She gasped and clutched my arm. "Robin, *look*! It's Shannon!"

I glanced back at Shannon. She was gazing intently at the clerk, a soft smile on her face as if she'd just seen something very pleasant. But then she began to change. Behind her wire-rimmed glasses her eyes took on a look of alarm. She seemed to be trying to cry out, but her lips barely moved. No sound came out! Shannon grabbed wildly at the clerk, but her arm made only a jerky motion and then grew stiff, stopping halfway out in the air. And her skin took on a plasticlike shine.

I couldn't move. My worst nightmare had come true.

Shannon Markoff had been turned into a mannequin right before my eyes!

Chapter

"We've got to get out of here!" I cried.

"I can't believe it. It's not possible," Lisa murmured. "It looked like . . ." She didn't finish her sentence. She just stared at me as if the whole thing was too much to comprehend.

"Believe it, Lisa," I said. "I know it's not possible, but that clerk turned Shannon into a mannequin!" I could hear the panic in my own voice. "What have I been telling you? Come on, Lisa. Let's go before the same thing happens to *us*!"

I tugged on her arm, but she didn't move. "I want to go, too. Really," she whispered. "But we can't leave Shannon here."

"She's a *mannequin*!" I insisted. "You didn't believe me at first. You thought I was making the whole thing up about Jamie and Aaron. But now

71

you've seen it with your own eyes."

"This is crazy," Lisa said, shaking her head. "It can't be happening. We've got to go into that store and find out for sure if that mannequin is really Shannon. I mean, maybe we just imagined it. Or it's a coincidence that the mannequin looks so much like Shannon. It *could* happen that way, you know." She didn't sound as if she believed what she was saying herself.

"No! No!" I shrieked. "You saw it happen. You know it's her."

"I know it looks like her from a distance," Lisa reasoned. "And I know it's wearing glasses like hers. But what if Shannon accidentally dropped her glasses, and a salesclerk found them and put them on the mannequin as a joke? And we're so paranoid that we thought that mannequin was a real person when we first got here?"

"Lisa, listen to me, you can't go back in there," I begged. She wasn't listening, though. She had brushed past me and was heading into the store.

I ran after her. I had to tell her about the boy in the video arcade and his blood-red eyes and hypnotizing gaze.

Lisa must have known I was following her, because she was moving awfully fast. The store was larger than I had thought when I first looked inside, and the mannequin Lisa was heading toward was near the back.

72

"Wait a minute," I called to her. "I'm coming, too."

She let me catch up, but she didn't look at me. She was staring at the display containing the mannequin. Her mouth was open, and her eyes bulged wide.

"Look," she whispered, her voice quivering. "It *is* Shannon. And look at the mannequin standing beside her. It's *Jamie.* Oh, Robin, I'm scared! What are we going to do?"

Just then I heard someone come up behind us.

"May I help you girls find something to try on?"

The blonde in the miniskirt stood between us and the door.

Chapter

"Um . . . we're about to leave, thanks," I said, and swallowed hard. Little icicles of fear raced up my back.

I moved away from the mannequins and pretended to be looking at a western shirt with fringe across the front. I kept my head bent toward the merchandise, but my eyes were searching the room, looking for the fastest route to the door.

"We have some terrific opening-day sales," said the girl, moving closer. "Maybe you'd like to try something on. I'd be glad to show you to the dressing rooms."

I exchanged terrified glances with Lisa.

"We'll let you know if we find something," I said stiffly. "Come on, Lisa, let's look over here."

My heart was pounding as I motioned for her to follow me. I knew we had to get out of the store,

75

but I was afraid to make any sudden moves. I didn't know what the blonde might do. I decided that our best bet was to keep pretending to look at clothes and gradually make our way toward the front of the store and the door.

Suddenly I realized that it had gotten deathly still. I glanced around. Lisa and I were the only customers in the place. There had been lots of people browsing among the merchandise a few minutes ago. Now there weren't even any other salesclerks around.

It was then I realized that mannequins were all over the store. There were displays of mannequins roping fake cows and riding fake horses. Others were showing off elaborate pairs of cowboy boots. I had never seen so many dummies modeling clothing in one store before in my life. My heart was in my throat. I moved closer to Lisa.

She was standing in front of a pair of mannequins, staring at them intently.

I glanced at them, too. One was wearing an oversize sleep-shirt with a cartoon character of a horse in a cowboy hat on the front. The other one had on pajamas.

Lisa squeezed my hand and whispered, "Doesn't the one in the sleep-shirt remind you of a girl in our social-studies class?"

I squinted and looked at it again. She was right. I didn't know the girl's name, but she was short

76

and really overweight. So was the mannequin.

I caught my breath. Who had ever heard of a short, fat mannequin! But then, who had ever heard of a mannequin wearing wire-rimmed glasses? Or having the face of someone I knew?

I looked slowly around the store, gazing at first one mannequin and then another. A lot of the faces were familiar. Kids from classes. Kids I saw in the halls. And every one of them was frozen into the form of a mannequin.

I started edging toward the door again, moving more quickly this time.

"Lisa, we've got to get out of here right now," I mumbled. "Before it's too late."

As I moved, I tried to keep as far away from the mannequins as possible. On all sides of me mannequins smiled at me with painted smiles, their eyes following me as I went past. Had some of them moved? Reached out hands as I went by? I didn't dare look back to find out.

Hurry! Hurry! I screamed inside my head.

The blonde was blocking the door. She didn't say anything. She just smiled and looked at us with her enormous blue eyes.

As much as I tried not to, I couldn't help looking back. And then I forgot about wanting to leave the store. Her eyes were so big and so blue that it was like looking into the sea. So peaceful. Like riding a raft away from the beach. Bobbing along in the gentle waves. Feeling the warmth of the sun. Wanting to stay there forever.

Suddenly something clicked inside my brain. This peaceful, drifting feeling was the same sensation I'd had in the arcade when I had looked into that boy's blood-red eyes. *Danger! Danger!* The words flashed like a strobe light in my brain.

"Lisa! Don't look at her eyes!" I shouted, clamping my own eyes shut. "That's how they do it! With their eyes!"

Chapter

19

Grabbing Lisa's hand, I pulled her away from the clerk. We ducked low and zigzagged through racks of clothing and behind display cases as we made a mad dash toward the back of the store.

"Where are you going?" Lisa called in a hoarse whisper. "We'll be trapped in here with that . . . monster!"

"I see a door back here," I whispered back. "It's our only chance."

"Girls! Girls, where are you?" The clerk's voice rang out in the silent store.

We froze behind a rack of skirts. My heart was pounding so loudly, I was sure she could hear it. Lisa's face was frozen in a look of pure terror.

"It won't do you any good to try to hide," the

blonde said. Her voice was soft and coaxing now. "I've closed the door to the mall and locked it. The three of us are all alone in the store," she purred. "It's only a matter of time until I find you. And I will find you."

I tried to swallow, but I couldn't. I held my breath, listening for what she would do next.

Suddenly there was a racket near the front of the store.

I raised my head and peered over the skirts. Her back was to us, and she was furiously pulling garments off the racks and dumping over display cases. The air was filled with the screech of hangers being raked across rods and with the sound of shattering glass.

She wasn't coaxing anymore. Her mood had changed. She was destroying the entire store in her frantic search for us!

"I'm going to find you!" she raged. "I'm going to get you!"

"Now!" I whispered to Lisa. "While she's looking the other way."

We dashed toward the door. What if it was locked? Where else could we go? The blond girl would have us cornered. We'd be goners.

I grabbed the knob and turned it. It was open! I pulled the door open enough for us to squeeze through and closed it securely behind us.

"Lock it!" urged Lisa.

"I can't!" I whispered frantically. "It doesn't have a lock!"

"Oh, my gosh! When she can't find us out there, she's bound to come in here," said Lisa.

My eyes darted around the room. No windows. No way out. It was just a small, cramped storeroom filled with boxes and boxes of merchandise.

"Maybe we could hide in a box," Lisa cried. Her voice was thin and squeaky with fright.

I shook my head. "There has to be a better place."

I slumped against the wall to catch my breath when I heard the blonde screaming again.

"You little brats! Where are you?" Her voice was coming closer. "You can't hide from me! *I'll . . . get . . . you!*"

My blood froze. There had to be a place to hide. There just had to!

"Look!" whispered Lisa. She was pointing to a stack of boxes. The outline of a door showed behind them.

Together we wildly threw the boxes aside. A sign on the door read Freight Entrance. My heart leaped. If we could just get through this door, we could surely find the back entrance to the mall and freedom!

The heavy metal door opened with a heart-wrenching groan. Had the blond girl heard it? There was no time to lose. We propelled ourselves through the opening as it clanged shut behind us.

We were out!

We were free!

Our moment of relief ended abruptly as we looked at our surroundings. Instead of the bright hallway leading to an outdoor loading ramp which we had expected, we were in a dimly lit passageway that slanted downward. A damp, moldy smell hung in the chilly air.

Clutching each other in terror, we crept slowly down the passage toward the dark unknown.

Chapter

Lisa peered fearfully around the passageway. "I don't like this," she said in a breathy whisper. "It's creepy, and I'm scared. I want to go home."

"Me, too," I said. "But you know we can't go back into that store. We don't have any other choice. We have to see where this goes."

It was as silent as a tomb as we crept along in the darkness. Still, I couldn't help glancing back over my shoulder every few steps to see if we were being followed. And I kept picturing Shannon, turning from a happy, smiling girl into a stiff, plastic mannequin with terror-filled eyes. And Aaron, struggling to cry out the instant before he was changed into a lifeless dummy. I couldn't let the same thing happen to Lisa and me—*no matter what*.

Just ahead I spotted another door. It was on the

left side of the hallway, the same side as the door we had come out of.

"Let's try it," I said.

"I don't know," said Lisa, hesitating in front of the door, her face filled with confusion. "What if that blonde is in there waiting for us? She's been showing up in a lot of different places."

And so have the clerk with the French braid and the boy from the movie theater and the video arcade, I thought, but I didn't say it out loud. Somebody had to make decisions, and Lisa was too terrified to make them.

"Maybe it goes into another store, and we can cut through it and get back to the main part of the mall. Then all we have to do is grab the next bus to town, and we're outta here," I said, trying to sound more optimistic than I felt. "Let's try it."

I could tell that Lisa didn't want to do it, but she watched silently as I reached for the doorknob. The door was locked!

"Darn!" I muttered. "Let's keep going. Maybe there's another door up ahead that isn't locked."

"Do we have to?" Lisa's eyes were pleading. "Couldn't we just . . . just . . ."

"Just what? Can't you see that there is nothing else to do?" I insisted.

This time as we moved along, Lisa stayed behind me. Seeing another door on the left, I surged forward.

84

"Wait for me!" called Lisa, reaching out and grabbing the back of my belt.

That door was locked, too, and the next one, and the next one. And all the time we had been moving downward, deeper and deeper into the dark innards of the mall.

"Robin, look. There's a door on the other side of the hall," Lisa shouted. Her words echoed off the heavy walls. "Maybe it goes to the outside!"

"And home free!" I added, speeding toward it.

Incredibly, the knob turned in my hand. Holding my breath, I inched it open.

Instead of daylight, all I saw was more darkness. My heart sank.

"We aren't outside yet," I said. "But we must be getting closer. Come on."

Lisa was trembling as I dragged her through the door, and she was whimpering softly.

"It'll be okay," I said, but in truth, I wasn't so sure.

Since we had been in the dimly lit passageway for so long, our eyes adjusted quickly to the room we were now in.

Something about it was familiar. I had the eerie feeling that I had been there before. I stared intently into the shadows.

"Oh, no!" I cried.

We were back in the storage room.

The one filled with mannequins.

Chapter

Looking around, I realized that there were at least twice as many mannequins in the room now as there had been that morning. They were heaped and piled everywhere. Their arms and legs were bent at odd angles and pointing every which way. Some of their heads lolled to one side or were turned around completely backward.

Lisa grabbed my arm. "Where did they all come from?"

Then, turning her frightened eyes on me, she stammered, "Do you think that they're . . . that they used to be . . . kids . . . like us?"

Or like Jamie. And Shannon, I thought. I didn't answer Lisa. The idea was too awful to think about.

While Lisa cringed by the door, I began walking

slowly among the mannequins. I didn't think I could stand to look at their painted faces, but I had to.

The room was deathly still as I tiptoed across the floor toward a pair of girl mannequins, sitting with their backs propped against the far wall and their legs straight out in front. Their heads were upright, and their blank eyes stared straight ahead. They made me think of puppets whose strings had been cut.

I inched forward, not wanting them to look like anyone I knew, but knowing they would. I stared at them in horror. "Lisa, don't look if you don't want to, but I've found Kitty Lopez and Diane Davies."

I closed my eyes, picturing the two of them looking at me in the food court. I had been so afraid that they would come over and ask what was wrong.

If only they had! I thought. *Maybe I could have warned them!* But deep inside I knew they wouldn't have listened.

"Are you sure it's them?" Lisa asked in a trembling voice.

"Positive," I murmured.

For the first time since I entered the mall that morning, I felt totally helpless. Trapped. And tears of frustration and dread made little rivers down my face. My mind was whirling as I imagined all of these boys and girls, innocently going to a store clerk for help, or to a ticket booth to get into the movies, or to the boy behind the counter in the video arcade for change. And looking into their eyes . . .

Chill out! I ordered myself. *Getting emotional will only make things worse.*

I moved on among the mannequins again, peering into their silent faces. Most of them were strangers, but lots of them weren't. A boy from my language-arts class was crumpled in a corner. Near him was Marti LaMaster, the pitcher on our school's softball team for girls; and Aaron Stemple, still wearing his Steelers sweatshirt, was stretched out on the floor.

"And here's Amy Hamilton and Kristin Bergner," I called to Lisa. "Remember how we saw them a few hours ago and asked them if they'd seen Jamie?"

Lisa nodded and covered her face with her hands. "Don't look anymore, Robin. Please." She sobbed. "I don't want to know who they are. I don't want to become one of them. I just want to go home."

A sudden noise on the other side of the room startled me. There was another door. It looked like the door we had come through when we entered this room earlier in the day. And someone was unlocking it.

Lisa had heard it, too. I signaled her. "Quick! Someone's coming! Lie down on the floor and pretend you're a mannequin!" I whispered.

From the look on her face I knew that she was too terrified to move. Grabbing her shirt, I pulled her down beside me. A second later the door opened.

"Keep your eyes open and try not to breathe," I murmured.

A blinding stab of light was the first thing that came into the room. My head was turned so that I could see the doorway out of the corner of my eye. Someone was coming in.

At first all I could see was a ghostly black silhouette. But as it came closer, I began to make out its features.

It was the girl with the dark French braid!

And she was carrying a mannequin under one arm!

Chapter

22

I wanted to jump up and run screaming from the room. But instead I held my breath and tried with every ounce of strength that I had to keep from trembling.

She was coming closer.

Beside me Lisa's hand moved!

Had the girl with the French braid seen it? I heard her chuckle to herself as she wandered around the room. "You poor kids," she said in a cold, sarcastic voice. "Look at all of you. What a shame you had to be sacrificed."

I thought I was going to faint. What did she mean, *sacrificed*? What had she and the others done to everyone?

The mannequin she was carrying dropped to the floor with a sickening thud. She pushed him aside with her foot as if he were nothing more than a bag of garbage.

My eyes flicked toward him for an instant. It was a boy with red hair, but I couldn't see his face. Frantically I racked my brain. *Do I know any red-haired boys?* I wondered. Right now I was too scared to remember anything.

Why wasn't she leaving? I thought with a jolt. She had pitched another mannequin into this storage room. So why didn't she go back into the mall? Why was she just standing there?

I didn't dare look at her. She might see my eyes move.

But what if she was looking at Lisa and me right now? What if she had noticed that our skin didn't shine like the plastic dummies lying all around us? And that there were no painted smiles on our faces?

Why didn't I remember to smile! I screamed inside my head.

She took another step toward us. And another. And another, until she was standing right beside me. Her feet were pointing to the left side of my head, the toes almost touching my hair. She was so close that I could hear her breathing.

My heart was racing. My lungs were bursting. I desperately needed to gulp in air. Every muscle in my body was screaming to move. *To run.*

Suddenly the door burst open again.

"What's taking you so long?" It was the blond girl in the miniskirt.

I could see her standing in the doorway, her chin raised angrily and her hands clamped against her hips.

"I was dumping another one of the little brats in here," spat out the girl with the French braid.

"Come on. I need you," commanded the blonde. "I had two of them trapped, but they managed to get away."

The girl with the French braid laughed contemptuously. "Not for long, they didn't."

She stomped toward the door in long, determined strides and slammed it behind her, leaving Lisa and me trembling in the dark.

Chapter

23

At first I couldn't move. Beside me I could hear Lisa crying softly.

"What are they going to do to us?" she said, sobbing. "When we were in the store and the blonde wanted us to try things on, all I did was look at her and I started feeling funny. You said something about her eyes."

I nodded and explained to her about the boy in the video arcade and how his blood-red eyes had put me into a sort of a trance.

"But who are they?" Lisa whispered. "And why are they doing this? Why are they turning all our friends into mannequins? How?"

"I don't know," I said. "All I know is that they're after us. We've got to get away while we still can."

"I'm so scared," whimpered Lisa. "We'll never get away."

"We can't give up now," I said. "Come on. Try to get up. We have to get out into the main part of the mall and find the exit. And we'll stay in crowds. Maybe they won't come after us if they can't get us alone."

I tried not to look down as we tiptoed toward the door. Mannequins were strewn across the floor like corpses.

The girl in the French braid had left in a hurry and had forgotten to lock the door. I opened it a crack and looked out into the brightly lighted hall with closed office doors on both sides.

"The employee entrance!" I cried. "If we can find it, we can get out without going through the part of the mall where the stores are."

Lisa nodded. "But which way is it?"

I looked up and down the hallway. Both directions looked the same. I couldn't remember which side the door had been on when we ducked into it. It had been only a few hours ago, but it seemed more like a year.

"Come on," I said. "We'll have to take a chance."

I took off down the hall. Lisa was right behind me.

"Why don't we try to find an empty office to hide in?" she called to me.

"That wouldn't solve anything," I called back over my shoulder. "We'd still be in the mall with them, and we couldn't stay in there forever. We'd have to come out sometime."

Rounding a corner, I saw a large door at the end of the hall.

We're out of here! I thought ecstatically. It was either the employees' door or the entrance to the mall floor. Either one was better than where we were now.

When I pushed open the door, my heart sank.

"Oh, no," cried Lisa. "We're back in the mall."

I blinked at the sight of the escalators moving slowly up and down, the waterfall tumbling into the goldfish pond, the laughing, talking shoppers lugging bags and packages. They were totally unaware of what was happening right under their noses. They had no idea that innocent kids were being turned into lifeless mannequins all around them.

We darted through the crowd, running without looking back until a pain in my side made me stop and lean against a jewelry-store window.

I bent over, holding my side, and let my chest heave until the pain stopped and I could catch my breath.

"We made it this far," I finally managed to say. "We're going to get away."

"Let's look for a pay phone. I'll call my dad to come after us," offered Lisa.

I shook my head. "We don't have that much

97

time. The buses run every fifteen minutes. Come on, let's hurry."

As I pushed myself away from the jewelry-store window, I could see someone coming out of the store. It was the girl with the black French braid!

"Come on in, girls. Wouldn't you like to try on some pretty earrings?" she asked sweetly.

"Lisa, don't look in her eyes," I warned as we hurried on past.

Two doors down the blonde in the miniskirt rushed out of a bookstore and shouted, "Come on in, girls. Everything's on sale today."

"Keep going," I ordered Lisa. "Faster."

As we passed an open-air T-shirt shop in the center of the mall, the boy from the video store blocked our way.

"Hey, I've got some great deals on some far-out T's! Come in and look!"

"No! No! We don't want any T-shirts!" I shouted.

"No T-shirts? How about playing a super new video game?" he said, laughing crazily. "Or maybe you'd like to go to a movie. They're all first-run hits." His eyes were wild, and he was lunging toward us.

"No! Leave us alone," I said, pushing him away and running.

"Let go!" I heard Lisa scream.

I looked back. The boy had grabbed Lisa. I saw her struggle wildly and break loose from his grip.

Lisa was crying as she ran toward me.

As we raced past the goldfish pond, she grabbed my arm and stopped.

"What's the matter?" I demanded. "Come on. Let's get out of here!"

Her face was ashen. "Oh, my gosh! Eric! I saw him go into a sporting-goods store called Extra Innings when you went into the video arcade and Shannon and I split up to shop. What if he's still in there?"

"Oh, no," I breathed. "We've got to find him and get him out of here, too. Do you remember where the store is?"

"I think so. It's . . . No, it's . . ." Lisa turned first one direction and then another. "There it is," she said, pointing up to the next level. "See the sign? It says Extra Innings."

I ran for the escalator, praying that Eric would be there and that he was all right. The ride up to the second level seemed to take forever. I could swear the escalator slowed to half speed as soon as we stepped on. When I got off at the top, I turned to tell Lisa to hurry.

I couldn't believe it. She wasn't there!

"Lisa!" I shrieked, jumping up and down to see better. "Lisa, where are you?"

An older couple who were stepping off glared at me.

I looked down the escalator as it continued its

slow rise to the second floor, where person after person got off and went on their way.

But Lisa wasn't with them. She wasn't among the crowd on the first floor waiting to get on the escalator, either.

She was gone.

Lisa had vanished. I was all alone.

Chapter

If they had gotten Lisa, they could get me, too. One of them could be standing near me right now. Waiting for me to look around. And when our eyes locked—

"No! No!" I cried.

I ran blindly through the throngs of shoppers. I had to get to Extra Innings and find Eric!

"Excuse me. Excuse me," I muttered over and over as I practically trampled people in my path. Some of them moved out of the way when they heard me coming, but others got angry.

"What a rude girl," I heard someone say.

"That's the younger generation for you," someone else said smugly.

If only they knew, I thought.

I stopped once beside a bridal shop to get my bearings. Without thinking, I glanced up at the bride in the window. Suddenly my eyes widened in alarm. Had she nodded and smiled at me! Was every mannequin in the entire mall under their power?

I tore off through the crowd again as fast as I could go, tripping over a baby stroller and almost falling on my face.

"Excuse me," I said to the mother, stopping only long enough to make sure the baby was all right.

I had to get help, but first I had to find Eric. I could see the sign for Extra Innings just ahead.

Fear was smothering me. I tried not to look at the mannequins in the store windows I was passing, but I knew they were moving. Smiling. Nodding. Reaching toward me. Their eyes followed me. Did that one raise her hand? Did another one blink?

I had to find Eric and drag him to the bus stop. We would get out of there as fast as we could, and on the bus I would tell him about Shannon and Lisa and all the others who had been discarded in the mannequin storeroom. He would believe me this time! And then later—a *lot later*—we would go back to the mall together, and we would figure out what to do.

Inside the front door to Extra Innings was the ski-equipment department. *Eric won't be here,* I thought as I hurried through. He loved to play tennis. I would probably find him in the tennis department.

I stood on tiptoes, trying to see which direction to go, but I couldn't spot any sign of the tennis things. I inched past the workout equipment, every nerve in my body alert.

"Eric," I called out, but my voice was small and thin. "Eric! Where are you?"

"Can I help you, miss?"

I froze. The voice was familiar. *Too* familiar. I was face-to-face with the same teenage boy who had been in Cinema Six. And in the video arcade. And the T-shirt shop.

He was smiling. But above his smile, his eyes glinted cold and hard.

I looked away quickly, but he stopped me with a hand.

"Can I help you, miss?" he repeated.

I swallowed hard. I couldn't wait around to find Eric. I had to get out of there!

I could hear my own ragged breathing as I began slowly to back away from the boy. I didn't dare look into his eyes. But I didn't dare turn my back on him either.

Suddenly I bumped against something. I turned my head slightly, catching sight of a tennis racket out of the corner of my eye. I let out a scream.

The racket was in a mannequin's hand.

And that mannequin looked exactly like Eric!

Chapter

25

I don't remember leaving Extra Innings. I don't remember racing through the mall. I don't even remember entering the bus-stop shelter and curling up in a ball in the corner. But when I finally got the nerve to open my eyes, that's where I was. And it was dark outside!

I glanced at my watch. It was almost time for Wonderland Mall to close for the night, and I was alone at the bus stop. In the silence I could hear the pounding of my heart. Nothing else.

I jumped up and raced to the window, looking toward the highway.

"Come on, bus," I whispered. "Get here. I have to get away. Oh, bus, please. Come on!"

I don't know how long I stood there, watching for the bus to approach, afraid that at any moment one of the freaks from the mall would come after me.

Finally I turned away from the window. I looked at my watch again and then at the schedule on the wall. The last bus should have been here five minutes ago. In twenty minutes the mall doors would be locked. If no more buses came, I would be stuck out here at the bus stop. Alone.

I couldn't take that chance. But what else could I do? I couldn't start out on foot. It was a long way into town, and the highway was dark and lonely. And there was no place else to hide. There was only one possibility left. I had to go back inside before the mall closed and find a phone. I would call home and ask Mom to pick me up.

"Then everything will be okay, and I'll be safe," I said out loud, trying to reassure myself.

My legs were almost too weak to hold me up as I went back inside. I looked around fearfully, but the three evil teenagers were not in sight. Then I hurriedly checked the directory. A bank of telephones was near the escalators.

I could hear the sound of my own footsteps echoing off the walls as I raced toward the phones. Few shoppers remained now, and in the silence the tiny waterfall by the fish pond in the gigantic center court sounded like Niagara Falls.

When I reached the bank of four phones, I couldn't believe my eyes. They were all occupied. Yet there were scarcely four more people still walking around in the mall.

Hurry up! I wanted to scream.

I paced back and forth for a couple of minutes, but no one hung up. Then I remembered that I had seen a second bank of phones on the map. They were at the far end of the mall.

I looked at my watch again. Ten minutes till closing time. I looked around frantically. Still no sign of the three teenagers.

This time my shoes clattered loudly on the concrete floor as I ran toward the phones, but I didn't care. I had to call home—and fast.

This phone bank was empty. I dug change out of my belt bag and shoved it into the slot on the pay phone. My fingers shook as I punched in the number and listened to ring number one. Two. Three.

"Come on, somebody!" I muttered under my breath. "Answer!"

Four. Five. What was I going to do if my parents had gone out? Who else could I call?

Glancing around in desperation, I stopped cold. The telephone receiver slipped slowly out of my hand and clunked against the wall. I could hear a tiny voice saying hello, but I was too horrified to move.

Directly across the hall from the bank of phones was the jewelry store Lisa and I had passed just before she disappeared. In the display case a mannequin head was wearing a glittering diamond tiara, a sparkling necklace of rubies and emeralds, and matching earrings.

The head had thick curly hair and a big smile.

I backed up to the wall in horror, sliding slowly down to the floor. "Lisa?" I whimpered.

I sat there staring at the head. Of all my friends that had come to the mall together, I was the only one left.

Just then I heard the mall's doors slam shut and the automatic locks clang into place.

Chapter

26

I rose slowly to my feet.

The corridors were deserted now. The sky-lights dark. Silence was everywhere. The mall was closed for the night.

But I was still in it. And I was alone. Alone with three deranged teenagers.

My throat tightened as I tiptoed along.

The main mall lights had been turned off, but inside each of the stores the mannequins in the windows stood out in eerie relief against soft security lights. Their arms were extended toward me as if they were motioning for me to join them.

Beyond the stores—what seemed like at least a thousand miles away—was the mall entrance. I took a deep breath and tried to run for it. Blood thundered in my temples, and all the nerves in my body were poised like porcupine quills.

Suddenly I spotted someone coming toward me from the opposite end of the mall. My heart jumped.

"Oh, please! Let it be a store employee! Or a security guard!"

I blinked and squinted through the shadowy light.

I raised my hand and started to yell.

My hand stopped in midair.

Walking toward me was the beautiful blond teenager in the miniskirt. She was hurrying straight at me!

I spun around and tried to run in the other direction. I needed to find another door!

Coming from that end of the mall was the salesboy. A cry escaped from my throat as I turned again. Looking up, I saw the girl with the black French braid riding down the escalator.

Slowly I became aware of a sound—a soft rustling that grew until I realized that it wasn't a rustling at all. It was voices. Whispers.

"Fa-gin. Fa-gin. Fa-gin."

The whispers sounded unbelievably familiar. I knew where I had heard them before. In the mall basement early that morning. It was when all my friends had already gone, and I was alone beside the crack that had mysteriously opened in the floor and had been cemented up again. I had thought it was the air-conditioning machines.

110

"FA-GIN! FA-GIN! FA-GIN!"

As the angry whispers swirled around me, I forced my legs to run. But as I ran, so did the mannequins. They started leaving their pedestals in the store windows and moving stiffly after me, like the monster in an old Frankenstein movie.

"FA-GIN! FA-GIN! FA-GIN!"

I lunged toward the double glass doors, praying that someone would be out there and I could call for help. Outside, only a lone car sat under a light post. It was empty. I could see the highway beyond. I could see *freedom*! If only I could get there.

My legs were pumping, my lungs screaming for air as I put every last ounce of energy I had into getting away.

I reached out, almost touching the door, when I skidded to a halt. The beautiful blonde, the salesboy, and the girl with the dark French braid had somehow blocked my way.

Every muscle in my body shuddered with exhaustion.

There was no escape. Nowhere to run.

I was trapped.

I turned slowly around to face the parade of mannequins coming in my direction. They had lost their stiffness now, and they danced toward me with outstretched arms.

To my horror, leading the parade was a mannequin with white-blonde hair, one with wire-rimmed glasses, a boy mannequin carrying a tennis racket, and a laughing jewelry-store head, floating and bobbing in the air.

112

Chapter

27

The blonde in the miniskirt snapped her fingers. The ghostly parade stopped on command. The whispers stopped too. It was deadly silent as the mannequins shuffled forward to form a circle around me.

I looked from one of my friends to another. The painted smiles remained on each of their faces, but above the smiles, their eyes had grown sorrowful. As I stared at Jamie, a tear rolled down her shiny plastic cheek.

"What do you *want*?" I screamed, turning to the three teenagers who had joined me inside the circle.

"Revenge," whispered the blonde.

"Wheels," said the boy.

"Life," said the girl with the French braid.

"I don't understand!" I cried. "Why are you doing this?"

The boy sneered. "We were too young to die when we got lost in Mournful Swamp."

"Our friends all grew up, but we didn't," said the blonde. Her voice sounded like a moan.

"It wasn't fair," snapped the girl with the French braid. "We want what we missed out on."

The blonde nodded somberly. "And all we got was a cold, lonely grave at the bottom of the Mournful Swamp ravine."

I blinked at them in astonishment. "I . . . I know who you are," I whispered. "You're the teenagers who disappeared in Mournful Swamp a long time ago."

"That's right," said the girl with the French braid. "The mall construction disturbed our grave and made us restless. We want to live again. To *party*." She looked at the boy and grinned.

"Yeah," he said, grinning back at her. "To get some wheels and cruise."

"And when the crack in the mall floor appeared right over our graves, we knew the perfect chance had come," said the blonde. "It was like a door opening up for us so that we could escape back into life again—the life we had missed."

"But to do it we had to trade our existence for yours," said the boy.

"Now it's your turn to spend eternity watching your friends laughing and having fun, while you stand silently by and watch," said the girl with the

French braid. She snickered. "After all, don't all teenagers come to the mall? You'll see everyone you know."

My heart was in my throat. "Do you mean that you're stealing back your lives by turning innocent kids into mannequins?" I asked incredulously. I looked back at the sea of plastic faces with their mournful eyes. "Into lifeless zombies?"

The blonde nodded and moved toward me. Her eyes were glowing with an unearthly brilliance. Her voice was low and menacing.

"And you're next, Robin Fagin."

Chapter

I tried to back away, but she kept advancing toward me. The other two ghosts were coming at me from each side.

I could feel their eyes burning into my face, but I didn't dare look at them. I knew what their eyes could do to me. Hypnotize me. Put me in a trance so that I would be in their power. And then, when I was helpless, they would draw the life out of me, leaving only a shell.

A mannequin.

Just like my friends.

Behind the ghosts, the mannequins stirred restlessly. Their arms moved stiffly up and down, and the smiling jewelry-store head nodded, as if agreeing that I was about to join her fate.

Then the whispers started again.

"*Fa-gin. Fa-gin. Fa-gin.*"

I clamped my hands over my ears to shut out the awful sound.

I was alone! There was no escape! No one to save me!

"FA-GIN. FA-GIN. FA-GIN."

The whispers had turned to shouts. The ghosts were nearer. Grinning.

The mannequins closed around me. Suffocating me.

"FA-GIN! FA-GIN! FA-GIN!"

I took a deep breath. I had to do something to save myself. There was only one chance.

"Stop it! I can help you!" I screamed.

Everything stopped. The ghosts stood facing me like stone statues. The mannequins were silent and motionless, as if someone had thrown a switch, shutting them down.

"How?" challenged the blonde. "How can *you* help *us?*"

I took a deep breath to slow the pounding of my heart. "Wheels!" I said. My voice boomed in the silent mall and echoed faintly off the skylights.

"Wheels?" the boy asked excitedly. "What do you mean, wheels?"

"I know where there's a car," I said. "You could cruise. Party. Really live again the way you want to."

"Where?" The boy looked eagerly around.

I hesitated. I couldn't tell them about the one

118

car left in the parking lot. They might go after it themselves and leave me here, after they transformed me into a plastic dummy. But if I could persuade them to open the door and follow me, maybe I could get away from them. Run for my life!

"I'll have to show you," I said in a faltering voice.

The ghost with the black French braid bounced up and down with excitement. "Oh, let's do it!"

"It would be like before," the blonde said breathlessly. "Like when we were *alive*."

"That's right," I said, trying to keep my voice steady. "You don't want to stay in this stupid mall, do you? Not when you could cruise all night long. Anywhere you wanted to cruise. For as long as you wanted to."

A faraway smile appeared on the boy's face, and his eyes danced, as if he were imagining it all.

I held my breath and listened to the pounding of my heart. He had to say yes. It was my only chance to escape. My only chance to stay alive!

"Okay," he said. "Let's go."

He shoved past me and pushed open the double doors. The security alarm blasted in our ears. He ignored it, stalking out into the night. I was right behind him. I could hear the other two ghosts following.

"There it is," I shouted, pointing to the car sitting

119

under the lamppost. "Go get it. It's all yours."

At the sight of the car, the boy broke into a run. He seemed to have forgotten all about me. Now was my chance!

I veered off toward the main highway and hurled myself into the darkness.

Maybe I could flag down a car. Hitch a ride into town. Get help.

Just then I heard the girls shouting.

"Look! She's getting away!"

"After her!"

I didn't dare look back. My legs were pumping like pistons. My lungs gasping for air.

The highway was still far away, and they were gaining on me. I could hear their feet pounding on the asphalt.

I ran on, praying I could make it.

Then I caught a faint sound on the night wind. A low moan that built into a wail.

"Ooooohhh! Aaaaawww!"

I glanced over my shoulder and gasped in horror. Three pairs of ancient gnarled hands reached out for me. Three wrinkled toothless faces gaped at me.

"Robin! Robin!" screamed the old hag in the miniskirt. Her once beautiful blond hair hung in long white tatters.

Skin was falling away from the face of the boy ghost, revealing ghastly patches of white skull. The fingers that reached toward me weren't fingers anymore. They were turning into bones.

The ghost with the French braid let out a blood-curdling scream and clutched her face as an eyeball popped out of its socket and rolled across the ground.

They had grown hideously old in the few seconds since they had left the mall, and they were disintegrating—all three of them—rotting right before my eyes.

But they still managed to stumble after me with amazing speed, screaming my name over and over.

Suddenly I tripped. My legs flew out from under me, sending me sprawling onto the ground. I struggled to get up. I could hear their pounding feet behind me! Coming closer!

They were there! I could see three ghoulish faces over me. Bony fingers forcing my face to turn toward theirs. Livid eyes staring into mine. The stench of the swamp gagged me as their hot breath wrapped around me like a blanket of decay.

I felt myself slipping away. Floating out of consciousness and into a world of darkness. I had failed. I was theirs.

Forever.

Chapter

Suddenly the air around me seemed to change and grow cooler. The smell of decay drifted slowly away.

I opened my eyes. A million stars twinkled above me. I wasn't in the land of blackness I had been heading toward a moment ago. I was still in the parking lot of Wonderland Mall.

Then something caught my eye. Movement. My heart jumped into my throat.

I raised my head and stared in amazement at three shadows, whirling at an incredible speed. They were hurrying away from me and toward the mall.

"Oh, my gosh!" I whispered aloud. "It's them! The ghosts!"

Suddenly I understood. They had strayed too far from their grave and from the life force they had stolen from my friends. Now they were trying to save themselves by getting back inside the mall!

I stumbled to my feet, holding my breath as they sped toward the same double glass doors we had come out of only moments before.

No! I screamed silently. *You can't make it back inside! You must be destroyed!*

As I watched, the figures began to change again. Withering like autumn leaves in a flame and falling to the ground into three small piles of ashes outside the doors.

Tears of relief and joy rolled down my face. They were gone, and I was alive!

I looked up at the sound of faint moaning. *Was it the wind?* I wondered, and shivered. *Or the last angry cries of the ghosts?*

An instant later a breeze picked up the ashes and swirled them one more time, whisking them past me in little dust devils and away into the night. As they blew by my face, I caught the distinct stench of the swamp.

Suddenly the mall doors burst open, and dozens of boys and girls raced out into the parking lot.

"Robin! Robin!"

Jamie was running toward me with her arms flung open wide. "I got to the mall late, and I couldn't find you! Where have you been?"

"It's a long story," I said, laughing and hugging her tightly. Shannon, Lisa, and Eric were gathering around me, too. And I saw Aaron Stemple and the girl from my social-studies class in the crowd. And Kitty Lopez and Diane Davies. Everyone was giggling and talking at once.

Shannon pushed her glasses up on her nose and looked around, frowning. "Hey, guys, it's night. I didn't realize we had been in the mall that long."

"Me, either," said Lisa. "My mom will kill me if I don't get home."

"And look," said Kitty. "The mall's *closed*."

I shook my head in amazement. They didn't remember being mannequins! They didn't remember anything that had happened to them!

The sound of a siren was building in the distance, and a moment later a police car with flashing lights turned into the mall's parking lot. I had forgotten all about setting off the security alarm.

There's going to be a lot of explaining to do, I thought with a sigh. But I certainly could never tell anyone the truth. Nobody would ever believe that something like this could happen, *not in a million years*.

Then I glanced at Eric. He looked back and smiled.

His dimple appeared like magic.

Here's a Sneak Preview of Bone Chillers #2: Little Pet Shop of Horrors. . . .

Cassidy Cavanaugh brought her bike to a skidding stop. She stared at the small red brick building. "Look at that pet shop," she said, pointing. "I don't remember seeing it before. Where'd it come from?"

She and her best friend, Suki Chen, were out riding their bikes. It was a scorching hot summer afternoon, and they were trying to cool off.

"Me either," said Suki. "It's weird. There was an empty lot there the last time we came by."

"Yeah, that's what I thought," agreed Cassie. "But they couldn't have built a whole building in one week. And look at the vines. They're growing all the way up to the roof. Even mutant vines don't grow that fast."

Suki shrugged and flipped her straight black hair over one shoulder. "Who cares? I'm roasting out here. Let's go back to my house and blast the air-conditioning."

Cassie shook her head and stared at the building. It looked old—really old. She wondered if maybe they'd built it with antique bricks to make it look that way.

"You just want to go home so you can practice gymnastics," she said to Suki. "I want to go check out the store. I bet they have some cute puppies in there."

It annoyed Cassie that gymnastics was practically the only thing Suki cared about. Especially since Cassie couldn't even do a decent cartwheel. Cassie was too big to be a gymnast anyway.

All the gymnasts Cassie had ever seen were small and cute, like Suki. None of them were tall and bony like Cassie. *I need binoculars to see past my knobby knees all the way to my feet—my huge feet*, she thought.

"You know I've got to practice for that meet next Saturday," complained Suki. "It's a really big deal."

"And you know how much I love animals," said Cassie. "I want to see what they've got in that store. It'll only take a couple of minutes."

"Oh, all right," Suki said. "But I'm out of there if they have any snakes. I *hate* snakes!"

They walked their bikes to the front of the store.

It wasn't much like any pet store Cassie had seen.

128

Usually pet stores had big windows, so that you could look inside and see all the cute, cuddly puppies and kittens. This one just had a bulletin board inside one small window. It had pictures of dogs and cats thumbtacked to it. It reminded her of the "WANTED" posters for criminals they had in the post office.

Cassie read a sign, which was posted over the bulletin board:

CUSTOM PETS
TELL US EXACTLY WHAT TYPE PET YOU'RE
LOOKING FOR, AND WE'LL FIND IT FOR YOU.
SATISFACTION GUARANTEED!!!

Suki opened the door, and Cassie followed her inside.

The walls of the store were lined with cages, but most of them were empty. A single light bulb was hanging from the center of the ceiling. It cast a dim glow over everything, making it hard to see. Cassie walked over to check out the animals in the cages.

"This is a pretty lame pet shop," said Suki. "They really don't have much."

Only three of the cages had dogs in them. Another held two kittens.

When they saw the girls, the dogs started frantically pawing at the doors to their cages. The kittens started meowing and walking in circles.

Cassie knelt down in front of a cage with a

Siberian Husky puppy inside. Its fur was soft and fluffy. "Ohhh, poor thing. He's lonely."

The husky pushed up against the door and looked up at Cassie. She stuck her fingers through the bars and scratched it on its neck.

The puppy whimpered.

"He's got the saddest eyes," Cassie cooed. "I'd love to take him home with me."

Cassie suddenly felt a tickle in the back of her nose.

"AH-AH-AH-CHOO!" Cassie sneezed. "Darn it! AH-CHOO!" she sneezed again.

"Bless you," Suki said. "With your allergies, Cassie . . . that puppy would probably make you sneeze yourself to death."

"Bless you!" said a voice.

Cassie rubbed her nose and turned to see who had said that.

Sitting behind the counter, on a stool, was a very pale and incredibly fat man. He looked like a giant bullfrog propped on a lily pad.

Cassie squinted in the dim light, trying to see the man's face.

His eyes were bulging out of their sockets. His mouth was wide and thin. He didn't seem to have lips. He was gross!

"Thanks," she murmured, trying to throw off the creepy feeling he gave her.

"My name is Mr. Willard. Can I help you young

130

ladies?" he wheezed from his perch on the stool.

"No, we're just looking," said Suki. "Come on, Cassie. You promised we'd just stay a minute."

"I'm sure I can show you a pet that would interest you," said Mr. Willard. Struggling to get down off his stool, he waddled toward them. "If one of these animals isn't satisfactory, I can get you any kind of pet you want," he said. "Any kind at all."

Cassie could smell his sour breath. And she couldn't help noticing his eyes. They were solid black and watery, like a giant bug's.

Cassie heard a whine behind her and looked back at the puppy. Was it begging to come with her?

"Come on, Cassie. You promised," said Suki tugging at her arm.

"Okay," Cassie answered reluctantly.

She looked over her shoulder as they left the shop. The clerk was staring at her with his black watery eyes.

"You'll be back," he said.

Then he laughed.

On the way to Suki's house, they passed by City Park. *I'd really rather ride my bike in the park than stay inside at Suki's. Who cares about the stupid old air-conditioning*, thought Cassie. When you pedal fast, the breeze keeps you plenty cool.

"Hey, David, come on! Let *me* play with it. Pleeeze!"

Cassie heard a boy's voice nearby. It sounded like some boys from her school. She and Suki stopped their bikes to see what was going on.

"As usual, David Ferrante's showing off for this friends," said Suki.

Cassie shaded her eyes from the bright sunlight. She could see David and four other boys from their class huddled in a circle. David was holding a small white box. Cassie noticed that the box had holes in its sides.

David opened the top just long enough for the others to peek inside. Then he slammed it shut.

"Come on, David. I didn't even get to see it," cried Max Neal.

"Me either," complained Todd Cook. "Keep the lid off longer."

"Too bad. It's my turn next," said Ken Coffey, elbowing his way closer to David.

"I wonder what he's got in that box," said Cassie.

"Who cares?" said Suki, heaving a bored sigh. "Maybe it's his brains. They're certainly tiny enough to fit in that box. Let's go. I can hear the air-conditioning calling me, can't you?"

"Get serious," said Cassie. "I've got to know what's in that box. Do you think David would let us see it?"

132

"Ca-*aassi!*" moaned Suki. "Have you totally lost it? You know the kind of stupid jokes David Ferrante is always pulling. It's probably something disgusting."

"I know, but . . ." said Cassie. She put her foot on the pedal to leave. Then she stopped. It really bugged her when people kept secrets from her.

David raised the lid a couple of inches, holding the box up so that Ken Coffey could peak in. The next instant he slammed the lid shut again.

"Aaaahiiieee!" Ken cried. "Totally cool! Let me see it again! Come on, David! Let me see it!"

"Now, I've *got* to find out what's in that box," Cassie said.

She pushed down the kickstand, angled the front wheel so that the bike would stand up on its own, and marched toward the group of boys.

They were so intent on the box that none of them noticed her.

"David, can I see?" she asked sweetly.

David looked up and grinned. "It's Hopalong Cassidy!" he teased. "Hey, everybody, say hi to Hopalong!"

Cassie's face turned bright red with embarrassment as the boys broke into wild laughter.

Shouts of "Hi, Hopalong!" filled the air.

Cassie *hated* it when David called her Hopalong. David knew that, so he did it all the time. It was even worse when he got other kids to say it, too.

133

"David Ferrante, you are such a jerk!" she yelled, spinning around and heading back for her bike.

"Hey, Hopalong, where are you going?" he called. "I thought you wanted to see what's in the box."

Cassie stopped. She knew that it was dangerous to trust David. But it was all she could do to keep from turning around.

"Come here," David coaxed. "I'll let you see if you want to. Don't you want to see?"

"Ignore him, Cassie," Suki warned. She had parked her bike and was heading toward them.

"Come on, Suki-Pukey. You can see, too," David said.

"Listen, you jerk!" Cassie cried, angrily advancing on David. "You—"

Suddenly David held the box out toward her and took the lid off. It was almost under her nose. She couldn't help but look inside.

"Eeeeyuk!" Cassie squealed.

A giant tarantula was staring back at her with beady black eyes! Its long hairy front legs waved as if it were reaching out for her.

The tarantula was lunging right at Cassie's face.

LITTLE PET SHOP OF HORRORS

For Coney, Lollipop, Maxie,
Heidi, and Duchess

Chapter

Cassidy Cavanaugh brought her bike to a skidding stop. She stared at the small red brick building. "Look at that pet shop," she said, pointing. "I don't remember seeing it before. Where'd it come from?"

Cassie and her best friend Suki Chen were out riding their bikes. It was a scorching hot summer afternoon, and they were trying to cool off.

"Me either," said Suki. "It's weird. There was an empty lot there the last time we came by."

"Yeah, that's what I thought," agreed Cassie. "But they couldn't have built a whole building in one week. And look at the vines. They're growing all the way up to the roof. Even mutant vines don't grow that fast."

Suki shrugged and flipped her straight black hair

1

over one shoulder. "Who cares? I'm roasting out here. Let's go back to my house and blast the air-conditioning."

Cassie shook her head and stared at the building. It looked old—really old. She wondered if maybe they'd built it with antique bricks to make it look that way.

"You just want to go home so you can practice gymnastics," she said to Suki. "I want to go check out the store. I bet they have some cute puppies in there."

It annoyed Cassie that gymnastics was practically the only thing Suki cared about. Especially since Cassie couldn't even do a decent cartwheel. Cassie was too big to be a gymnast, anyway.

All the gymnasts Cassie had ever seen were small and cute, like Suki. None of them were tall and bony like Cassie. *I need binoculars to see past my knobby knees all the way to my feet—my huge feet,* she thought.

"You know I've got to practice for that meet next Saturday," complained Suki. "It's a really big deal."

"And you know how much I love animals," said Cassie. "I want to see what they've got in that store. It'll only take a couple of minutes."

"Oh, all right," Suki said. "But I'm out of there if they have any snakes. I *hate* snakes!"

They walked their bikes to the front of the store.

It wasn't much like any pet store Cassie had seen. Usually they had big windows so that you could look inside and see all the cute, cuddly puppies and kittens. This one just had a bulletin board inside one small window. It had pictures of dogs and cats thumbtacked to it. It reminded her of the wanted posters for criminals they had in the post office.

Cassie read a sign that was posted over the bulletin board:

CUSTOM PETS
TELL US EXACTLY WHAT TYPE PET YOU'RE LOOKING
FOR, AND WE'LL FIND IT FOR YOU.
SATISFACTION GUARANTEED!!!

Suki opened the door, and Cassie followed her inside.

The walls of the store were lined with cages, but most of them were empty. A single lightbulb was hanging from the center of the ceiling. It cast a dim glow over everything, making it hard to see. Cassie walked over to check out the animals in the cages.

"This is a pretty lame pet shop," said Suki. "They really don't have much."

Only three of the cages had dogs in them. Another held two kittens.

When they saw the girls, the dogs started frantically pawing at the doors to their cages. The kittens started meowing and walking in circles.

Cassie knelt down in front of a cage with a husky puppy inside. Its fur was soft and fluffy. "Ohhh, poor thing. He's lonely."

The husky pushed up against the door and looked up at Cassie. She stuck her fingers through the bars and scratched it on its neck.

The puppy whimpered.

"He's got the saddest eyes," Cassie cooed. "I'd love to take him home with me."

Cassie suddenly felt a tickle in the back of her nose.

"AH-AH-AH-CHOO!" Cassie sneezed. "Darn it! AH-CHOO!" she sneezed again.

"Bless you," Suki said. "With your allergies, Cassie, that puppy would probably make you sneeze yourself to death."

"Bless you!" said a voice.

Cassie rubbed her nose and turned to see who had said that.

Sitting behind the counter on a stool was a very pale and incredibly fat man. He looked like a giant bullfrog propped on a lily pad.

Cassie squinted in the dim light, trying to see the man's face.

His eyes were bulging out of their sockets. His mouth was wide and thin. He didn't seem to have lips. He was gross!

4

"Thanks," she murmured, trying to throw off the creepy feeling he gave her.

"My name is Mr. Willard. Can I help you young ladies?" he wheezed from his perch on the stool.

"No, we're just looking," said Suki. "Come on, Cassie. You promised we'd just stay a minute."

"I'm sure I can show you a pet that would interest you," said Mr. Willard. Struggling to get down off his stool, he waddled toward them. "If one of these animals isn't satisfactory, I can get you any kind of pet you want," he said. "Any kind at all."

Cassie could smell his sour breath. And she couldn't help noticing his eyes. They were solid black and watery, like a giant bug's.

Cassie heard a whine behind her and looked back at the husky puppy. Was it begging to come with her?

"Come on, Cassie. You promised," said Suki, tugging at her arm.

"Okay," Cassie answered reluctantly.

She looked over her shoulder as they left the shop. The man was staring at her with his black watery eyes.

"You'll be back," he said.

Then he laughed.

Chapter

On the way to Suki's house they passed by City Park. *I'd really rather ride my bike in the park than stay inside at Suki's. Who cares about the stupid old air-conditioning?* thought Cassie. *When you pedal fast, the breeze keeps you plenty cool.*

"Hey, David, come on! Let *me* play with it. Pleeeze!"

Cassie heard a boy's voice nearby. It sounded like some boys from her school. She and Suki stopped their bikes to see what was going on.

"As usual, David Ferrante's showing off for his friends," said Suki.

Cassie shaded her eyes from the bright sunlight. She could see David and four other boys from their class huddled in a circle. David was holding a small

7

white box. Cassie noticed that the box had holes in its sides.

David opened the top just long enough for the others to peek inside. Then he slammed it shut.

"Come on, David. I didn't even get to see it," cried Max Neal.

"Me, either," complained Todd Cook. "Keep the lid off longer."

"Too bad. It's my turn next," said Ken Coffey, elbowing his way closer to David.

"I wonder what he's got in that box," said Cassie.

"Who cares?" said Suki, heaving a bored sigh. "Maybe it's his brains. They're certainly tiny enough to fit in that box. Let's go. I can hear the air-conditioning calling me, can't you?"

"Get serious," said Cassie. "I've got to know what's in that box. Do you think David would let us see it?"

"Ca-*aassi!*" moaned Suki. "Have you totally lost it? You know the kind of stupid jokes David Ferrante is always pulling. It's probably something disgusting."

"I know, but . . . ," said Cassie. She put her foot on the pedal to leave. Then she stopped. It really bugged her when people kept secrets from her.

David raised the lid a couple of inches, holding the box up so that Ken Coffey could peak in. The next instant he slammed the lid shut again.

"Aaaahiiieee!" Ken cried. "Totally cool! Let me

8

see it again! Come on, David! Let me see it!"

"Now, I've *got* to find out what's in that box," Cassie said.

She pushed down the kickstand, angled the front wheel so that the bike would stand up on its own, and marched toward the group of boys.

They were so intent on the box that none of them noticed her.

"David, can I see?" she asked sweetly.

David looked up and grinned. "It's Hopalong Cassidy!" he teased. "Hey, everybody, say hi to Hopalong!"

Cassie's face turned bright red with embarrassment as the boys broke into wild laughter.

Shouts of "Hi, Hopalong!" filled the air.

Cassie *hated* it when David called her Hopalong. David knew that, so he did it all the time. It was even worse when he got other kids to say it, too.

"David Ferrante, you are such a jerk!" she yelled, spinning around and heading back for her bike.

"Hey, Hopalong, where are you going?" he called. "I thought you wanted to see what's in the box?"

Cassie stopped. She knew that it was dangerous to trust David. But it was all she could do to keep from turning around.

"Come here," David coaxed. "I'll let you see, if you want to. Don't you want to see?"

"Ignore him, Cassie," Suki warned. She had parked her bike and was heading toward them.

"Come on, Suki-Pukey. You can see, too," David said.

"Listen, you jerk!" Cassie cried, angrily advancing on David. "You—"

Suddenly David held the box out toward her and took the lid completely off. It was almost under her nose. She couldn't help but look inside.

"Eeeeyuk!" Cassie squealed.

A giant tarantula was staring back at her with black beady eyes! Its long, hairy front legs waved as if it were reaching out for her.

The tarantula was lunging right at Cassie's face.

Chapter

3

"**G**et that thing away from me! Get it away!" Cassie shrieked, throwing up her hands and backing away from the boys.

She backed right into a giant tree. She couldn't escape as David shoved the box in front of her face.

Cassie stared in horror at the huge black tarantula. It stared back at her, its long legs preparing to jump.

She screamed and pressed against the tree. Her eyes bugged out, and her heart pounded in her chest.

"Stop it, you moron!" yelled Suki. "Come on, Cassie. Let's get out of here." She turned a back flip. And another. And another until she was several feet away.

Cassie wanted to run, too, but she was paralyzed with fear.

David laughed.

All around her the boys were shouting.

"Chicken!" called Ken. "Hopalong Cassidy's a chicken!"

"Yeah," yelled Todd, making clucking noises. "And Suki-Pukey's gonna puke!" He stuck a finger down his throat, belching and gagging.

"Hey, David, that's enough. Close the box, will you?" said Max. "What if she dies of fright or something?"

"Now who's a chicken?" David spat out.

Max shrugged. "You've already scared them. It's not fun anymore."

Reluctantly David closed the lid and pulled the box from under Cassie's nose.

She opened her mouth to thank Max, but he shot her a warning look before she could say anything.

"David got the tarantula at that new pet shop over there," Max said quickly. He was pointing toward the pet shop that Cassie and Suki had just come from.

"It's a really neat place," said David. "The sign in the window says they'll get you whatever kind of pet you're looking for, and they guarantee it. And that's what I did," he bragged. "I went in two days ago and told them I wanted the *biggest* and *hairiest* and *ugli-*

12

est tarantula they could find." He smiled. "Then this morning they called me and said they had him. Isn't he great!"

"We saw the sign," said Suki. "And we went in. It's no big deal. They don't even have many pets."

"I thought girls were supposed to be smart." David smirked. "Let me explain it to you really slowly. You tell the guy in there what you want, and he special-orders it for you," David said, taking forever.

Suki stuck her tongue out at him.

Cassie shrank back against the tree as David opened the box again.

He took the spider between two fingers, and held it over his head so everyone could see. Its legs wiggled and batted the empty air.

"I'm naming him Igor," David said, grinning slyly.

He put the tarantula on his shoulder and lurched forward, limping and dragging one foot across the grass in a perfect hunchback imitation.

"Don't do it!" said Cassie as he inched closer to her.

He had one hand raised like a claw. His face was twisted into a hideous grin.

Behind him the other boys giggled and slapped each other's backs.

"*David Ferrante, you'd better not!*" squealed Cassie.

13

Before she could move. David shouted, "And I got Igor to scare the daylights out of girls—*like this!*"

He reached up and plucked the spider off his shoulder. With a sweeping motion he pitched it at Cassie.

She heard herself shrieking at the top of her lungs as the hairy monster landed on her arm.

"*Get it off! Get it off!*" she cried, shaking her arm and flinging the tarantula onto the ground.

"Come on!" shouted Suki, grabbing Cassie's arm and pulling her away from the tree. "Let's get away from these idiots!"

Cassie stumbled after Suki. As she hurried toward her bike, she glanced back over her shoulder.

The boys were laughing. "Hopalong Cassidy is a chicken!" yelled one.

"Suki-Pukey is gonna puke!" shouted another.

Jumping on their bikes, the girls rode away as fast as they could.

Chapter

4

The girls parked their bikes in Suki's driveway and hurried inside to the basement playroom. The furniture there had been pushed against the walls and the rug rolled up. A mat had been placed on the floor so that Suki could practice her tumbling routines.

Cassie sat down on a huge beanbag and watched as Suki went through her warm-up exercises. She was still furious at David Ferrante.

"I almost died when that spider landed on my arm. That David Ferrante is so stupid," she huffed.

"Tell me about it," said Suki, rolling her eyes. "If those boys call me Suki-Pukey one more time, they're going to be really sorry," she grumbled, doing the splits.

"I've never heard of a pet shop that took orders like that, have you?" Cassie asked, changing the subject.

Suki was doing walkovers now, so she was upside down. She shook her head, her hair twirling on the mat. "It sounds weird to me. What if somebody wanted a hippopotamus?"

Cassie giggled. "Or a giraffe?"

"Hey, I've got an idea," cried Suki, bouncing upright again. "We could order an anteater the next time we want to go on a picnic."

"I wonder if they'd take him back after the picnic was over," Cassie said.

"What about a tyrannosaurus?" Suki chuckled. "Maybe we could get one and sic it on David."

"Yesss!" said Cassie, punching her fist into the air.

"Or a raptor," yelled Suki. "Like in *Jurassic Park*!"

The girls broke up laughing, and Suki did three fast back flips.

Cassie grew serious again and said to Suki, "Can you believe how cute that husky puppy was? I felt so bad, seeing him locked up in a cage in that shop." Cassie sighed, remembering the puppy's pleading eyes. "My parents won't let me have a pet because of my allergies. Every time I'm around cats and dogs, I sneeze my head off. I guess my mom and dad are afraid that if we had a pet, my allergies might turn into asthma."

16

"I heard that there are certain kinds of dogs that no one is allergic to," said Suki. "I saw something about it on TV. I don't know what breed they are, but I'll bet the guy at that pet shop could tell you. Maybe he'd even order one for you. Why don't you ask him?"

A vision of Mr. Willard waddling toward her sprang into Cassie's mind. She shivered again at the memory of his fleshy, ghostly white skin and large watery eyes. And the way he smiled—it gave her the creeps.

That's ridiculous, she thought. *He's probably a really nice man.*

Jumping to her feet, she said, "Come on, let's go there right now. I want to find out what kind of dogs there are that don't make people sneeze."

Suki shook her head. "Bummer, Cassie, I'd love to, but I really need to practice for the meet on Saturday. My tumbling routine stinks, and I'm competing against Laura Carter. You know she's the best tumbler in the county."

Cassie left Suki's house a few minutes later and rode her bike back to the pet shop. Parking on the sidewalk, she stopped to read the sign once more.

CUSTOM PETS
TELL US EXACTLY WHAT TYPE PET YOU'RE LOOKING
FOR, AND WE'LL FIND IT FOR YOU.
SATISFACTION GUARANTEED!!!

17

Maybe . . . just maybe . . . Mr. Willard can find me a dog I won't be allergic to, Cassie thought happily. She opened the door and went inside.

The room was still dark and gloomy. Cassie noticed that it smelled bad, too. Mr. Willard was perched on his stool at the back of the store. The corners of his mouth turned up in a wide grin when he saw Cassie.

Cassie glanced at the cages and saw that the husky was gone. She was happy that the puppy found a home.

"Can I help you, miss?" Mr. Willard asked.

"I hope so," said Cassie, rubbing her nose. Another tickle was starting up.

"My friend told me that there were certain kinds of dogs that people who are allergic—ACHOO! Excuse me," she said, feeling her nose stop up. "Dogs that don't make people sneeze," she added quickly. "Do you have any?"

Mr. Willard inhaled deeply. It sounded like air escaping from a leaky balloon.

"There are a number of short-haired breeds that people with your problem can own," he wheezed.

He put his fingers together like a church steeple and peered over them at her. His black watery eyes stared directly into hers.

Cassie suddenly realized that Mr. Willard hadn't blinked once since they'd been talking. *That's weird,* she thought. *This whole place is weird!*

"I don't happen to have any in stock at the moment," he continued, "but if you'd care to fill out an order form, I could get one for you in a couple of days."

Cassie's heart leaped. She reached for the ballpoint pen he was handing her. Then her hand froze.

"I've got to talk to my parents first," she said, sighing. "They wouldn't like it if I ordered something without telling them. But you're sure you could get a dog that won't make me sneeze?"

The corners of his mouth turned up ever so slightly. "Absolutely. I can fill any order. Some just take more time than others. Ask your parents to call me here at the store if they want more information."

"Thanks," said Cassie. "I'll go home and talk to them right now."

She skipped toward the door, feeling happier than she had in a long time. *I might get a dog,* she sang to herself. *A cute little puppy even.*

Suddenly she heard a deep, menacing growl behind her. She whirled around in horror.

A huge black dog was coming through a door at

19

the back of the store. It let out another low, rumbling growl. Its lips were rolled back, baring long white fangs.

It was rushing straight at Cassie!

Chapter

5

"**G**RRRRR!"

Cassie froze as the snarling dog came bounding across the room. Its eyes were fixed on her throat. She ducked her head and threw up her arms to protect herself.

"Cuda! Halt!" shouted Mr. Willard. He grabbed the dog by its spiked collar and pulled it to a stop.

Cassie stood shaking with fear at the massive dog. It was just inches from her.

"Bad dog! Bad Cuda!" Mr. Willard scolded. He looked at Cassie with his black, unblinking eyes. "My apologies, miss. This is Barracuda. He needs a little training." He paused to catch his breath.

Cassie gulped. She knew that barracudas were mean and dangerous. That they had razor-sharp teeth that could cut you to shreds in an instant.

21

She shot a fearful look at Cuda's fangs.

"He's one of our custom-ordered watchdogs. His new master is on his way to pick him up," Mr. Willard wheezed. "I don't know how he got out of the back room."

Cassie's heartbeat was slowly returning to normal. She nodded and murmured, "That's . . . that's okay."

As she turned to leave, she felt a soft tap on her leg and jumped. Startled, she looked down. Cuda was reaching out a paw to get her attention. To her amazement he suddenly didn't seem vicious at all.

He whimpered softly and lay down on the floor at her feet. Wiggling to get closer, he looked up at her with huge brown eyes. He seemed to be pleading, the way the husky puppy had.

How could I have ever been afraid of him? she wondered.

"Good doggie," she said softly. She knelt beside him and stroked his head. He whimpered again and pressed closer to her. The sound he was making was strange. Almost as if he were trying to talk. "What is it, Cuda? What are you trying to tell me?" Cassie asked.

Mr. Willard jerked Cuda's collar and tried to haul the dog to its feet and away from her. "Back, Cuda! Get into the back room right now!" he ordered.

Cuda planted his back end firmly on the floor and braced himself against the pull. He looked at Cassie with wide eyes and made the funny sound, only louder this time.

"Arroaroro!"

Gripping Cuda's collar tightly, Mr. Willard huffed and puffed and began dragging the huge dog toward the back of the store.

"It's okay," Cassie insisted, following them. "I'm not afraid of him. Honest."

Mr. Willard ignored her.

Cuda looked over his shoulder and rolled his eyes back at Cassie. He let out a piteous wail. Cassie stood there, her hands over her mouth. Her heart was breaking at the awful sound. She watched the tortured dog helplessly.

"Please don't hurt him," she cried as Mr. Willard shoved Cuda through the door and slammed it.

Tears in her eyes, she hurried out of the store. All the way home the dog's sorrowful whine echoed in her mind. The eerie feeling about the pet shop and Mr. Willard grew bigger and bigger. She could see his cold smile and black watery eyes dancing in her mind.

Why had he been so mean to Cuda?

Poor Cuda, she thought. *I know he was trying desperately to tell me something. But what?*

Chapter

"**A**bsolutely not," Cassie's father said. Cassie had asked him as soon as she got home from Custom Pets if she could get a puppy. "Those salesmen will tell you anything. All they care about is making you buy something."

"That's right, dear," said Mrs. Cavanaugh, shaking her head and frowning. "And your health is our biggest concern."

"But Dad, Mom," Cassie pleaded. "It's not just *his* word. Suki's the one who told me about dogs that are okay for people with allergies. She heard all about it on television. The dogs don't shed at all. That's what makes people sneeze," Cassie explained. She could tell that her parents weren't convinced. It was time to beg. "You know I only went to the pet shop in the first place to find out if Suki was right. And Mr. Willard said she was. Just talk to Mr. Willard. Please. Please. Oh, *please*."

"Sorry, Cassie," said her father. "Our decision is final." He picked up the evening newspaper and settled into his favorite chair.

Cassie's shoulders slumped. She knew the subject was closed.

During the next few days she tried hinting about how nice it would be to have a puppy. All she got were icy stares. At the breakfast table on Saturday morning she decided to give it one last try.

"Mom, Dad, just think how much fun it would be to have a sweet little puppy around the house. They're good for security when they grow up, you know, as watchdogs. And they love you no matter what you do. They never get crabby and they make you feel good and they—"

"*Cassie,* will you drop the subject, *please*?" Her mother gave her a sympathetic smile. "Look, honey, we know how much you want a dog, okay? But we honestly don't think it would be for the best."

Cassie nodded and pretended to pat her mouth with her napkin. She was about to cry, and she didn't want her parents to see her chin quivering.

A little while later she got on her bike and headed for the pet shop again. She had called Suki to see if she wanted to come along. When Mrs. Chen answered the phone, though, she reminded Cassie that Suki had a gym meet.

As she rode through the park, Cassie told herself that she was just going to the pet shop to tell the salesman the bad news. Deep down inside she knew she was hoping that he had actually gone ahead and ordered her a puppy. If he had, maybe she'd be able to take it home on a trial basis. Then she might be able to convince her parents to let her keep it.

"Sorry," said Mr. Willard. "I don't order a pet until I have an order form filled out and a deposit paid. And if the person ordering the pet is a kid, it has to be signed by the kid's parents."

"Oh," Cassie said. She let out a big sigh, and tears came to her eyes. It was no use. She would never get a puppy.

She glanced around at the cages, feeling sadder than ever. The dogs and kittens that had been there were all gone now, and a lonely-looking basset hound sat staring out of its cage at her. It was funny how many cages the store had and so few animals.

She glanced toward the door to the back room. Had Cuda's new owners picked him up? She hoped so. Mr. Willard was definitely not nice to him.

She walked over to the basset's cage and stuck her fingers in. It immediately started licking them.

"You're nice, too," said Cassie. "And I bet you'll get a good home real soon."

Suddenly a terrible wail filled the air, making the hair on the back of Cassie's neck stand up. It sounded like a cat. A cat that was in pain.

Cassie looked toward the back door as the cat yowled again. It was the same room where Mr. Willard had taken Cuda. Cassie had an eerie feeling that Cuda had been trying to tell her something. Had he been afraid to go in there?

She glanced at Mr. Willard. He was sitting with his back to her, looking at some papers. How could he not have heard the cat?

She started to call out to him but was cut short by the cat yowling again. It was obviously in pain, and it was also obvious that Mr. Willard wasn't going to do anything about it.

If he doesn't care, I'll find out for myself what's going on, she thought angrily.

She tiptoed over to the door and pressed her ear against it. The cat cries were coming more softly now, but there was misery in the sound.

Cassie slowly turned the knob. She started to push the door open. Suddenly someone grabbed her from behind!

28

Chapter

7

Strong hands spun Cassie around.

"That room's private!" shouted Mr. Willard.
"Where do you think you're going anyway?"
His face had turned beet-red, and his eyes bulged
out of their sockets. She could smell his sour breath.
He was breathing in fast wheezes.

"I . . . I was looking for a rest room."

"It's back there." He pointed to a door near the
fish supplies. He pulled a key out of his pocket.
Then he locked the door Cassie had been trying to
enter.

Cassie ducked into the rest room and leaned
against the wall. "That's it! This is the last time I
come here," she muttered to herself. "That man is
such a creep!"

She couldn't hear the cat's crying anymore, but

29

it didn't make her feel any better.

There's definitely something weird about this place, Cassie thought.

In case Mr. Willard was listening, she ran water in the washbasin to make him believe she was washing her hands.

Leaving the rest room, she walked quickly toward the exit. But she suddenly heard a familiar voice and stopped. It was David Ferrante. She ducked behind a display of dog food to listen.

"I accidentally sat on my tarantula," David said. "So I want a new pet."

Cassie clamped a hand over her mouth to keep from bursting out laughing. The thought of David sitting on his revolting spider and squashing it to death was too funny. She buried her face in her hands to muffle the sound of her giggles. But the more Cassie tried to stifle her laughter, the funnier it got.

Then she heard a woman talking.

Peering around the dog food, Cassie saw David kneeling in front of the basset hound's cage. His parents were at the counter with Mr. Willard. She couldn't hear all of what they were saying, just a few words: "dog," "golden retriever," "pet." And it looked as if Mrs. Ferrante was filling out a form. The next thing Cassie knew, David and his parents left the store.

Cassie hesitated a moment to give the Ferrantes time to get in their car and drive away. She didn't want David to know she had been there listening when he confessed to squashing his spider.

When she was sure they had had enough time, she hurried for the door.

Mr. Willard looked up at her. A weird smile spread slowly across his face. He raised his eyebrows and his eyes seemed to sparkle.

Suddenly the room felt hot and stuffy. There was a strange humming sound in her head. She felt dizzy.

Cassie stopped and shook her head, trying to make the sound go away. Her breath was coming in short gasps. "What's going on?" she whispered. "What's happening to me?"

She looked at Mr. Willard. His smile covered his entire face. His watery eyes had turned even blacker.

The heat was sapping Cassie's strength. She turned back to the door. It looked miles away.

"You don't look well, miss," she heard Mr. Willard say. "Here, drink this. It'll make you feel better."

She looked at the glass he was holding out to her. It was filled with a pink liquid.

She hesitated. She was awfully thirsty. Maybe it would help.

Cassie took the glass and swallowed some of the bright-pink liquid. It tasted good—cool and sweet. She gulped down the rest.

"Thanks," she said, and started toward the door again.

Her legs felt as if they were made of lead. It took all her energy to put one foot in front of the other. The hum in Cassie's head grew louder, and the room spun even faster.

One step. Two steps. Cassie stopped and rocked back and forth, trying to keep her balance.

Cassie sank slowly to the floor and closed her eyes. Crackling noises in her ears were drowning out all the other sounds. She felt so tired.

Then everything went black.

Chapter

assie felt as if she were trapped in a whirlpool, struggling to the surface from the depths of a deep black sea. The closer to the surface she got, the brighter it became. The hum in her head slowly faded away.

"It's okay, Cassidy. Everything's fine, girl."

Her eyes fluttered open, and she looked up into Mr. Willard's smiling face. He was reaching toward her. He had something in his beefy hand. *It was a dog collar!*

"Good girl, Cassidy. Good girl," Mr. Willard said in a soothing voice. "You'll be going home soon."

Cassie cringed as Mr. Willard's hand came closer. Trying desperately to back away, she bumped to a stop against something hard. She looked around in a panic. There was nowhere to go! She was in a small metal cage. Mr. Willard fastened the collar around Cassie's neck. Then he slammed the cage door closed and locked it.

"No!" Cassie yelled at him. *"Don't! There's been some mistake!"*

But no words came out. All that came from Cassie's mouth were loud barks.

She tried again. *"Let me out of here! I want to go home!"*

"Shut up your stupid yapping," shouted Mr. Willard.

"Please let me out of here! My parents will be looking for me if I'm not home immediately, and then you'll be in big trouble!"

Mr. Willard's eyes narrowed. He reached through the bars and grabbed the collar, pulling Cassie forward until her nose was mashed against the bars.

She yelped with pain.

"Didn't you hear me?" he said, clenching his teeth and putting his face close to hers. His breath smelled worse than ever. "You'd better shut up, or I'll beat you within an inch of your life."

Cassie looked into his watery black eyes. She knew he meant what he said.

He let go of her collar. With a massive effort he struggled to his feet. He stood glaring down at her.

She didn't dare move. Or make a sound. Her

heart was racing. Cassie had never been so frightened in her life.

She looked down at her arms, and a shudder went through her body. They were completely covered with thick blond fur. She looked at her hands. But all she saw were furry paws! She crossed her eyes and looked down her nose. The tip of it was much too far away—and it was *black!*

Cassie turned and looked behind her. Her body was long and hairy. At the very end of her body Cassie saw—a tail!

Oh, no! she thought. *I'm a—I'm a dog! A half-grown golden retriever. And I'm locked in a cage!* She was a prisoner. Helpless. She couldn't even *talk.*

"One more custom pet, ready for delivery," Mr. Willard said. A sinister smile spread across his fat face. "Oh, what a story you could tell if you could talk, Cassidy." He cackled wildly. "But no one will ever understand your miserable barking."

He threw back his head and laughed hysterically. His huge belly bounced with each chuckle. Mr. Willard was still laughing as he waddled across the store and disappeared into the back room.

Frantically Cassie threw herself against the cage door, trying with all her might to get out. She pawed at the lock, but without fingers she couldn't begin to open it. She bit at it in frustration. That didn't work either. In her desperation she rammed the bars over and over with her shoulders until she was aching and bruised. Finally she sank to the floor in defeat.

She was a dog!

And she was trapped.

Chapter

Cassie rested her head on her front paws and gazed sadly through the bars.

Were the animals that had been in the cages before custom pets, too? she wondered. She looked at the basset hound. It was lying in the corner of its cage looking back at her.

Cassie opened her mouth, then stopped herself. If she tried to communicate with the basset hound, Mr. Willard would hear. She was scared he'd make good on his threat to beat her if she barked.

If I'm a custom pet, I wonder who ordered me, Cassie thought. *Will it be somebody mean, like Mr. Willard? Will whoever it is be able to understand me and realize that I'm not really a dog?*

Finally, exhausted from trying to escape, Cassie drifted off into a fitful sleep.

A little while later she was startled awake by a noise. She pricked up her ears and shot a quick look in the direction it was coming from.

David Ferrante and his parents were coming in the front door.

"Where is she?" David shouted excitedly. "I want to see her."

Mr. Willard was sitting on his stool again. "Hold your horses, young man. Your parents and I have a little business to take care of first."

"I'm not paying for the dog until I see it and make sure it's what I ordered," boomed Mr. Ferrante.

Mr. Willard shrugged and climbed down from his stool. He motioned for them to follow him and headed straight for Cassie!

Oh, no! she thought with a jolt. *Not David Ferrante's pet! Anything but that!*

She looked around wildly. There was no way to escape. David spotted her and ran to her cage.

"Wow! That was fast. This is her, all right. Exactly the kind of dog I want!" He knelt down and wriggled a hand through the bars.

Cassie backed away, huddling in the corner in terror.

David noticed the nameplate on her cage. He stared at it, and then at her.

"Hey, cool! Her name's Cassidy? I know a girl at school named Cassidy." He chuckled. "And she looks just like you, girl!" he said, pointing a finger in the cage. "She's got a big nose and big feet, too."

"David, what a mean thing to say," his mother scolded.

"Well, it's true," David said defiantly. "She even has the same color hair."

His words hit Cassie like a thunderbolt. *You creep!* she thought angrily. *How dare you say I look like a dog!*

Looking David straight in the eye, Cassie bared her teeth and let out a low growl.

Suddenly Mr. Willard's face appeared in front of the bars. "You'd better not let her get away with growling at you like that," he warned. "She's still young, and she needs plenty of discipline. There's not many things worse than a dog that won't behave."

Cassie could feel the hair standing up all along her spine.

"You don't have to worry about that," Mr. Ferrante assured him. "She'll get plenty of discipline once we get her home. My wife and I were against getting a dog, but David talked us into it. I guarantee you that dog will behave."

Cassie watched as David's father dug out his credit card and followed Mr. Willard to the counter. They were going to pay for her. Buy her just as if she were a sack of groceries.

You can't do that! I'm a girl, not a dog! she wanted to cry out. But she didn't dare make a sound.

Cassie watched as David picked up a leash. She had the feeling that her troubles were just beginning.

Chapter

All the way home Cassie tried to tell the Ferrantes what had happened. But no matter how hard she tried, no one seemed to understand what she was saying.

"I'm not a dog!" Cassie shouted from the backseat. *"I'm a girl! The man in the pet shop gave me something bad to drink, and I passed out. When I woke up I looked like this. Like a dog. Please! Please help me!"* she cried, pacing back and forth across David's lap. He kept trying to hold her down, but each time she struggled free.

"David, will you shut that dog up, for Pete's sake," Mr. Ferrante ordered. "How do you expect me to drive with that yapping in my ear? We're going to have a wreck!"

"Sure, Dad," replied David. He caught Cassie by

41

the collar and pulled a ball out of his pocket. "Good, Cassidy. Settle down, girl. Look. I got you a ball."

He poked the lime-green tennis ball into Cassie's mouth. *He's probably expecting me to chomp down on it so that we can play tug of war,* she thought. *Fat chance!*

The ball was all fuzzy. And it tasted gross! Cassie spat it out and watched it roll under the front seat. *Quadruple yuck. Good riddance.*

David fished it out from under the seat. He held it toward her again. "Come on, girl," he coaxed. "Let's play."

Cassie looked at the ball in disgust. It was covered with spit and had picked up globs of dirt and dried grass from the car floor. There was no way she was going to put that filthy thing in her mouth!

"Here, girl, here. Catch." David pitched the ball into the air. It hit Cassie on the head. Then it bounced off Mrs. Ferrante's shoulder and landed in the front seat.

"David, you know better than to throw a ball in the car," Mrs. Ferrante said.

"Aw, Mom," said David. "I was just playing with Cassidy so she wouldn't bark."

"Well, keep the ball in the backseat," she warned. She glared at Cassie as if to warn her, too.

Cassie was glad when the car finally pulled to a

stop in the Ferrantes' driveway a few minutes later.

Maybe when they open the car door, I can make a break for it, she thought.

But her hopes were dashed immediately. The instant her feet hit the ground, David grabbed her leash and began dragging her toward the house. The tightness of the collar made her stick her tongue out. She had to trot to keep up as he raced through the house to the kitchen.

"Are you hungry, Cassidy?" he asked. "How about some water? Mom and Dad say if I'm going to have a dog, I have to take care of it. I'm going to take the best care of you in the world."

While he was talking to her, he was filling two big plastic bowls. One had water in it, and the other had revolting-looking dry dog food. Then he set the bowls on the floor and stood back, beaming proudly.

"There you are, girl. Go ahead. Have some."

Cassie looked first at David and then at the bowls.

"But they're on the floor! You can't expect me to eat on the floor!" she shouted.

David swooped down and clamped Cassie's mouth shut with both hands. He squeezed so hard, tears of pain spurted into her eyes.

His eyes were wide with concern. "Shhhhh! No

more barking," he said. "Don't you understand? My parents don't even like dogs. You'd better watch it, or we'll both be in trouble."

Cassie wriggled out of his grasp and headed for the living room. She had never been more frustrated in her life. All she wanted was to get away by herself and bawl her eyes out in peace. She looked first one way and then the other to be sure the coast was clear. Then she jumped up on the sofa and curled up in a ball. If she pretended to be asleep, David might leave her alone.

"Get that dog off the furniture!"

Startled at the sound, she looked up to see Mrs. Ferrante standing in the doorway. David came barreling into the room and grabbed Cassie by the collar and hauled her off the couch.

"Bad dog!" he yelled. "Bad Cassidy!"

This is so humiliating, Cassie thought. *I hate being a dog!* She didn't want to eat on the floor. And she didn't want to sit on it either. It was hard, and the scratchy living-room carpet was making her itch all over.

"*Won't anybody listen!*" she wailed. "*I'm not a dog! I'm a girl!*"

Just then Mr. Ferrante charged into the room. His fists were clenched. His face was a beet-red.

Cassie lowered her head and tucked her tail between her legs. Mr. Ferrante was headed straight for her.

"Let me at that dog!" he cried. "*I'll* make her shut up for good!"

Chapter

"Wait, Dad! Don't hurt her," David pleaded. He jumped in front of Cassie and put his arms around her protectively. "I was just going to take Cassidy for a walk."

For the first time since she had known him, Cassie actually appreciated David. For an instant she almost liked him.

"You'd better get her out of my sight fast if you don't want to see me teach her a lesson she won't forget," snarled Mr. Ferrante. "I'll never understand why we let you talk us into buying a dog." He frowned as he watched David fasten the leash to Cassie's collar and lead her out the door.

She followed David at a run, afraid even to look back. As soon as they were outside, she looked up at David and wagged her tail. She started to say thanks but remembered that it would just come out a bark.

"Let's go to the park," David said, patting her on the head. "I want to show you to my friends."

Cassie's heart leaped. She knew all those kids. Maybe she could make one of them understand her.

But as she trotted along at David's heel, her optimism gave way to other problems. The pavement was so hot that it burned the soft pads on the bottom of her feet. Pesky bugs whizzed around her nose and dug into her coat, making her neck itch so badly that she had to stop. She tried to reach a front paw up to scratch, but her leg wouldn't bend in that direction. Then she remembered she didn't have fingers, just short furry toes! Frustrated, she sat down on the hot sidewalk and scratched her neck with a back leg.

Yuuuck! she thought. *Fleas!*

They came to a street crossing where the traffic light was red. As they waited for it to change, Cassie peered fearfully from behind David's legs at the cars zooming by. They loomed like huge monsters, belching foul-smelling exhaust fumes, their horns blaring. They were terrifying!

She was trembling and her tail was tucked between her legs when the light finally turned green. She didn't want to go into the street.

48

What if she got run over? It happened to dogs all the time.

"Come on, Cassidy," David urged, tugging on her leash. "It's okay."

She stepped gingerly off the curb, casting a fearful glance at the cars. Their engines growled like tigers about to spring. The smell of exhaust stung her nose. What if one of the cars shot ahead? She'd be killed!

Traffic was never this scary when I was a girl, she thought.

David yanked on her leash. Cassie pulled back, but he dragged her away from the curb and out into the intersection.

Cassie looked up at the grilles of the cars waiting to come at her. There was no turning back. She leaped forward, almost jerking David off his feet, and ran for the opposite curb.

"Geez, Cassidy," said David, rubbing the hand that had been holding the leash. "You just about tore my hand off."

Safely on the other side, they strolled along a residential street that was shaded by giant trees. Cassie relaxed a little and thought about what she would do when they got to the park. It was obvious that barking wouldn't do any good. She had found that out the hard way.

Maybe I can do some kind of trick, she

49

thought. *Something that dogs don't usually do. But what?*

She was trotting along, trying to think of a good trick, when she glanced up the sidewalk. Coming straight toward her and David was a grouchy-looking man leading a huge black rottweiler.

The dog was wearing a spiked collar. He bared his fangs and began growling when he spotted Cassidy.

Uh-oh, Cassie thought, feeling suddenly panicky. *I must be in his territory or something. Whatever it is, he definitely doesn't like me!*

Suddenly the dog lunged and broke loose. Snarling furiously, he raced for Cassidy!

Chapter

12

assie stared in horror at the charging dog. He had a bloodthirsty look in his eyes. His jaws were open wide, showing long white fangs. Saliva drooled from his mouth. She froze with fright. Her heart pounded as he came bounding toward her. She could almost feel his teeth ripping into her throat.

David yelled and pulled frantically on her leash. But the rottweiler was almost on them. There was no escape.

Cassie crouched low and scrunched her eyes shut, waiting for him to slam into her.

Nothing happened.

Opening one eye, she peeked out. The huge black dog had stopped in his tracks just inches from her. He was looking down at her, twisting his head first one way and then another.

With a little whimper he lay down in front of her and rested his nose on his paws. Their noses were almost touching. His eyes were soft and pleading.

Cassie raised her head and blinked in surprise. Her heart began to slow down. She didn't know what had made the rottweiler stop; she was just thankful to be alive.

Cassie looked at the huge black dog more closely. Had she seen him before? Yes! In Custom Pets.

It was Cuda!

"What's the big idea of letting your big old vicious dog attack my little Cassidy!" demanded David. "She's just a pup. He could have killed her!"

The man knitted his eyebrows together angrily and shook his fist at David. "Don't raise your voice at me, you young hoodlum. I've seen you around before. You're nothing but a troublemaker."

Neither of them seemed to notice that Cassidy and Cuda weren't fighting.

"Oh, yeah? Well, you'll have plenty of trouble if your dog hurts my dog," countered David.

Cassie felt a rush of excitement. Cuda seemed to recognize her. *If only I can communicate with him,* she thought.

While David and the man continued yelling at each other, Cassie stood up and bent over Cuda.

52

"Cuda? Is that really you?" she asked.

Cuda jumped to his feet and began wagging his nub of a tail furiously. His mouth was open in what resembled a big grin. His eyes sparkled at her brightly.

Cassidy wagged back. *He understands,* she thought happily.

"I'm so glad to see you," she said.

Cuda touched his nose to the tip of hers. She had seen dogs do this before. It was how they made friends.

If he barks back, will I know what he's trying to say? Or will it only sound like barking to me? she wondered. *I sure hope not. I have so many questions to ask him.*

"I'm scared," Cassie said. *"I don't understand what happened to us. Do you? Is there any way we can get back to our human bodies?"*

Cuda's eyes lit up, as if he knew exactly what she was saying.

Just then the grouchy man grabbed Cuda's leash. "Come on, Cuda. Let's get out of here and finish your walk," he grumbled, jerking the dog away. "I've had enough of this rude boy and his yapping dog."

Cuda looked alarmed. He tried to resist, but the man was too strong and dragged him along the sidewalk.

"Cuda, say something!" cried Cassie.

Cuda opened his mouth to bark, but before anything could come out, the man jerked on his leash again, choking off the sound.

"*David, come on! Let's go after them!*" Cassie insisted. She tugged on her own leash and leaned in the direction Cuda was being taken. "*I have to talk to Cuda.*"

"Easy, Cassidy. Easy, girl. Don't be afraid. He won't hurt you now," David said. "I made sure of that."

Cassie jumped up, putting her front paws on David's chest. She looked him straight in the eye. "*No! No! You don't understand!*"

David pushed her down. "Don't bark in my face, you stupid dog," he said in a disgusted voice.

Cassie was frantic as she watched the man lead Cuda around the corner and out of sight.

What will I do now? she thought desperately. *Cuda is the only one who understands me. He might know what happened to us. What if I never see him again?*

Chapter

"**C**ome on, girl," said David, heading down the street. "Let's go to the park."

Cassie took one last look as Cuda and his master disappeared around a corner. Her heart sank. There was nothing else she could do. She trotted after David.

By the time they reached the park, she was miserable. She was hot from running in a fur coat in the blazing summer sunshine. Bugs were dive-bombing her face, getting in her eyes and flying up her nose. She was so thirsty that her tongue was hanging out the side of her mouth, almost dragging on the ground.

David must have noticed, because he tugged on her leash and said, "Hey, Cassidy. Here's a puddle. Get a drink."

Cassie's eyes widened in horror. A puddle! He didn't really expect her to drink filthy, muddy water that people had walked through!

"Get serious!" she cried. *"There's got to be a drinking fountain around here somewhere."*

"Barking's just going to make you thirstier," said David, shaking his head and frowning. "I don't know about you, Cassidy. You don't act very smart."

She made a low growl rumble in the back of her throat. She was getting tired of David again.

"Are you going to get a drink, or aren't you?" David asked impatiently. "I haven't got all day, you know."

Cassie lowered her head, slinking toward the puddle. *What if I get sick?* she thought as she stared down into the brown water. She lowered the tip of her tongue into it. At least it felt cool. Closing her eyes, she lapped up a mouthful and gulped it down quickly.

Quadruple yuck!

It tasted awful! And it left a layer of grit all over her tongue.

"Come on, Cassidy, let's go," David urged. "I think I hear some of the guys at the baseball diamond."

Cassidy trudged after him, hoping there would be some shade near the diamond where she could stretch out on her stomach and cool off.

"Hey, look, everybody! Ferrante's got a dog!" Ken shouted the instant they came in sight of the ball field.

"Hey, yeah! Look!" yelled Todd. "He's neat. Where'd you get him?"

"Here, boy. Here, boy," called Max.

"She's not a boy, she's a girl," David corrected him. "I got her at the same pet shop where I got Igor."

"You mean the custom pet shop?" asked Todd. "Cool! Did you order her, too?"

David nodded as the boys all crowded around Cassie.

"Wow! She's a beauty. What's her name?" asked Max, kneeling down and gently stroking her head.

David burst out laughing. "You're not going to believe this, but she already had a name when I got her. It's Cassidy. You know, like Cassidy Cavanaugh in our class at school."

"Yeah, I can even see the resemblance," said Ken, chuckling.

"Me, too," said Todd, making a silly face at Cassie.

All the boys were laughing now, and Cassie wished that she could hide somewhere. Even more than that, she wanted desperately to get off the leash

57

and run for home. "Here, Cassidy. Here, girl. Fetch!" yelled Todd.

Cassie looked up to see a stick flying past her nose and soaring into the air. She watched as it arched upward, hanging there for an instant, and then plummeted to the earth.

"She's not very smart, is she?" asked Todd.

"Hey, you stupid dog, don't you even know what 'fetch' means?" cried David.

"She's not full-grown yet," said Max. "Maybe she hasn't been taught how to fetch."

Cassie cast a grateful look in Max's direction. *He's the only intelligent one here,* she thought.

"I've got an idea," said Todd. "You show her how it's done, David. I'll throw the stick again, and you run over and pick it up in your mouth and bring it to me."

Todd broke up laughing at his own joke, and Ken and Max did, too.

David wasn't laughing. His face had turned bright red and was filled with rage.

"That's not funny," he said. "She'll learn how to fetch—right now!" He picked up a stick and stomped toward Cassie.

Cassie tucked her tail and looked up at him in terror. Even though he had been extra nice to her when his parents got angry, she had seen David do mean things before. She wasn't sure what to expect.

David waggled the stick under her nose. "You see this? It's a stick!" he said in a commanding voice. "You got that? It's a *stick!*"

Cassie looked at the stick and then back at David.

"I'm going to throw it, see. And you'd better go get it and bring it back to me if you know what's good for you."

I know I ought to do what David says, thought Cassie, *but I just can't fetch a dumb old stick. It's humiliating. I'm a girl, not a dog!*

David raised his arm and let the stick fly. "Go get it, girl. Show them how smart you are."

Cassie planted her bottom firmly on the grass.

"Cassidy!" shrieked David. "I said fetch!"

Her heart was pounding, but she didn't move.

Suddenly David went into a rage. "I told you to fetch, you dumb mutt!" He raced toward her, stopping and pulling back his foot to kick her.

Cassie closed her eyes, waiting for the blow.

"Stop! Don't you kick that dog, David Ferrante! You'll hurt her!"

Cassie couldn't believe her ears. It was Suki! And she was riding her bike up the path straight toward them. *She'll help me!* Cassie thought with a rush of hope. *She'll know it's me!*

"Look out. Here comes Suki-Pukey," Ken said sarcastically. "Oh, boy, am I scared."

"Me, too," said Todd, giggling. "She's prob-

59

ably mad enough to puke all over us."

Cassie broke loose and took off at a run for Suki. *"Suki! Suki! It's me, Cassie!"* she shouted. *"You've got to help me! The man at the pet store turned me into a dog!"*

Suki's expression changed to shock and then horror as Cassie sprinted toward her. Her mouth fell open, and her eyes widened with fright. Suki tried to jerk her bike around but lost her balance and tumbled to the ground, getting her feet tangled.

"David, call off your dog!" she screamed.

Cassie was standing over her now. *"No, Suki. It's me!"* she cried. *"You've got to help me! Please!"*

"Get her away from me! She's going to bite!" Suki cried hysterically. She scooted away from Cassie.

Cassie could hear David and the others running toward her, shouting at her. But suddenly it didn't matter. It didn't even matter if David kicked her or Mr. Ferrante beat her when they got home.

Suki Chen had been her best friend forever, and even *she* didn't recognize Cassie.

Even worse, Suki was afraid of her!

Cassie felt her heart breaking into little pieces.

Chapter 14

For the next few days Cassie was so busy surviving, she didn't have time to think about Suki or Cuda. She was having enough trouble adjusting to her life as a dog.

For one thing, there was the food. She had refused to touch the dry dog food in the bowl on the floor. One sniff had told Cassie that it would taste unbelievably gross. To make things worse, Mrs. Ferrante cooked the most delicious-smelling meals in the world.

The first night Cassie was there, Mrs. Ferrante made fried chicken. And mashed potatoes and gravy. And apple pie. When Cassie smelled them, she thought she would die.

She had lain on the living-room floor, with her nose resting on her front paws just inside the kitchen. Her mouth watered as she took in the delicious aromas. She had sent pleading look after pleading look in David's direction, but he hadn't noticed. She hadn't been given a single bite.

The second night David's mother fixed potato salad while Mr. Ferrante cooked hamburgers outside on the grill. This time Cassie managed to get her whole body into the kitchen and whimpered softly. Still David didn't notice or toss her even the tiniest morsel.

By the third night she was desperate. It got even worse when David answered the front door and a delivery boy handed him two huge pizza boxes. She trotted behind David, sniffing the air, as he carried them into the kitchen.

"Which would you rather have, David, sausage or pepperoni?" asked his mother when the Ferrantes were seated. The spicy aroma filled the air, making Cassie's mouth water furiously.

She managed to sneak all the way into the dining area and under the table while the family's attention was on the pizza. Putting her chin on David's leg, she looked up at him with the saddest eyes she could make.

David couldn't help noticing her. He darted quick looks at his parents and slowly lowered the pizza wedge back to his plate. Quickly ripping off a piece, he jabbed it into Cassie's mouth and went on eating as if nothing were going on under the table.

Cassie almost died of happiness. The flavor was heavenly. Thick, creamy cheese, tangy tomato sauce, and spicy pepperoni.

"More," she whimpered softly. *"Please, David, another piece."*

David gave her another. This time it was just a flavorless half-moon of crust. *Oh, well,* she thought. *At least it's better than dog food.*

She had eaten four bites of pizza and two crusts when David's father accidentally dropped his napkin on the floor. Bending over to retrieve it, he came eye to eye and nose to nose with Cassie.

"Da-*vid!*" he roared, exploding upward and bumping his head on the table. "Are you feeding that dog off the *table?*" he said, rubbing his head.

David turned pale. "I . . . I just gave her a little bit," he fumbled.

Underneath the table Cassie trembled in fear.

"David, wash your hands immediately," ordered his mother. "That dog has probably licked your fingers."

David scooted his chair out and left the table.

"I'm warning you for the last time, David, that

dog has got to learn some manners," shouted his father.

At the same instant, Mr. Ferrante grabbed Cassie by the collar. Dragging her out from under the table, he zoomed across the room, pulling her with him.

"When you're hungry, you eat this," he ordered. He pushed her nose painfully into the hard pellets of food in her food bowl.

"And, David, if you want to keep this dog, you'd better make sure she stays away from the table at mealtime. And that's final!"

Cassie started to yell at them again and tell them for the millionth time that she was a girl, not a dog. But she didn't.

Get real, she told herself. *They can't understand me. And as far as they're concerned, I am a dog!*

Reluctantly she began eating the food in her dish. She was desperately hungry, and she had to eat something. Even if it was out of a bowl on the floor.

The dry dog food tasted like cardboard. It tasted like sawdust. It tasted like ground-up rocks. Cassie looked over at the bag. It had a picture of a rare piece of steak on it. The words "Your Dog Will Love Puppy Bits!" were printed in yellow letters.

Right, Cassie thought. *I really love this junk.*

The dry food stuck in Cassie's throat, but she kept eating. Unless she wanted to starve to death, it was all she could do.

Chapter

15

"In my day a dog was a *dog*," Mr. Ferrante said one evening at the dinner table.

Cassie was lounging on the living-room floor enjoying the mouthwatering aroma of lasagna wafting in from the kitchen. His words rudely interrupted her thoughts of the fabulous bites she knew David was squirreling away for her in his napkin.

She raised her head and frowned at Mr. Ferrante through the open doorway. *Uh-oh,* she thought. *I don't like the sound of this.*

"Yes, siree, when I was a boy, the old saying 'man's best friend' really meant something," he went on. "None of this business of a dog lying around in the air-conditioning getting fat and lazy. *My* dog was a crackerjack of a hunting dog. That's why I named him Cracker Jack," he said proudly. "Old Cracker Jack slept in the barn and never set foot in the house."

"Yeah, but Cassidy's a house dog," said David.

"What do you mean, Cassidy's a house dog?" Mr. Ferrante asked in amazement. "She's a golden retriever, isn't she? How do you think the breed got its name?"

"Because they're good hunting dogs," replied David, sounding bored with the whole idea. "Not Cassidy, though. I tried to teach her to fetch a stick at the park the other day. She was too dumb to catch on."

David's words stung Cassie.

I am not dumb! What's dumb is fetching a stupid stick. And I'm not fat and lazy, either!

"Honey, you know you could use a day off from work," David's mother said to her husband. "Why don't you and David take Cassidy out to Uncle Charlie's farm tomorrow and teach her to hunt. I'll pack you a big lunch to take along. It might help you and Cassidy get better acquainted and learn to like each other. All three of you would enjoy it."

Cassie groaned silently. *Fat chance of Mr. Grouchy and me getting along!* she thought.

"That's not a bad idea," Mr. Ferrante said, his

voice rising in anticipation. "How about it, David?"

"I guess so," David answered.

Cassie crawled under a chair in the living room and listened with dread to David's father making plans.

The next morning came too soon for Cassie. It was dark when Mr. Ferrante loaded the back of the family car with duck decoys, their lunches, and two gun-carrying cases. She hadn't seen him so happy. She, on the other hand, was miserable at the thought of wading in water to retrieve cold, dead birds.

When they arrived at Uncle Charlie's farm, Mr. Ferrante stuck shotgun shells in the holders on his khaki hunting jacket. Then he took a monstrous-looking shotgun out of one carrying case and a smaller one out of the other. He gave the small gun to David.

Shifting his red hunting cap on his head, he slapped David on the back good-naturedly. "This was a great idea, son. Are we gonna have fun today, or what?"

Next he stuck two fingers in his mouth and gave a shrill whistle. "Head 'em up, and move 'em out," he commanded cheerfully.

Cassie lay down in the grass and watched as father and son started off down an old wagon track.

They hadn't gone far before they realized she wasn't with them and turned around.

"Cassidy! Here, girl," Mr. Ferrante called.

She didn't budge.

"Come on, Cassidy," David called. "It's going to be fun."

Cassidy ignored them, scratching a flea bite near her tail instead.

Mr. Ferrante hurried back to where she was lying. He grabbed her by the collar and gave it a sharp jerk. "Get moving, Cassidy. It's time you earned your keep."

Cassie trailed along reluctantly, her tail down. Before long she realized—even though she would never have admitted it to the Ferrantes—she was beginning to enjoy the fresh morning air. The sun had come up and was burning the dew off the grass. The air was crisp.

Just as she was beginning to forget why they had come, there was a loud whir of wings, and four birds flew up right under her nose. Cassie tangled her feet and fell over herself trying to jump out of the way.

"Fire just in front of them!" commanded Mr. Ferrante.

Two thunderous BOOMS! went off behind Cassie. She leaped forward and almost collapsed out of fear.

"Go get 'em, Cassidy!" yelled Mr. Ferrante.

She looked back at him in amazement. Her heart was pounding so hard, she thought it would jump right out of her body. But she didn't move.

"Didn't you hear me, Cassidy? Fetch!" he cried, waving the barrel of his gun first in the direction of the fallen birds and then toward her.

She trembled as she stared down the gun barrel. Was he pointing it toward her on purpose? she wondered. Would he actually shoot her if she didn't go get the birds?

She decided not to wait around to find out.

Her ears still ringing from the blasts, Cassie ran across the field to the edge of a small lake where she had seen one of the birds go down. It was lying crumpled in the shallow water, its neck twisted back. Its beautiful feathers were in disarray. It looked disgusting.

She circled it. Did he honestly expect her to pick it up? *In her mouth?*

Cassie looked back at Mr. Ferrante. His gun was still pointed toward her.

She cautiously stuck one paw into the water. It was cold. She glanced back at Mr. Ferrante and David again. They were still watching her.

Slowly Cassie eased herself into the muddy water and nuzzled the dead bird with her nose. It was soft.

71

Eeee . . . YUUCK! It was still warm! *Quadruple yuck!* she thought.

She looked back over her shoulder again. Mr. Ferrante was watching every move she made.

Turning back to the bird, she gingerly took it in her teeth by the tip of one wing. She almost gagged a hundred times as she carried it, dangling from her mouth, back across the field. She dropped it twenty feet away from David and his father.

"Don't put it down there, bring it here, you dumb dog," called Mr. Ferrante.

Cassie turned her back on him, refusing to listen. She had had enough! What's more, she wasn't about to be a part of killing poor animals just for sport. After all, she was an animal herself now, too!

"I don't think Cassidy likes hunting," David said. "Can't we go home now?"

"Of course not," huffed his father. "We're here to have *fun*."

Mr. Ferrante got angrier and angrier each time he shot a bird and Cassie refused to go after it. He didn't seem to notice that David had stopped shooting. Finally he loaded everything back into the car.

It was a very quiet trip home.

That night Cassie had to sleep in the basement.

Chapter

16

The next evening Cassie was resting on the floor beside the sofa when the local news came on television. She had never been much of a news fan, but her ears pricked up when she heard the announcer say, "Local police have joined in the search for a missing twelve-year-old girl. Cassidy Cavanaugh, known to her friends as Cassie, has not been seen since Saturday morning, when she left home to go shopping."

Cassie jumped to her feet and ran to the set. *"Look!"* she shouted. *"That's me they're talking about! That's my picture they're showing on TV!"*

Mr. Ferrante slammed his hand down on the table beside his chair. "Shut that dog up, David," he roared. "I can't hear a thing they're saying."

"Hush, Cassidy," said David. His eyes were on the set. "A girl from my school is missing. Her name's Cassidy, just like yours. She's in my class."

"Of course she is, you jerk," Cassie shouted, running in circles around the room. *"I'm Cassidy. Look at me. Remember how you said I looked like the Cassidy in your class? Long nose. Blond hair. David, it's me!"*

Running to the television set again, she rose up on her back legs, pawing desperately at the screen. *"Here I am!"* she cried in frustration. *"I belong to David Ferrante, and I'm a dog! Why can't anyone understand me?"*

"Didn't you hear me? I said shut up!" David warned. He pulled her away from the set and grabbed her nose, squeezing it shut so that she couldn't bark. "If you don't be quiet, I'm going to have to get you a muzzle."

Tears of pain squirted out of Cassie's eyes. Her pride hurt even worse. *How dare David squeeze my nose!* she thought indignantly. *I was only trying to tell him something. Something important!*

Cassie lay awake all night at the foot of David's bed. She had to find some way to make him pay attention to her. To understand. Barking certainly wouldn't do it. She had found that out the hard way.

74

There must be something else I can do to get his attention, she thought. *But what?*

It was almost morning when an idea came to her. She would get his attention, all right. She was so angry and so frustrated that it didn't matter what happened. She would get it good.

She waited until the house was empty. David was playing at a friend's house. His father had gone to work, and his mother was grocery shopping. The timing was perfect.

Cassie started in David's closet. She dug through the mound of dirty clothes, the empty potato-chip bags, the catcher's mitt and soccer ball, until she found what she was looking for.

David's prize basketball sneakers!

She dragged one of them out into the middle of his bedroom floor and growled at it as if it were her biggest enemy.

Just wait until he sees this, she thought, her eyes gleaming and her fangs bared.

Cassie lunged at the shoe, grabbing it in her teeth and snarling as she shook it and wrestled it around the floor. The next instant she dropped it.

Pee-YEW! she cried. *It stinks!*

She sat back on her haunches and looked at the sneaker. She didn't know if she could bring herself to do what needed to be done. It was just too smelly.

Holding her breath, Cassie grabbed the shoe again. Her sharp teeth punctured the soft leather. Next she held it tightly with her front paws, tearing and tearing at the tongue until it was in shreds.

This is starting to be fun, she thought gleefully. *Now for the serious part!*

She plunged her nose into the shoe, jerking out the inner lining and spitting it out an instant later.

Wow! It tasted ten times worse than it smelled!

As soon as she had finished destroying the sneaker, Cassie barreled into the table beside David's bed, sending his model-airplane collection all over he floor. Then she rolled on every one of them, smashing them into a million slivers of wood.

Next she pulled the covers off his bed, ripping open his pillow and watching as a cloud of white feathers burst into the air and settled over everything like a gentle snowfall.

There! If that doesn't get his attention, nothing will, she thought, surveying the destruction with satisfaction. *Now maybe he'll try to understand me!*

Curling up in a ball in the middle of the disheveled mound of sheets and blankets, Cassie fell into an exhausted sleep.

Chapter

17

"**O**bedience school!" David's father thundered when he got home from work and heard about Cassidy's latest escapade.

Cassie was hiding under David's bed. When she heard his enraged voice, she scooted deeper, burying herself among the dirty socks and forgotten toys that littered the floor.

Her plan had backfired. David hadn't gotten the message. He had scolded her for messing up his things. To make things even worse, now she had to go to *obedience school*.

"You'll go with her, David, and learn how to control her," Mr. Ferrante continued, "and you'll start tomorrow."

Cassie shivered nervously as Mrs. Ferrante dropped her and David off the next day at obedience school. Before they left home, David had replaced her leather collar with a choke-chain training collar that could be jerked painfully if she disobeyed. She shook her head back and forth, trying to adjust to the weight of the chain.

The classes were being held in the park across the street from Custom Pets. Cassie looked fearfully at the vine-covered building, wondering if Mr. Willard was watching.

But she didn't have much time to worry about it. A dozen or so dogs and their owners were already crowded around the instructor. David led her over to the group.

Cassie looked up at the instructor. Her heart skipped a beat. He was a big, burly man with a crooked nose and massive arms. His mouth seemed to be turned downward in a permanent frown. He reminded her more of a lion tamer than a dog trainer.

David must have noticed how mean he looked, too. He leaned down to Cassie and said, "He looks like he wrestles alligators for a living. You'd better do everything he tells you, girl."

The instructor held up a hand. "Okay, everybody. Time to get started. My name's Bruiser, and I'm going to teach you how to control your dogs."

Bruiser! Cassie thought with alarm. He obviously had gotten the name for a good reason.

"Everybody line up in front of me with your dogs," he ordered. "The first thing we're going to learn is sit and stay. And remember, *absolutely no barking.*"

Cassie trotted meekly along at David's side as they joined the line that was forming in front of Bruiser. If she could have crossed her toes for luck, she would have. Instead she promised herself that she would do exactly as she was told. She certainly didn't want to attract the wrath of Bruiser or make David yank on the choke collar. He had demonstrated at home how it would tighten up and choke her when he pulled on her leash.

As soon as they were in line, Cassie glanced around at the other dogs. There were two poodles, a miniature schnauzer, another golden retriever, and—

Her heart leaped with joy. At the end of the line was a grouchy-looking man and a black rottweiler wearing a spiked collar. It was Cuda!

Instantly Cassie forgot all about Bruiser. *"Cuda!"* she called out joyfully. *"It's me, Cassie. Remember? From the pet—"*

A sharp pain in her throat cut off her words.

"Shut up, Cassidy," David whispered loudly. "Bruiser said no barking."

79

Bruiser was glaring at them. "Control your dog, young man."

"Yes, sir," David said meekly. He was holding the choke chain so tight, Cassie could barely breath. It was so tight, her tongue was hanging out of her mouth.

Cassie obeyed Bruiser completely and sat and stayed four times before she dared look down the line at Cuda again. He was looking back! Giving her a big doggie smile!

In spite of the warnings she jumped to her feet, wagging her tail furiously and pulling on the leash.

"Cuda! Say something to me. I need to talk to you!"

A sudden pain in her throat reminded her of her mistake. But this time it wasn't David pulling on her leash.

Bruiser had grabbed it and was jerking furiously. "Sit!" he commanded, shoving her rear end down and pulling up hard on her collar.

Cassie was filled with panic. It hurt. What was he doing? Why wouldn't he let go!

The pain made lights explode before her eyes like fireworks. She couldn't breathe and her lungs screamed for air.

She had to make him stop. She had to get away.

80

Frantically she lunged, sinking her teeth into his arm. An instant later she felt a sharp crack on the head.

Everything went black.

Chapter

18

"**E**xpelled! What do you mean, Cassidy was expelled from obedience school?" Mr. Ferrante asked between clenched teeth. His face was purple with rage. Cassie wouldn't have been surprised to see fire and smoke pouring out his nose.

But for once she couldn't care less that David's father was furious. Her head throbbed so badly, it made her eyes cross. And a lump the size of an egg was rising behind her left ear.

Mr. Ferrante threw up his hands after he heard David's explanation of what happened. "Bit the instructor! What will that dog do next?"

"But, Dad, it wasn't Cassidy's fault. Bruiser was being mean," David said. "He really hurt her."

His father began pacing the floor. He glared

83

first at Cassie and then at David.

"Suppose the man sues. What will we do then?"

"Maybe if you just pay for his stitches," David offered.

"So now he's got stitches!" cried Mr. Ferrante. "And I suppose he'll have to take a tetanus shot and be tested for rabies. Do we get to pay for that, too? No way. I've had it. This dog goes back to the pet store right now, and we're demanding our money back."

Cassidy's ears pricked up, and she forgot all about her headache. The thought of returning to Custom Pets terrified her. There was no telling what evil things Mr. Willard had in the back room or what he might do to her if the Ferrantes brought her back and asked for a refund.

"Please, Dad," cried David. He dropped to his knees beside Cassie and put his arms around her. "Don't make me take Cassidy back to the pet shop. *Please!* She's the only dog I've ever had, and I *love* her." He buried his face in her fur and nuzzled her. Looking up into David's face, Cassie saw his eyes were brimming with tears. To her surprise she felt an unexpected rush of affection for him. *Maybe he isn't a total jerk, after all*, she thought. She gave his cheek a big slurpy kiss.

84

What's the matter with me? she thought with a jolt. *I just kissed David Ferrante! I would never do a thing like that in a million years. Besides, I don't want to be his dog forever. I want to go back to being a girl!*

"I think you'd better take Cassidy out in the backyard for a little while, David, and let your father and me discuss the situation," suggested Mrs. Ferrante.

"Okay," David said. "Come on, Cassidy. Let's go out and play."

David picked up his basketball and made shots while Cassie stretched out under a shade tree. Every once in a while she glanced nervously at the back door of the house. David's parents were in there deciding her fate, and there wasn't a single thing she could do about it!

After a while, when they still hadn't come out, she shifted her attention to a dripping water faucet that was making a big mud puddle beside the back door. Drip. Drip. Drip. The hypnotic dripping made her feel sleepy. Drip. Drip. Drip. Her eyelids started to droop.

Suddenly they popped open again. She looked closer at the puddle. Paw prints! She had made them when she and David came outside.

Cassie jumped to her feet and ran to the mud. *I've finally found it!* she thought gleefully. *A way to make them understand!*

She glanced around the yard. David had stopped shooting baskets and was building a model airplane on the picnic table. *Good,* she thought. *He won't notice what I'm doing until I'm finished.*

She stood back, looking over the soft, damp earth like an artist studying her canvas. Then she started to work.

She pawed at the mud for a long time, working hard to get it just right. Her front toes didn't move as easily as fingers, and she had to smooth over what she was doing and start again. Her frustration almost caused her to give up, but the thought of Mr. Willard and Custom Pets made her keep going.

When she was finished, she stood back and proudly looked over what she had done. With the jab of a paw, she put a dot over the letter *i.*

She grinned. Written in the soft, dark mud were the words:

HELP! NOT DOG! GIRL!

Chapter

19

Cassie watched the back door expectantly. David's parents had been inside an awfully long time. One of them had to come out soon.

Time dragged on. Even David was beginning to fidget and toss worried glances at the door.

Cassie looked again at the words she had written in the mud:

HELP! NOT DOG! GIRL!

Pretty impressive, if you ask me, she thought proudly.

Finally the back door opened, and Mrs. Ferrante stepped out onto the porch.

Cassie shot to attention.

"Time to come in for supper, David," she called.

"But, Mom. What about Cassidy?" David asked. "Did you and Dad make up your minds? Can I keep her? Please?"

Cassie pricked up her ears.

"We'll talk about it at dinner, dear," she replied. Her voice gave no clue as to what had been decided. "Hurry in now, and don't forget to wash your hands."

She turned to go back inside without so much as a glance in Cassie's direction or at the mud where Cassie had written the message.

Cassie jumped up. *"Hey, look over here! I wrote you a message! You've got to read it! Please!"*

"Doesn't that dog know how to do anything but bark?" Mrs. Ferrante asked with disgust.

Galloping over to the back porch, Cassie stood up on her back legs in front of Mrs. Ferrante and pawed at the air. *"Come on,"* she insisted. *"Follow me. I've got something to show you!"*

When Mrs. Ferrante didn't make a move to follow her, Cassie ran to David, jumping on him and almost knocking him down.

"Don't let her go in! Make her look at the mud. If you come, maybe she'll follow!" she cried. Cassie grabbed his pant leg in her teeth and pulled him toward the mud.

88

"Cut it out, Cassidy," cried David. He swatted at her and tried to pull his pant leg out of her mouth. "The more you bark, the more Mom and Dad are likely to send you back to the pet store. Don't you know anything, you stupid dog?"

Cassie held on tight and pulled him toward the mud.

David shrugged at his mother. "I think there's something Cassidy wants to show us."

"What on earth?" grumbled Mrs. Ferrante, frowning. She came down the porch steps.

She was coming, too! It was only a matter of minutes—seconds maybe—until the truth would come out. Surely they would want to help her. Together they could find a way to turn her back into a girl again.

Cassie trotted over to her message. *"See?"* she asked, running in circles. *"Do you understand now?"*

Mrs. Ferrante stopped and stared at Cassie in surprise.

Suddenly Cassie was dizzy with hope. Had David's mother read the message already? Even a split second of waiting seemed like an hour.

"Look at that dog!" cried Mrs. Ferrante. "She's covered with mud! It's all over her paws and in her coat. Even her nose is muddy! I'll not allow her to step one foot into my clean house.

She'll have to sleep in the yard tonight!"

With that Mrs. Ferrante spun around and marched to the house, dragging David along by the arm.

Cassie watched in disbelief. She lowered her head and tail. *It's no use, she thought. I'll never make them understand. I'll be a dog forever.*

Chapter

20

Cassie spent the night curled up under a bush in the backyard. She scratched her fleas and worried. She was scared. What if they decided to send her back to Custom Pets? She pictured Mr. Willard's black watery eyes staring at her, his cold smile just before he gave her the pink liquid to drink.

Cassie remembered the painful wail of the cat. What cruel things was he doing to animals in the back room?

David had come out once before dark to pat her head and mumble that she'd better be awfully good. He'd had a pretty tough time talking his parents into giving her *one last chance*.

Cassie felt so helpless.

She finally managed to fall into a fitful sleep

91

filled with nightmares about Custom Pets.

As the sun rose, a cardinal woke Cassie. It was sitting on the tall wooden fence and singing its heart out.

She was so groggy she couldn't remember where she was at first. Then she spotted the bird and the fence, and the hopelessness of her situation came rushing back to her like an avalanche. She was David Ferrante's dog. She had been banished to the backyard for the night because she had muddy paws.

She was still staring at the bird and the tall wooden fence when a new idea began tickling the edges of her mind.

Why didn't I think of it before! she thought. *I'm a dog, so why can't I dig my way out under the fence?* she asked herself in amazement. She cocked her head to one side and sized up the soft dirt along the fence. *It doesn't look like too difficult a job. If I'd started digging last night, I'd be free by now.*

Cassie trotted across the backyard to the corner farthest from the house. Maybe it wasn't too late. No one was up yet in the house.

Finding an extra-soft spot in the dirt, she started digging furiously. Her front paws moved like twin whirlwinds. Dirt flew three feet into the air behind her. Best of all, the hole was quickly getting deeper and deeper.

Cassie knew freedom was on the other side. She would run as fast as she could to her own home. Surely, in some way, she would be able to make her parents understand it was her in this dog body.

Just a little bit farther, and her tunnel would break through to the other side. She was almost there. She could see a tiny pinhole of light. She dug harder and a hole opened up. In another minute she would be able to squeeze through and run for home.

She was so intent on digging that she didn't hear the back door open and Mrs. Ferrante come out onto the porch. And she didn't see the look of shock and horror spread across her face.

"Cassidy!" Mrs. Ferrante screamed. "You're digging up my flower bed! Oh, no. My beautiful flowers are ruined!"

Cassie froze, her paws stretched into the hole and her nose buried in loose dirt.

David and his father had heard the commotion, and now they were outside, too. All three were running across the backyard toward her. She could feel the earth vibrating as if three giant dinosaurs were thundering down on her.

Cassie backed out of the hole. Her tail was tucked firmly between her legs as she desperately looked for a place to hide. She wanted to cry. She had come so close to freedom.

"Come back here, you worthless mutt!" ordered Mr. Ferrante, stomping after her. His fists were clenched. His face was purple with rage. "This is it! The last straw! Finished! You're going back to the pet store right now. And this time I mean it!"

She knew her fate was sealed. Not even David could save her now.

Chapter
21

With a feeling of dread Cassie climbed into the rear seat of the car. She was going back to Custom Pets. Mr. Willard would be furious when the Ferrantes returned her and demanded their money back. He would take his anger out on her.

Cassie could still see the fat man leering at her through the cage bars. She could hear him threatening to beat her if she didn't stop barking. That had been bad enough. What would he do to her now?

Beside her in the backseat, David hugged her and cried into her fur.

"I'm going to miss you, Cassidy," he said, wiping his nose on the tail of his shirt. "I really *really* am."

To Cassie's surprise she realized she would miss him, too. A little bit, anyway. He wasn't the same obnoxious David she had known at school. The show-off. The troublemaker. The jerk.

He had loved her and had tried to take good care of her. He had even continued to give her food in his napkin when nobody was looking. Saying good-bye to David was going to be harder than she ever would have imagined.

Sighing sadly, she licked his salty face.

Mr. Ferrante found a parking space in front of the pet shop. David led her out of the car and toward the store. Cassie wondered if he could hear her heart beating. Pounding in terror.

She was trembling as they went through the door. She said a silent prayer that Mr. Willard would be gone, replaced by someone kind and gentle with animals. Someone who might be able to help her. Someone who could make her a girl again.

Her heart sank. Mr. Willard had his massive body planted on the stool behind the counter. He looked at them with his watery black eyes when they walked in.

He put down his paperwork and smiled at the Ferrantes.

"Hello, folks. Welcome to Custom Pets. How can I . . ."

His smile faded and his lips set in a hard line as he recognized them. His eyes bulged wider as he glared first at Cassie and then at David's father.

"Something wrong with your dog?" Mr. Willard demanded.

"She's a no-good worthless mutt, that's what's wrong!" snapped Mr. Ferrante.

Cassie's insides were churning as Mr. Willard wheezed and slid off the stool. He came from behind the counter and grabbed the leash from David's hand. Jerking her hard, he hauled Cassie to a cage and forced her inside. Then he slammed the door and locked it.

"Now tell me what the problem is," he said, lumbering across the floor toward David's parents.

David had lingered near the cage. "I'm sorry, Cassidy," he whispered. He reached a hand between the bars to rub her head.

Cassie whimpered softly.

"David!" Mr. Ferrante called. "Get away from that dog right now."

David sighed deeply. " 'Bye, Cassidy. I love you." Tears were in his eyes. He wiped them with his shirtsleeve as he slowly backed away.

Cassie's heart ached as she watched him go. Suddenly, being David's dog didn't seem so bad.

Pacing back and forth in the tiny cage, she

strained to hear what was going on. But they were too far away for her to make out much of the conversation, except for an occasional burst from David's father. "Stupid fleabag." "Barks like an idiot."

Her only hope was that Mr. Willard would refuse to take her back and she could return home with David.

If that happens, I'll never ever bark again, she promised herself. *I'll be the best dog in the world. I'll fetch, and roll over, and bring Mr. Ferrante his paper, and—*

The sudden sound of the cash register slamming shut broke into her thoughts.

"Sorry you folks got a rotten dog," Mr. Willard called out with a hearty laugh. "That happens sometimes. But don't worry. I'll take care of her myself."

Cassie listened in terror as the door closed behind the Ferrantes. Mr. Willard came out from behind the counter and headed toward her.

An evil grin spread across his fleshy face.

Chapter 22

Mr. Willard stood over Cassie's cage, blocking out what dim light there was in the room. His watery eyes were as cold and hard as a black night. His nostrils widened as his face slowly contorted into an expression of rage.

"So . . . you couldn't handle it, huh?" he asked, sneering. "You had to blow it. Well, we'll just have to do something about that, now, won't we, Cassidy?" His warm, sour breath spread over her like a putrid blanket.

"*Let me out of here!*" she cried. "*You can't keep me here! I'm a girl, not a dog! And my parents are looking for me. And the police. And if you don't let me out of here, they're going to catch you. And put you in jail!*"

"You can bark your head off, as far as I'm con-

99

cerned," Mr. Willard said. "It won't do you any good. No one can understand a word you're trying to say. But you already know that, don't you?"

He laughed. It sent chills down Cassie's spine. It made the fur rise on her back.

Cassie backed as far as she could into the corner of her cage. She rolled herself up into a quivering ball and shut her eyes tightly.

She was helpless. Totally at his mercy. She wished she could disappear.

The cage moved and she opened her eyes a slit.

Mr. Willard had picked up the cage. Cradling it against his huge body, he shuffled across the room.

"I think it's time you and I went into the back room," he said with a sinister laugh.

Cassie's heart stopped. *The back room!*

That's where he had taken Cuda.

And that was where the cat had been crying so pitifully.

And that was also the room Mr. Willard had stopped her from entering the day David and his parents ordered a golden retriever.

It was where Mr. Willard had turned her into a dog!

When they reached the door, Mr. Willard balanced the cage on his knee. Digging in his pants pocket, he pulled out a key. He unlocked the door and pushed it open.

Cassie glanced fearfully into the room. It looked like an ordinary storage room. It was filled with cases of dog food, bags of cat litter. All the supplies one would expect to find in the back room of a pet shop. There was also a sink in one corner with a coffeepot on the drain board. Beside the sink was a long table.

Cassie's heart lurched. It reminded her of an examining table she'd once seen in a veterinarian's office.

With a grunt Mr. Willard heaved the cage onto the table. He put his face up close to the bars. His bad breath oozed into the cage.

"I'll bet you'd like for me to turn you back into a girl, wouldn't you, Cassidy?" he asked in a sticky-sweet voice.

Cassie jumped up, wagging her tail furiously, and cried. *"Oh, yes! Yes, please! Oh, please let me be a girl again! I'll never tell anyone what happened here. I promise. Just let me be a girl again!"*

He closed one eye. He had an amused look on his face. "Of course, we both know I couldn't do that, don't we?" he said.

"Yes, you could! You could!" Cassie whined, and gave him a pleading look. Her feet pranced in ex-

citement. *"I promise you could! I can keep a se-cret! I swear!"*

He chuckled softly. "It doesn't do you any good to bark at me that way. Even I can't understand a word you're saying."

Cassie raced around her cage in circles crying, *"You've got to let me out of here! I want to go home!"*

Mr. Willard wheezed deeply. "I suppose there's just one thing to do. Since nobody wants you . . . I'm going to have to put you to sleep."

Chapter

Cassie watched in horror as Mr. Willard opened the cabinet under the sink. He pulled out a vial of medicine and a syringe.

"It's just a little shot," said Mr. Willard. "It'll hardly hurt at all."

He tipped the medicine vial upside down and stuck the syringe needle into it.

The syringe slowly filled with a clear liquid. Cassie couldn't believe what was happening. She really was going to be put to sleep.

Mr. Willard smiled and hummed to himself as he put down the medicine vial and pointed the syringe upward. He squeezed one lone drop out of the tip of the needle. The poison glistened in the light for an instant. Then it rolled down the shaft of the needle and disappeared.

"Well, Cassidy girl, it looks like everything's ready," he said. "Just relax and be a good dog. There's nothing you can do. You may feel a little sting at first, but it will all be over before you know it."

Was this what had caused the cat's terrible wailing? Cassie wondered.

Fear clogged her throat, choking off her breath. She watched Mr. Willard put the syringe down beside the sink and open the door to her cage. She shrank as far back as she could, but his hand shot inside and grabbed her collar.

A deep growl rose in Cassie's throat. She planted herself firmly, bracing herself against his pull.

He jerked hard on her collar but couldn't budge her.

"I'm warning you!" he snarled angrily. The rolls of fat on his face and neck were turning red. "I'm trying to make this as easy on you as I can."

Cassie growled louder and bared her fangs. Her mind was spinning as his massive hand pulled at her. Veins bulged on his arm just inches from her nose.

"Come *out* of there!" he commanded.

Cassie sank her teeth into his arm as hard as she could.

"Yooowww!" Mr. Willard screamed.

She held on, dangling from his arm as he yanked it out of the cage.

"Get off me!" he shrieked, trying to shake her loose.

Cassie dropped to the floor, scrambled to her feet, and raced for the door.

She could hear him cursing behind her.

The door was open a crack. That was all she needed. She could crash through it and into the main part of the store. She would hide somewhere—*anywhere*—until a customer opened the outside door. The final door to freedom . . . and home.

"Come back here, you mangy hound," cried Mr. Willard. "I'll teach you to bite me!"

She heard things being knocked over and his heavy steps behind her. Cassie made a final sprint toward the door.

Suddenly a hand shot out above her and the door slammed shut inches in front of her nose. Unable to stop, Cassie went crashing into it.

Dazed and trembling, she lay by the door.

"Don't think you can get away from me, you stupid mutt." Mr. Willard stood over her, laughing insanely. He held the syringe in one hand. Blood ran down the other and dripped from his fingertips onto the floor.

Cassie knew it was all over.

Chapter

24

Mr. Willard's huge body moved in slow motion. He bent over Cassie. The evil grin on his face chilled her to the bone. Warm blood from his arm splattered onto her coat. He was wheezing hard.

Cassie's eyes opened wide in terror as the syringe full of poison came closer and closer, the tip of the needle nearer and nearer. Mr. Willard's hand reached out to grab her collar again.

Gathering her strength, Cassie jerked away and jumped to her feet.

Mr. Willard lunged for her.

She dashed between his legs and scampered under the examining table, pressing up against the wall.

He let out a yowl of anger.

107

Bolting upright, Mr. Willard lost control of his immense weight. He fell off balance. He tried grabbing for a stack of dog-food cases to steady himself and dropped the syringe. An instant later he lost his grip and came crashing to the floor.

Mr. Willard lay sprawled out like a giant beached whale.

"Don't think you can outsmart me!" he screamed.

His feet and arms were flailing in the air.

Then he started rolling from side to side like a huge turtle as he tried to get up. "You can't get away!"

Suddenly Cassie spotted the syringe. It was lying on the floor halfway between herself and the bellowing man. She knew what she had to do.

Mr. Willard had managed to get to his hands and knees and was huffing and puffing to catch his breath. Cassie crept out from under the table. She crawled across the floor, keeping an eye on him.

Reaching out a paw, she touched the syringe. It felt ice-cold and evil. It was all she could do to keep from pulling her paw back in horror. But she forced herself not to.

She silently rolled the syringe away from Mr. Willard. She had to hide it, but where? Her heart was beating wildly.

Glancing around quickly, she saw a stack of cat-litter bags in the center of the room. Her paw was trembling as she edged the needle between two of them. Could she push the syringe far enough in between the bags that it would be hidden from sight?

Out of the corner of her eye she could see Mr. Willard struggling to his feet.

Hurry! Hurry! she screamed inside her head.

Using her nose, she pushed the syringe until it was almost out of sight.

Would he see it? She had to draw his attention away! Slinking quickly across the floor on her stomach, Cassie headed for a dark corner. Mops and brooms were leaning against the wall. Maybe she could get behind them. Hide for a little while. Buy herself some time to think. To come up with a plan.

With a gigantic heave Mr. Willard exploded off the floor. He twisted his head first one way and then another, shrieking, "Where are you? I know you're in here somewhere!"

Cassie cringed, shivering behind the cleaning equipment. Mr. Willard was in a wild rage. He stomped around the room, cursing and swiping merchandise onto the floor.

"Come out, you stupid dog! There's no way you can get away from me! *I'm going to get you!*"

He was making his way around the room more slowly now. He was looking behind every box, under every piece of furniture, and into every space big enough for a dog to slip into.

Coming closer and closer to Cassie.

Chapter
25

Suddenly Mr. Willard spotted Cassie hiding among the mops and brooms. His black eyes glinted brightly as he let out a hideous cackle of delight.

"So . . . my . . . poor . . . little . . . Cassidy. You thought you could get away from me, did you?"

He threw back his head and roared so hard, his body shook like an immense bowl of Jell-O. His laughter echoed off the walls and bounced around the room.

"Well, I've got you now, you mutt," Mr. Willard said, toppling over a stack of dog-food cans that stood in his way. They clattered to the floor.

Cassie peered up at him through the tall handles of the mops and brooms. They closed her into the corner like prison bars. Her teeth were chattering. It felt as if her heart were going to pound its way out of her chest.

"What did you do with my needle?" Mr. Willard demanded. He kicked aside cans and threw a chair out of the way as he advanced toward her. "I know you did something with it. It couldn't have disappeared into thin air."

Cassie fought to keep her eyes on his face. If she looked away, she might accidentally let her eyes linger on the cat-litter bags. Then he'd realize the syringe was hidden there.

Mr. Willard stopped, closed one eye, and studied her for a moment. Then he chuckled.

"Think you're smart, eh?" Waddling across the room, he opened the cabinet below the sink. Bending down, he pulled out the vial of poison and *another syringe!*

Cassie let out a howl. *Owww-wowww-owww.*

"Hah! You didn't think I only had one, did you?" he asked without looking at her. His attention was focused on filling the syringe.

"Be prepared!" he said, laughing. "They taught me that in Boy Scouts. Probably surprises you to know that I was once a Boy Scout, doesn't it?" He giggled crazily to himself.

Then he turned toward Cassie.

With a yelp Cassie exploded through the brooms

and mops, sending them flying in all directions.

She careened around the crowded storage room, dodging through bags of pet food and litter. Under the table and out again, slipping and sliding and scattering cans as Mr. Willard chased her.

She could hear his thundering footsteps.

She felt his doughy hands grabbing at her.

"Stop!" he shouted. "It won't do you any good to run!"

Around and around the room she went, crashing into boxes, scattering a display of dog toys.

Mr. Willard was right behind her, throwing things out of his way.

Cassie leaped over more boxes.

"Stop!" cried Mr. Willard. He was panting and wheezing heavily. "Stop this instant!" he yelled, but his voice was getting fainter. His footsteps slower.

Finally Mr. Willard leaned against the examining table. His huge body was heaving as he gasped for air. His face was glowing bright red from exhaustion. Sweat dripped off the end of his nose. His shirttail was pulled out. His clothes were soaked with perspiration.

With a shaky hand he pulled a handkerchief from his back pocket and mopped his face.

"I said stop!" he tried to cry out again. But his voice was barely above a whisper. His chest was

113

heaving even harder now, and he was holding his side.

Across the room Cassie peered at him from behind a box. Her own breath was coming in ragged gasps. Her tongue was dripping.

What was he going to do now? Was he just pretending to be tired? Was he actually planning another way to trap her?

She looked around quickly. What could she do? *There was no place else to hide!*

Suddenly Mr. Willard shoved himself away from the examining table and stomped to the door. The poison-filled syringe still glinted in his hand.

When he reached the door, he turned around. "I'm going to get help," he wheezed. "And when I get back . . . *you are dead, Cassidy.*"

Chapter

26

The instant the door slammed behind him, Cassie began pacing back and forth, looking for a place to hide, a way out.

What am I going to do? she screamed inside her head.

She looked around helplessly. Mr. Willard wasn't the only one who was tired. She was exhausted. Her legs trembled so much that she could barely stand. Her head throbbed. Her dry tongue lolled out of the side of her mouth. With help he wouldn't have any trouble catching her and putting her to sleep!

She sagged to the floor to rest a moment and wait until her breathing slowed to normal.

I can't give up! I can't! she told herself stubbornly. *I've got to keep going.*

It took all her energy to struggle to her feet. Frantically she circled the room again, looking for a way out. Hot, thirsty, and desperate, she pushed boxes of dog food away from the wall with her shoulder. She knocked over stacks of cat-food cans and looked under furniture.

It's no use! I'm trapped! she whimpered.

The only door led into the main part of the store, where Mr. Willard was getting help. There was no other way out.

Unless . . .

Cassie looked up.

High up on the wall, near the ceiling, was a tiny window she hadn't noticed before. Dull sunlight was barely able to shine through the grimy pane.

She studied the window for a moment. There was a handle on the bottom near the sill.

Cassie looked down at her paws. *I don't have any fingers!* she moaned. *Even if I could get up to it, I couldn't open it.*

Still, she had to try. She couldn't just stay there and wait for Mr. Willard to come back with help. To come back and put her to sleep.

There was a rickety table beneath the window. On top of it were a few sheets of paper and a fancy cut-glass bottle.

Cassie crouched low and then jumped.

Landing on the table, she slipped on the papers

and scrambled to regain her balance. She held her breath as the table swayed wildly. First to the left and then to the right. Finally it stopped. She breathed a sigh of relief.

Cassie looked up slowly to keep from shaking the table. Her heart sank.

The window was still too far away!

She inched closer to the wall, stopping to steady herself each time the table wobbled.

She pricked up her ears. She froze, listening. What was that sound? Was it Mr. Willard coming back or the table bumping against the floor? Or was it her pounding heart?

Slowly Cassie put her front paws against the wall and stood up on her hind legs. She edged her paws closer and closer to the window.

She stretched upward, straining every muscle. Farther. Farther, until one paw touched the sill.

But she still couldn't reach the handle.

Cassie pressed her tummy against the wall and stood on her toes, stretching as far as she could reach.

Please, she prayed silently, *please let me make it. Only . . . a . . . little . . . bit . . . farther.*

Cassie held her breath as she squeezed out the last bit of stretch she had in her.

She could feel the handle now.

She was touching it!

She tried to wrap her paw around it. Almost. Almost.

Suddenly the table wobbled. Her feet flew out from under her, and she came crashing down.

Oh, no! she cried.

The table swayed wildly, tipping from side to side like a boat in a storm.

Cassie tried to steady it but couldn't.

Suddenly she heard a sickening snap as a table leg broke. The table tilted, sending her sliding and clawing off the edge and down onto the floor.

The fancy cut-glass bottle flew in the air. It landed on the floor and shattered into a million pieces, splattering liquid everywhere.

Cassie lay in a heap, her head resting on the broken table. She looked back up at the window. It might as well be a million miles away.

It's no use! she thought. *He'll be back any minute. I'm finished.*

Sighing deeply, she dropped her head again to await her fate.

She felt a dampness under her chin and rolled her eyes to see what it was. Her big pink tongue was as dry as cardboard.

One last little drink to quench my thirst, she thought. She gently lapped at it, not worrying about drinking in slivers of broken glass. What difference did it make now?

The taste surprised her. *That's good,* she thought, lapping at it again. It was sweet and cool.

When every single bit of the liquid was gone, Cassie stumbled to her feet.

Swaying, she shook her head. She was suddenly dizzy.

She spread her feet to brace herself. The room started spinning. A loud humming noise started in her head.

Cassie tried to take a step, but it was all she could do to move her feet.

She leaned against the wall as sleepiness came rolling over her like giant waves.

I can't resist anymore. I give up. Her mind was almost too groggy to form the thought.

She was falling. Spiraling downward into darkness. But as her eyes closed, she remembered.

Cassie knew in that instant where she had tasted the liquid before!

When Cassie opened her eyes, she was sprawled across the floor. The storage room was deathly silent.

She raised her head and listened hard. Nothing. Had something happened to Mr. Willard?

She felt better, stronger. Her heart leaped. Maybe she could still get away!

She pushed herself up onto her hands and knees.

Hands! Knees!

Cassie gasped and looked down at herself.

Hands! Arms! Legs! Feet! No paws! No furry legs! She looked behind her.

Yessss! No tail!

"I'm a girl again!" she cried in disbelief.

She held her hands up in front of her eyes, wiggling her fingers and giggling.

121

Next she ran her hands down her long legs. Feet! I've got real girl-type feet! She crossed her eyes to see and gingerly patted her nose, her cheeks, her mouth.

She was normal! She felt giddy.

Cassie threw back her head and laughed out loud.

Then the memories came flooding back.

The sweet-tasting liquid she had lapped off the floor. She remembered now that it was pink! It was the same liquid Mr. Willard had given her when she was turned into a golden retriever.

"Here, drink this. It'll make you feel better," Mr. Willard had said.

She had felt dizzy. Had heard the humming sound. Then everything had gone black.

And when she had awakened . . . she was a dog!

That was how Mr. Willard got his custom pets! He found people who looked like the animals people ordered and changed them with his liquid.

It was impossible, but it had to be true. When she drank the liquid the second time, it changed her back into a girl.

Cassie scrambled to her feet. There was no time to lose. She had no idea how long she had been out.

She looked down at her body.

"Oh, no!" she whispered. "What did he do with my clothes?"

Frantically, Cassie looked in the cabinet under the sink. Nothing.

She looked on shelves and in drawers.

Then she saw a large cardboard box sitting next to the door. She opened it quickly and pulled out shirts, pants, blouses, and shoes. Halfway into the box she found her things. She put them on quickly.

Mr. Willard could come barging in any minute. With help. To put her to sleep.

Would it matter to him that she was a girl again? she wondered. Would it make him change his mind about killing her? Probably not, now that she knew his secret. Especially when he would have a syringe filled with poison in his hand.

Cassie headed for the door and stopped in her tracks. She could hear voices out in the pet shop.

"Back here! Come on!" It was Mr. Willard's voice. She heard footsteps outside the door. "Hurry!"

Whirling around, Cassie dashed for the window. She looked for something to climb up on. The table she had used before was a broken mess.

Frantically she shoved it out of the way and pushed a cart loaded with dog-food cases under the

123

window. She scrambled onto the boxes and reached the window easily!

Grabbing the handle, she tugged hard. The latch didn't give.

Stay cool! she told herself.

She put all her weight on it. This time the latch popped!

Cassie pushed the window open and wiggled through it—at the same time, she heard the storeroom door bang open.

She started to run. She ran across the park. Down sidewalks. Around corners. In and out of traffic.

She was *free!*

She was going home!

Chapter

28

As she ran, Cassie kept looking over her shoulder. Any minute she expected to see Mr. Willard's hulking form lumbering after her. Blood dripping from his arm. The poison-filled syringe held high in his hand.

But as she moved farther and farther away from Custom Pets, she began to relax. Even if he came after her, he'd be looking for a half-grown golden retriever. And he couldn't run that fast or far.

As she turned a corner, Cassie noticed a gray-and-white cat sitting on the branch of a tree. She stopped with a jolt when the cat let out a long, pitiful yowl.

Oh, my gosh, she thought. *That cat sounds just like the one in the back room of Custom Pets.*

Walking to the tree, she peered up at the cat. "Kitty, kitty," she called.

"Meooow," cried the cat.

Cassie swallowed hard. "Are you okay, kitty?" Looking around to make sure no one was near, she added in a whisper, "Are you trying to tell me something? Did you used to be a person?"

The cat blinked its eyes and looked back at her, but it didn't make a sound.

"Wag your tail if the answer is yes," she whispered again.

The cat just stared at her.

Cassie hurried on, feeling a little foolish. At the same time, she couldn't shake the eerie feeling that the cat may have come from Custom Pets. Maybe there were lots of kids like herself who had been turned into animals. What about the other clothes in the box?

Would she be able to tell if she saw an animal from Mr. Willard's store? And would she be able to communicate with it? She had never found out if Cuda had understood her.

A little farther along the street a teenage girl was coming toward her. She was walking a champagne-colored poodle on a leash.

Cassie stared at the dog as it came closer. It had a blue satin bow in its hair. It looked perfectly content as it trotted along beside its mistress. As it got near, it looked at her and let out a little yip.

Have you always been a dog? Cassie wanted to ask. As they passed, the dog looked back at her.

Are you trying to send me a message? Cassie wondered.

All the rest of the way home she kept an eye out for Cuda. *Poor Cuda,* she thought. *I'll bet he was a person and Mr. Willard turned him into a dog.*

But who was he before? she wondered. *Was he my age? I'll try to find him in a day or so,* she promised herself. *At any rate, one thing is certain. I'll never set foot in Custom Pets again!*

127

Chapter

29

Cassie and her parents talked late into the night. They were so glad to have her home, they believed her story about having amnesia and not knowing where she had been. She knew it was a far-out story, but it was the best she could do. There was no way she could tell them the truth. She could hardly believe what had happened herself.

The next morning was Saturday, and she hurried to the phone to call Suki. She was dying to tell her best friend that she was home.

It seemed like a whole lifetime had passed since she'd last seen Suki. Cassie listened excitedly as the phone rang. One ring. Two rings.

"Come on, Suki," she whispered anxiously. "Be there."

Cassie could scarcely hide her disappointment when Mrs. Chen answered and said that Suki had gone out.

"But she'll be so happy to know that you're home safe and sound," said Mrs. Chen. "I'll have her call you the moment she gets home."

After they hung up, Cassie wandered restlessly around her bedroom. Her mind was filled with disturbing images: Mr. Willard chasing her around the storeroom with the syringe filled with poison. Obedience school and Bruiser. Hunting birds. Eating dog food out of a bowl on the floor. Quadruple yuck!

There was a soft tap on her door.

Her mother called, "Cassie, may your dad and I come in? We have a little surprise for you."

"Sure," said Cassie, swinging the door open for them.

Her mouth dropped open, and she gasped with pleasure when she saw what her mother was holding.

"A dog!" she cried. "Isn't she cute. Whose is she? Where did she come from?"

"She's yours, sweetheart," said her dad. "She's a Pekingese, and we knew you'd love her."

"While you were missing, we talked over our objections to a pet. We decided we were being overprotective," said her mother. She put the fluffy little dog in Cassie's outstretched arms. "We knew how badly you wanted a dog, so we went to a pet shop a few minutes ago and got her for you. We hope you like her."

Cassie took the squirming bundle of fur in her arms. The little dog's eyes were sparkling. She licked Cassie on the cheek and then hopped out of her arms, barking a high-pitched little bark.

"Thanks, Mom. Thanks, Dad. She's beautiful, and I love her already."

As soon as her parents left her room, Cassie knelt to the floor beside her new pet.

"You are absolutely the *cutest* dog I've ever seen!" she said. "I'll have to think of a perfect name for you."

The little dog was a bundle of energy. She bounced up and down and raced around and around the room.

Cassie bent double with laughter. "You're so funny! You remind me of my best friend, Suki."

Suddenly the little dog stopped running. It looked up at Cassie with pleading eyes. Then without warning it turned a perfect back flip.

Cassie stopped cold and stared at the dog.

"Suki!?"

HERE'S A SNEAK PREVIEW OF BONE
CHILLERS #3: BACK TO SCHOOL

Fitz Traflon scowled into the trash can. Running across the top of the junk inside was a giant brown cockroach. Fitz held the empty peanut-butter jar directly over it.

"Bombs away! *Boom!*" he said as he dropped the jar.

He picked up the jar and looked under it. The cockroach's antennae were still moving, so he squashed it.

Most of his buddies were fascinated by bugs, but not Fitz. He hated them.

He picked up the peanut-butter-and-jelly sandwich he had been making and stuffed it into his bulging backpack. With his luck, it would be squashed, just like the cockroach, by lunchtime. A brown-and-purple gooey mess.

"I can't believe it's my twelfth birthday *and* the first day of school. What a *rotten* way to spend my birthday."

Fitz trudged out of the house and down the sidewalk. He was thinking about all his other birthdays.

They had each fallen a day or two before the start of school. They had been *fun*! Parties with cake and presents and all his friends. Trips to the water park or the zoo. Never before in his life had his birthday fallen on the crummy first day of school.

He was still grumbling to himself when he arrived at Maple Grove Middle School. He stopped on the sidewalk and looked at the two-story red-brick building. It looked just like it had last year.

Like a prison.

Fitz sighed and shoved his hands in his pockets. He hated school. Same old stuff year after year. Except each year it got harder. He had hoped all summer that school would be different this year.

Fun, maybe.

Different, at least.

Obviously he was going to be out of luck.

"Hey, Fitz! Guess what?"

He looked around to see Sarah Cherone and Lexi Palmer rushing toward him.

Oh, no. Not those two, Fitz thought.

They were giggling and gushing.

"Hi, Fitz," said Sarah. She batted her eyelashes at him the way she always did. It was disgusting. Then she and Lexi giggled again.

"Hi," he mumbled.

134

"You're never going to believe this," Lexi went on breathlessly. "Tell him, Sarah."

"Yeah, Fitz. Our school has a new cook!"

"Big deal," he replied. "Who cares about a crummy cook?"

"You will when you see her," Lexi assured him. "This cook is seriously weird."

"Her name's Miss Larva Webb, and she's got—" Sarah went on, but Fitz tuned her out.

He couldn't stand to listen to her. She bugged him all the time. Fitz hated all girls, but he hated Sarah the most.

"Hey, Traflon. Over here."

Brian's voice cut into Fitz's thoughts.

"What's up?" he called as he hurried toward Brian.

"Have I ever got something to show you," Brian said excitedly.

"What is it?" Fitz asked as he trotted beside his best friend.

"You'll see," said Brian.

"Hey, Brian. What's the big mystery? Come on, tell me," Fitz insisted.

"You've got to see it yourself to believe it," said Brian.

The moment Fitz realized they were heading toward the cafeteria, he tugged on Brian's sleeve. "This doesn't have anything to do with the new cook, does it?" he asked.

Brian nodded. "Wait 'til you see her."

"Come on, Brian," Fitz insisted. "Give me a break. What's the big deal about a cook?"

Brian pushed open the double doors to the lunchroom and shoved Fitz in. He pulled Fitz down behind a table and pointed toward the cook who was polishing the empty steam tables with a cloth.

Fitz rolled his eyes in exasperation. He'd seen cooks before. Lots of them. And this one didn't look that different. She was an older lady with white curly hair. She was wearing a white apron, and a tall chef's hat was perched on her head. The strangest thing about her that Fitz could see was the large dark sunglasses she was wearing.

"She looks pretty normal to me, except for the glasses," Fitz whispered.

Suddenly he did a double take.

The cook was wearing a weird-looking necklace. It was a chain with lots of little baubles hanging from it.

He frowned. "Am I seeing things?" he whispered, squinting at the necklace. The baubles seemed to be moving.

Fitz raised his head so that he could see better. His eyes flew open in alarm. The baubles on her necklace were *bugs*.

And they were alive!

BACK TO SCHOOL

In memory of the real Miss Buggy Webb,
my seventh grade teacher, who taught me about
insects in a much nicer way.

Chapter
1

Fitz Traflon scowled into the trash can. Running across the top of the empty cans and cartons and congealed spaghetti inside was a giant brown cockroach. It was at least as big as Fitz's thumb. He wrinkled his nose in disgust. Then he held the empty peanut-butter jar directly over it.

"Bombs away!" he said as he dropped the jar.

He picked up the jar and looked under it. The cockroach's antennae were still moving. Aiming carefully, he shoved the jar into the garbage as hard as he could. Then he lifted it once more, surveying the now-smushed cockroach with satisfaction.

Most of his friends were fascinated by

bugs, but not Fitz. He hated them. He didn't really know why, but he'd been completely disgusted by anything creepy or crawly ever since he could remember.

Grabbing his peanut-butter-and-jelly sandwich from the counter, he stuffed it into his bulging backpack. With his luck it would be as smushed as the cockroach by lunchtime. A brown and purple gooey mess.

"Who cares?" he muttered under his breath. "I can't believe it's my twelfth birthday *and* the first day of school. What a rotten way to celebrate."

As Fitz headed for the back door, his mother looked up from the crossword puzzle she was working on at the kitchen table. "Have a nice day, dear," she said cheerily.

"And happy birthday, son," added his father, setting down his coffee cup and smiling at Fitz over the top of the newspaper.

Fitz grunted, then he trudged out of the house and down the sidewalk. He was thinking about past birthdays. Every year until now, his birthday had fallen a day or two before the start of school. It had been an awesome way to celebrate the end of summer vacation—his parents always took

6

him and a group of his friends to the amusement park or some other fun place. But today the only place he was going was to school. Ugh.

He was still grumbling to himself when he arrived at Maple Grove Middle School. He stopped on the sidewalk and looked up at the two-story red brick building. It looked just like it had last year.

Like a prison.

Fitz sighed and shoved his hands into his pockets. He hated school. Every year it was the same old stuff—except that every year it got harder and harder. He had hoped all summer that this year things would change—that school would be fun, maybe. Or at least different somehow.

But as he stared at the familiar grim front of the school building, he had a sinking feeling that he was going to be out of luck.

"Hi, Fitz! Guess what?"

He looked around to see Sarah Cherone and Lexi Palmer rushing towards him. Sarah had curly blond hair and was kind of chubby. There were two things she liked. One was food—and the other was Fitz.

Sarah's best friend, Lexi, had straight brown hair, was thin, and wore glasses. Fitz didn't really know her very well. All he knew was that she was kind of a nerd. She had all kinds of allergies, and half her school lunch was always vitamins and pills.

"Hi, Fitz," Sarah said again. She batted her eyelashes at him the way she always did. It was disgusting. Then she and Lexi giggled.

"Hi," he mumbled, feeling grumpier than ever. The last thing he wanted to do on his birthday was get stuck talking to Sarah. That was even worse than having to go to school. Well, almost.

"You're never going to believe this," Lexi said breathlessly. "Tell him, Sarah."

"Yeah, Fitz. Our school has a new cook!"

Fitz frowned at her as if she'd lost her mind. "Big deal," he replied. "Who cares about a crummy cook?"

"You will when you see her," Lexi assured him. "This cook is seriously weird."

"Her name's Miss Larva Webb, and she's got—" Sarah went on, but Fitz tuned her out.

He couldn't stand to listen to her. She bugged him all the time. The year before, she had told his best friend, Brian Collins, that she liked Fitz. She was always passing him stupid notes in class. Sometimes they had hearts drawn on them. Stupid hearts with stupid arrows stuck through them. Fitz hated all girls, but he hated Sarah the most.

"Hey, Traflon. Over here."

Brian's voice cut into Fitz's thoughts. He spun around, breaking into a grin—his first smile of the day. Good old Brian. He'd save Fitz from the girls' ridiculous gossiping about the new cook.

"What's up?" Fitz called as he hurried toward Brian.

"Hey, happy birthday, man. I've got something to show you," Brian said excitedly. "Come on."

"What is it?" Fitz asked as he followed his best friend toward the school building.

"You'll see," said Brian.

"What's the big mystery?" Fitz asked. He wondered if Brian had some kind of surprise birthday present for him inside. Maybe this birthday wouldn't turn out to be a total loss. Fitz eagerly tried to figure out what the surprise could be. "Come on, tell me," he begged.

"No way. You've got to see it yourself to believe it," said Brian, pulling open the heavy front door and hurrying inside.

The moment Fitz realized they were heading toward the cafeteria, his heart sank with a thud. "This doesn't have anything to do with the new cook, does it?" he asked.

Brian nodded and grinned. "Just wait until you see her."

"Give me a break, Brian," Fitz said, his bad mood returning instantly. "What's the big deal about a stupid new cook?"

Brian pushed open the big double doors to the lunchroom and dragged him inside. Pulling Fitz down behind a table, Brian pointed toward a pudgy woman who was polishing the empty steam tables with a cloth. Her back was to them, but Fitz could hear her humming tunelessly as she worked.

Fitz rolled his eyes in exasperation. The cook was an older woman with curly white hair. A white apron was tied around her ample waist, and a tall chef's hat was perched on her head. She didn't look much different from any other school cook Fitz had ever seen—although when she turned her head a little, he noticed that she was wearing large dark sunglasses.

"She looks pretty normal to me, except for

the glasses," Fitz whispered. "Maybe she's blind or something."

"She's not blind. But just wait until she turns around," Brian urged, his eyes glittering.

Fitz shrugged, rolled his eyes, and waited. Finally the woman turned to dip her rag into a bucket behind her, and Fitz did a double take.

The cook was wearing a weird-looking necklace. It was a chain with lots of little baubles hanging from it. And the baubles seemed to be moving!

Fitz frowned. "Am I seeing things?" he whispered, squinting at the necklace.

Brian shook his head. "No way."

Fitz raised his head to get a better look. His eyes widened, and he gasped in horror. The baubles on the cook's necklace were *bugs.*

And they were alive!

Chapter 2

"Let's get out of here," Fitz whispered to Brian under his breath.

Brian nodded. But at that moment the cook looked up and spotted them.

"Boys, I'm so glad you came by to say hello," she exclaimed happily.

She was smiling. She looked like somebody's grandmother, except for the sunglasses—and, of course, the wiggling bugs around her neck. The sight of the necklace made Fitz's skin crawl.

"Come over here, boys, and introduce yourselves," she ordered.

Fitz and Brian hesitated for a second. But then they did as they were told.

As they got closer to the cook, Fitz stared at her necklace. The bugs seemed to have stopped moving. In fact, the more closely he inspected them, the more they looked like little plastic models.

How could I have thought they were alive? he wondered.

"I see you like my necklace," said the cook. "Pretty little things, aren't they?" She held it up so they could see. The bugs were made of plastic.

"You didn't think they were real, did you?" she asked Fitz, turning to look at him. Or at least Fitz assumed she was looking at him. With those huge dark glasses covering her eyes it was hard to tell. For a second Fitz had the eerie feeling that the huge, round black lenses *were* her eyes.

He suddenly realized he was staring openmouthed at the necklace. He shook his head, feeling a little dizzy.

The cook laughed out loud. "Oh, my! That's funny. Of course they're not real. They'd never allow me to bring bugs into the kitchen. Everyone knows bugs and food don't mix!" She laughed even harder at that.

Then, turning serious, she went on. "My

13

name is Miss Larva Webb. But you boys can call me Miss Larva. I hope we can become great friends."

Fitz was still staring at the necklace. He couldn't tear his gaze away from it. He saw that there was a long-legged praying mantis near the center and a couple of fat grasshoppers on either side. There were wasps, termites, and a dragonfly up one side of the chain, and a few beetles, a moth, and a giant water bug on the other side. Fitz had never seen anything like it.

Suddenly he felt Brian nudge him.

He shot a quick look at his friend, who nodded toward the cook's smiling face.

"Young man, weren't you listening? I said, I hope we can be great friends."

Fitz gulped nervously and tried once again to see her eyes through the dark lenses of her sunglasses.

"Uh, yeah, um, me too. N-nice to meet you, Miss Larva," he stammered.

"My name is Brian Collins," Brian told the cook politely. "He's Fitz Traflon."

"I see you're still admiring my necklace, Fitz. I'm very flattered. You see, I made it myself. Isn't it lovely?" Miss Larva said proudly. "I'm an amateur entomologist—a

14

bug person. I've been studying insects from the time I could crawl. I've learned some fascinating things in that time." She touched the necklace lovingly. "Including how to make friends with all the dear little bugs. This necklace reminds me of them when we can't be together." Her voice was almost a purr.

Fitz backed slowly toward the door. "Um, your necklace is really nice. We'd better get going now," he said. He knew his voice was shaking. "Nice to meet you Miss Bug—er, Miss Larva."

"Yeah, nice to meet you," echoed Brian.

The boys exchanged looks of relief as they headed for the cafeteria door.

Suddenly something darted across the floor in front of Fitz.

"Yuck! A cockroach!" he cried. Racing after it, he smashed his foot down on top of it and heard a soft squishing sound. "I hate cockroaches," he mumbled with a shudder as he stood over the oozing, flattened bug and watched it flail its tiny legs jerkily in the air.

"What have you done!" shrieked Miss Larva. She rushed over to the squished cockroach and dropped to her hands and

15

knees. "That's Gregory! He's one of my pets!"

Fitz watched in disbelief as the cook prodded the roach with the tip of her fingernail. The sight made him want to vomit.

"Gregory? Gregory, my sweet?" Miss Larva cooed softly. "It's Mommy. Give me a sign that you're alive, my baby."

The cockroach slowly kicked two of its legs. Once. Twice. And then the legs stopped, frozen in midair.

"Gregory?" Miss Larva cried. "Don't die. You can't die. *Please* don't die!"

She gently poked at the insect again, but there was no response. His legs were still.

She gently picked up Gregory and laid him inside one cupped hand. Then, with tears streaming down her face, she slowly got to her feet and carried him over to the lunchroom counter. She pulled a paper napkin out of a holder and folded it into a small square. Tenderly she put Gregory down on the napkin and gave a soft sigh of resignation.

Then, her face smoldering with rage, she whirled to face Fitz. As she did, her dark glasses slipped down her nose.

"*Murderer*," she hissed.

16

Fitz stared at her, unable to speak. Her eyes, clearly visible for the first time, were burning into his.

He stepped back, his heart pounding. Miss Larva's eyes were different from any human eyes he had ever seen. He wanted to look away, but he couldn't. He stared into them, seeing that each of her unusually large pupils was made up of hundreds of tiny little eyes, each looking in a slightly different direction.

Where had he seen eyes like that before? Then he remembered—he'd seen them in a close-up photograph in his science book last year. *Miss Larva's eyes looked just like the eyes of a fly.*

17

Chapter
3

"Didn't I say you'd have to see her to believe her?" Brian asked as soon as the boys were out in the hall again.

"Yeah," replied Fitz. "She's really weird. Did you see her eyes?"

Brian shook his head. "Nah, I was too busy looking at the bugs on her necklace. I almost thought they were alive when I first saw them. But even though they're only plastic, it's still pretty wild! Can you imagine any other adult wearing something like that?"

Fitz opened his mouth to tell Brian about the cook's eyes and then stopped himself. Now that he was away from the cafeteria, it didn't seem real. Maybe he'd just imagined that her eyes looked like the eyes of a fly. After all, he was still pretty shaken up by his two roach encounters that day. He decided to do his best to forget all about Miss Larva Webb.

That morning Fitz had a hard time concentrating on school. For one thing his teacher, Mrs Dewberry, assigned Sarah Cherone the seat directly in front of him. As she flounced over to her seat and flashed him a grin, Fitz sighed. It was going to be a long year.

It was bad enough that Sarah couldn't sit still and that her wiggling caused strands of her short, curly blond hair to bounce in front of his eyes like springs. But to make it worse, she was constantly looking over her shoulder and batting her eyes at him.

Once when the teacher's back was turned, Sarah spun around and gave him a toothy grin. "Have you seen the new cook yet, Fitz?"

Fitz heaved a bored sigh and looked at the ceiling. He didn't answer. Finally she took the hint and turned around again.

He was glad. But Sarah's comment started him thinking about Miss Larva. He shook his head as he remembered how he had almost called her Miss Buggy to her face. Still, it would have been a better name for her.

What kind of weirdo wears bugs on her necklace and keeps a cockroach named Gregory for a pet? he wondered. *And those eyes!* He couldn't stop the shudder that ran through him when he thought of her buggy fly eyes—even though by now he had almost convinced himself that he'd imagined the whole thing.

The morning seemed to drag on forever. English was boring. Math was boring. But in the middle of social studies, Fitz began to notice an appetizing smell drifting into the classroom. He sniffed the air curiously.

Is it my imagination, he wondered, *or do I smell pizza?*

He looked at the clock above Mrs Dewberry's desk. It was almost time for lunch.

Fitz took a deep breath, inhaling the delicious aroma. It was definitely pizza. But it didn't smell like the crummy pizza the cafeteria usually served. The crust on that pizza had been tougher than cardboard, and the cheese had tasted like plastic. That pizza had been one of the reasons Fitz had started bringing his lunch from home.

But this pizza smelled delicious.

Closing his eyes, Fitz began daydreaming about thick, tangy tomato sauce and spicy pepperoni. This was more like it—the perfect birthday lunch. He couldn't believe his luck. His stomach was roaring by the time the lunch bell rang.

He had bolted out of his seat and pushed his way to the door before he remembered he had brought his lunch. Sighing, he went back to his desk and pulled out his smushed and soggy sandwich and walked to the lunchroom. The closer he got to the cafeteria, the better the pizza smelled.

"Some birthday lunch," he grumbled. He wished he had enough money to buy a slice of pizza, but his pockets were empty.

"Smells good, huh?" Brian asked sadly when he and Fitz found a table.

Fitz nodded and gazed longingly toward some kids at the next table who were eating pizza. "Get a load of that," he said. "Look how big and thick those slices are."

"Yeah," Brian agreed, nibbling halfheartedly on his bologna sandwich. "And there's so much cheese on them that it strings out as far as their arms can reach."

"Yeah," said Fitz enviously.

"I'll tell you one thing, if Miss Larva is

21

this good a cook, I'm not bringing my lunch tomorrow." Brian pitched his sandwich onto the table in disgust. "Are you?"

"I dunno," muttered Fitz. He couldn't help remembering how much Miss Larva liked bugs and how much he hated them. And he also remembered how she had yelled at him for stepping on her pet cockroach.

I'm not sure I could eat anything Miss Buggy cooked, no matter how good it looked, he thought.

Just then the kitchen door swung open, and Miss Larva came marching out. There was a big smile on her face, and her chef's hat sat high on her head. She was carrying a huge three-tiered cake on a gigantic platter in front of her. The cake looked fantastic. It was over four feet high, and every layer was slathered with thick white frosting.

To Fitz's amazement Miss Larva marched straight over to where he was sitting and set the cake squarely in front of him. His mouth dropped open. Written on the cake in fancy letters were the words:

HAPPY BIRTHDAY, FITZGERALD
TRAFLON III

22

Fitz looked at the cake, then at the cook, and then back at the cake again. Miss Larva was beaming at him expectantly.

"Brian, did you tell her it's my birthday?" he demanded in a whisper.

"No way," Brian insisted. "You'd have heard me if I had, dude."

By that time the other kids in the cafeteria had spotted the cake and were gathering around the boys' table.

"Hey, Fitz," shouted Jeff McCormick. "How about a piece?"

"Yeah, Fitz. I hope you're going to share," said Sarah, gazing hungrily at the towering cake from the next table, where she was sitting with Lexi.

"Of course he's going to share," said Miss Larva. She produced paper dessert plates and extra forks from the large pockets of her apron and began cutting the cake into pieces.

Mrs Dewberry stood up at her table and clapped her hands. "Let's all sing 'Happy Birthday' to Fitz," she suggested with a smile.

Fitz looked around in amazement as the entire lunchroom began singing to him.

Maybe this isn't going to be such a bad birthday after all, he thought.

When the song was finished, Miss Larva held up her hand for silence. "The birthday boy gets the first bite," she announced loudly.

There were a few groans from the crowd, but most kids held up their forks to signal that they were waiting.

"Go ahead," urged Sarah.

"Yeah, hurry up so we can eat ours," said Brian. "It looks awesome."

The cake looked so delicious, his mouth was watering. Fitz pushed all the doubts he'd had about Miss Larva to the back of his mind. He scooped up a bite of cake on his fork. "Hey, look. It's got chocolate chips in it," he cried, popping the cake into his mouth and swallowing it.

"Oh, no, those aren't chocolate chips," said Miss Larva, shaking her head. "They're much better for you than chocolate chips." A grin spread across her pudgy face. "They're chocolate-covered ants!"

"Ha-ha," said Jeff McCormick, rolling his eyes as he wolfed down his slice of cake. "Good one, Miss Larva!" The rest of the kids started laughing, too.

All except for Fitz. He was too busy gagging.

Chapter
4

Fitz stuck his finger down his throat and retched. But nothing came up. He thought about dozens of chocolate-covered ants swimming around in his stomach. He retched harder.

Lexi was giving him a disgusted look from the next table. Fitz noticed that she hadn't touched her slice of cake. He figured she must be allergic to it, like she was to just about everything else.

Fitz was about to stick two fingers down his throat when Miss Larva climbed onto a chair and held up her hands for silence.

"Children, listen to me!" she shouted. "I want you to know that ants are dear little creatures while they're alive. But once they die, and their little bodies are dipped in chocolate, they make wonderful food. And so do many of our other little six-legged friends—fried grasshoppers, for instance. Why, in many parts of the world they're considered a delicacy."

Fitz stopped trying to throw up and listened. Everyone else was listening, too. He noticed some of the teachers exchanging smiles. The principal, Mr Gladstone, winked at Mrs Dewberry and chuckled.

"And best of all," Miss Larva went on, stabbing the air with a finger for emphasis. 'Best of all, boys and girls, they are *protein*, the building blocks of the body. They are very nutritious. Now, isn't that wonderful?"

"Thank you, Miss Larva, for that very interesting bit of information," said Mr Gladstone with a grin. By this time most of the kids and teachers were laughing. Some of them applauded when Miss Larva gave a little bow and headed back toward the kitchen.

Fitz stared down at the cake on his plate. Had Miss Larva really been kidding about the chocolate-covered ants? Most of his classmates seemed to think so. Many of them had already returned for second or even third helpings of the cake. Fitz had to admit that the one bite he had taken had tasted pretty good. Actually, it had tasted terrific. He picked up his fork, and he finished his cake in three more bites. But he secretly picked out the chocolate chips and hid them in his napkin—just in case.

The next day a lot of kids who normally brought their lunches from home were in the line to buy lunch, including Brian.

Fitz had thought about it that morning, but he still didn't quite trust Miss Larva. Once again he brought a peanut-butter-and-jelly sandwich from home. He didn't want to eat anything else the new cook made until he knew more about what she was putting into the food.

He clutched his sandwich and watched as Miss Larva filled other students' plates with big juicy cheeseburgers and french fries. Fitz's mouth watered furiously.

"Not a bad-looking burger," he said, looking at Brian's plate. "But I'd rather have my lunch."

"Uh-huh," said Brian, giving Fitz a skeptical look. "Sure you would."

Fitz grinned slyly. "Didn't you hear that Miss Buggy's french fries are really fried grasshoppers?"

"Cool," said Brian, popping one of his fries into his mouth and chewing noisily. "Grasshoppers are the building blocks of the body, you know." He grinned, revealing the partially chewed contents of his mouth. Fitz's stomach gave a shudder. Was it his imagination, or did the chewed-up french fry look a little green?

"Forget it," Fitz said, looking away.

But Brian wasn't through. "See, what Miss Larva does," he said, "is she grinds up the grasshoppers in this big meat grinder. Then when she's got this big mushy mess, she shapes it to look like french fries and cooks them. Yum yum." He popped another one into his mouth.

Fitz made a face. "Yeah, well, I wouldn't put it past Miss Buggy," he muttered, staring down at his sandwich.

Brian stared straight at Ftiz for a moment and frowned. "You're just jealous, man. It's nobody's fault but your own that you're missing out on this great food. Now, quit calling her Miss Buggy and pass the mustard."

Fitz looked around for the mustard, but there wasn't any on the table. "You'll have to borrow from another table," he said.

Brian picked up another long, golden french fry and stuffed it into his mouth. Fitz watched Brian chew his french fry. He looked at Brian's burger. The smell was driving him crazy.

"How'd Miss Bug-Larva know my full name was Fitzgerald Traflon the Third?" asked Fitz. "Did you tell her?"

"How could I have?" said Brian. "I told you, you were with me in the kitchen, remember? Now, come on, where's the mustard? I need it for my burger."

Usually there was salt, pepper, mustard, and ketchup on each lunch table. Fitz glanced around at the other tables. There was salt, pepper, and ketchup on all of them, but no mustard.

"I guess you'll have to go ask for some," said Fitz with a shrug.

Brian got up and hurried over to the cook, who was still standing behind the steam table. Fitz was left alone at the table.

Maybe I could steal one french fry, thought Fitz. *Brian would never know.*

Fitz's hand was inching across the table

toward the biggest fry on the plate when he heard Miss Larva let out a roar.

"*Mustard!* How dare you ask for mustard?" she shouted. Her face was beet-red, and her hands were clenched into fists. "I never allow mustard in my cafeteria. It's *terrible* on food. Now, go eat your lunch!"

Fitz pulled his hand away just in time as Brian raced back to the table.

"Did you see that?" Brian asked in astonishment, glancing back at the cook. "What tripped her trigger? All I did was ask for mustard."

"Who knows?" said Fitz with a shrug. "Maybe she's having a bad hair day or something." He stared at Brian's french fries. Even without mustard he'd rather have Brian's lunch than his own. His peanut-butter sandwich was sticking to the roof of his mouth like concrete.

Maybe tomorrow, he thought hungrily.

Chapter
5

The next morning Lexi stopped Fitz as he was coming into the playground.

"Can I talk to you for a minute?" she asked.

Fitz rolled his eyes. He had enough problems. He had decided to bring his lunch from home again today, and now he was regretting it. He was already in a bad mood, and talking to a girl wasn't likely to help.

"What do you want?" mumbled Fitz. He realized he'd never really talked to Lexi before unless Sarah was there, too.

"You aren't going to buy your lunch today, are you?" Lexi asked urgently.

Fitz frowned. "What's it to you?"

"I was just wondering," said Lexi, looking a little hurt.

Fitz instantly felt guilty for snapping at her. He wished she would go away and leave him alone, but she just stood there staring at him.

Finally he sighed and said, "No, I brought my lunch."

"I'm glad," said Lexi, looking relieved.

"Why do you care?" Fitz asked, a little curious in spite of himself.

Lexi held out her hand. In it were four dark-red specks. They looked like dead ants.

"What's that?" asked Fitz, leaning forward for a closer look.

"They're insects. They belong to the genus . . ."

"Whoa, you're as bad as Miss Buggy!" said Fitz, backing away from her. "They're ants!" *Why does she have to be such a nerd?* he wondered. "Don't give them to me. I don't want them."

"I wasn't going to give them to you. I just wanted you to see them," she replied irritably.

"So I see them. So what?"

"I took some of the chocolate chips from the birthday cake Miss Larva made you the other day," she explained. "These were in them. She wasn't kidding."

Fitz did a double take. He stared at the dead ant bodies in Lexi's hand. "No way," he said.

"Way," she replied, looking smug. "I just thought you should know. I don't know about you, but I'm certainly not going to eat any of Miss Bug—er . . . Miss Larva's cooking."

Fitz looked at her in disbelief. Was Lexi making this up? Or had there really been ants in the cake? Things were getting weirder and weirder. He mumbled something about having to get to homeroom and hurried away. When he glanced back over his shoulder, though, Lexi was still staring after him.

At lunch that day Fitz watched as the students and teachers crowded into line. Miss Larva was behind the steam table as usual, serving up heaping portions of tacos, refried beans, and rice.

When Brian came out of the lunch line, he hurried over to the table and sat down across from Fitz. He immediately started digging into his food without even saying hello.

Fitz looked nervously at the food on Brian's plate. Were the little lumps in the beans really beans—or were they some kind of beetle? And the rice. Were all those little white grains really rice—or could they be maggots?

Fitz tried to put those crazy thoughts out of his mind. Brian's plate wasn't full of beetles and maggots. It was full of beans and rice. Still, Fitz had seen maggots once when he had forgotten to empty a can of fishing worms for a couple of weeks in the summertime. And that was exactly what they had looked like—a can full of squirming grains of rice.

While Brian wolfed down his food, Fitz munched halfheartedly on his sandwich and cautiously looked around. Ordinarily the room was filled with the sounds of kids talking and laughing as they ate. But at that moment all the kids had their heads down and were shovelling food into their mouths in silence. Even the teachers were stuffing tacos into their mouths as fast as they could.

He scanned the room for Lexi. She was sitting at a table with Sarah, and she was watching the others eat, too. She noticed Fitz looking at her and she shrugged. Then she popped one of her allergy pills into her mouth.

Miss Larva was standing behind the steam table, beaming benevolently at the students and teachers. She sighed and absently removed her sunglasses to wipe them off.

Suddenly she saw Fitz looking at her. Her smile froze as she stared back at him.

Even from that distance he could see the hundreds of tiny irises of her fly's eyes glaring at him. Her eyes seemed to have grown larger since the first time he'd seen them. He wanted to look away, but he couldn't. His gaze was fixed on those eyes.

A moment later a sudden motion across the room finally dragged Fitz's attention away. It was Lexi. She was standing up, her face a ghostly white. Instantly Fitz understood. Lexi was staring at Miss Larva's eyes, and there was a look of terror on her face.

Chapter
6

After lunch Fitz followed Brian to the tray-return window.

Before he put his tray through the window, Brian licked the remaining beans off his plate. He grinned at Fitz. "Awesome," he said. "You really ought to try Miss Larva's cooking, Fitz. You don't know what you're missing."

As they headed for the exit, Fitz spotted a hand-printed sign tacked to the bulletin board just inside the door. "Hey, Brian. Check it out," he said. The boys stopped to read the sign.

ATTENTION ALL STUDENTS

Come to the cafeteria after school today

and learn all about some new and

wonderful creatures.

You'll be amazed!

You've never seen anything like them before!

Miss Larva Webb

"Wow, what do you think that's all about?" Brian asked excitedly.

Fitz shrugged. "I dunno," he said. He was still thinking more about Lexi and Miss Larva's weird eyes than about the sign.

"Are you going?" asked Brian.

"No, I've got better things to do after school," Fitz replied. "Are you?"

"Sure. I wouldn't miss it for anything," Brian said. "I can't believe you don't want to go."

The bell rang before Fitz could answer. All through his afternoon classes Fitz couldn't stop thinking about Miss Larva. Now that Lexi had seen her eyes, too, Fitz knew that they had to be real. He wondered whether he should tell his parents or Mr

Gladstone. But he decided that if he tried to tell them the new school cook had eyes like a fly, they would just think he was crazy. He had to find out more about Miss Larva first. And the best way to do that, he realized, was to go to the meeting in the cafeteria after school.

As soon as the final bell rang, Fitz hurried to the cafeteria. There he spotted Brian at a long table near the front.

Brian looked surprised for a second and then gestured for Fitz to join him. There was only one empty seat left at the table, and Fitz squeezed through the crowd and dropped into it.

"Thought you weren't coming," said Brian. He grinned slyly. "I guess you just couldn't resist Miss Larva's charm, could you?"

"Chill out, okay?" Fitz retorted. He looked around the room. It looked as though every student in the whole school was there.

Suddenly the doors to the kitchen swung open, and Miss Larva came bumping into the room, her arms loaded with small wire cages. Each cage was covered with cloth, hiding what was inside.

Brian leaned closer to Fitz. "What do you

think she's got in those cages? Something weird?"

Fitz shook his head. "Couldn't be any weirder than she is," he muttered.

Miss Larva set the cages in a row on a table. Then she bent over each of them, cooing softly as if she were talking to the creatures inside.

Fitz squirmed uneasily in his seat and glanced to his right. Lexi was sitting across the aisle next to Sarah. She was staring at Miss Larva's cages.

"Maybe Miss Buggy's got Gregory's brothers and sisters in those cages," Fitz whispered to Brian. "What if she turns them loose and lets them crawl all over everybody?" Fitz had meant it to be a joke, but he was embarrassed to hear that his voice was shaking.

Luckily, Brian didn't seem to notice. "Cool," he whispered back with a grin, his eyes fixed on the cages.

"She probably has them all named, like Timothy and Robert and Jordan, and she'll throw a fit if anyone says something mean about one of her babies," Fitz went on, more to himself than to Brian. He shuddered.

"Check it out," whispered Brian. Miss

Larva was holding up her hands for attention. Instantly all eyes were on her.

Fitz looked her over closely. She was wearing her sunglasses as usual, and the plastic bugs on her necklace swung around as she moved her arms.

"Thank you for coming, boys and girls," Miss Larva began. "As many of you already know, I'm an amateur entomologist—a bug person."

Laughter rippled through the crowd.

"I study insects," she went on. "I also study spiders. I hope this program and many more like it will inspire some of you to become interested in my fascinating hobby."

Murmurs raced through the room like wildfire.

"Ugh."

"No way!"

"Get serious."

Miss Larva smiled patiently. When everybody was quiet again, she continued. "Many people fear insects needlessly. Actually, most are quite harmless. The dear little creatures are fun to watch and easy to get acquainted with. Why, I'll bet there are some of you who've had ant farms, so you know that already."

"No way," mumbled Fitz to himself. He would never have an ant farm.

"But most of all, they are fun to experiment with," the cook said. She paused for a moment to let this statement sink in. "Yes, that's what I said. They're fun to experiment with, and I'm going to show you the results of some of my finest experiments."

Fitz exchanged nervous glances with Brian. Neither boy could imagine what was coming next.

The cook picked up one of the cages, but didn't remove the cloth cover. "My greatest joy is crossbreeding. That means I take one kind of insect and breed it with another kind to see what kind of amazing and fascinating creature I will get. For instance . . ." She held the cage high so everyone could see, and pulled off the cover with a flourish.

Fitz gasped. "Whoa, Brian, look at that thing!"

". . . I crossed a tarantula and a centipede, and look what I got," said Miss Larva proudly.

She reached into the cage and pulled out

41

a huge wiggling insect. Its body was long and narrow like a centipede's, and it had at least a hundred legs. But those legs were long and extremely hairy. The insect was black all over and stood more than two inches tall.

"Cool," said Brian, leaning forward for a better look. "Hey, Fitz. Check it out."

But Sarah had quite a different reaction. She let out a bloodcurdling scream and clutched at Lexi's arm. "Oh, yuck!" she shrieked. A few other kids squirmed and giggled nervously.

For once Fitz had to agree with Sarah. "Gross," he whispered to himself.

Brian's hand shot into the air. "Miss Larva, how do you do a thing like that?"

"That's my secret," she replied with a mysterious smile.

Next she brought out a creature with six long thin legs and graceful red, gray, and white wings. "This, boys and girls, is a cross between a spider and a butterfly." She opened yet another cage. "And here is a combination wasp and grasshopper." The angrily buzzing insect hopped across the table, making Fitz jump with alarm.

As quickly as she had brought them out,

Miss Buggy whisked the creatures back into their cages and covered them with cloth again.

When that was finished, she took a deep breath. "And now, children, for some really exciting news."

Fitz stared at her, watching her face take on a strange glow.

When she spoke again, her voice vibrated just above a whisper. "Very soon you will all help me with the greatest experiment I've ever conducted. I can't tell you about it now, but very soon you'll understand."

All the kids started whispering excitedly. All except Fitz. He shivered at her words. Miss Larva's mouth was turned up in a big smile. And the bugs on her necklace seemed to move just a little bit.

Chapter
7

"Hey, did you hear that?" Brian asked excitedly as the two boys headed for home a few minutes later. "Miss Larva said we're going to be part of her greatest experiment ever. Doesn't that sound cool?"

"I guess so," Fitz answered nervously. But deep down inside he wasn't so sure.

"I hope she'll let me cross a scorpion with something," said Brian. "They're wild. Maybe I'll cross a scorpion with a—"

"Listen, Brian, I need to talk to you about Miss Buggy," Fitz broke in. "She's . . . well, she's spooky. She might even be dangerous. Have you ever noticed her eyes?"

"What about her eyes?" snapped Brian. "Who can see them behind those sunglasses she's always wearing? And I told you to quit calling her Miss Buggy."

"Okay, okay. So you've never seen her eyes. Believe me, Brian, they're not the least bit normal."

Brian gave him a skeptical look. "What are you talking about?"

Fitz took a deep breath. He knew it was going to be hard to explain. "The pupils, they're . . . well, the pupils are like . . . like a fly's eye. They're made up of all these little eyes. Honest. If you look real close, you'll see it for yourself."

Brian threw back his head and roared with laughter. "Traflon, you're a nutcase! *Eyes like a fly?* That's a good one. How'd you think that up?"

"I didn't think it up," Fitz replied angrily. "You don't have to believe me. Go see for yourself."

"Sure, I'll just go ask her to take off her sunglasses so I can check out her fly eyes," Brian said sarcastically. He chuckled again. "You're really losing it, dude. In the meantime don't bad-mouth Miss Larva, okay? She's cool, and her cooking is even better than my mom's. Her burgers and fries are out of this world, even without mustard. As a matter of fact, I've decided that hers are the only ones I'm going to eat from now on."

Fitz didn't answer. There was no use talking to Brian. He was obviously too carried away with Miss Buggy's weird experiments—not to mention her cooking— to listen to reason.

The next morning at school Fitz tried to talk to some of his other friends about Miss Buggy, but none of them would listen either. Every time he brought up her name, kids would start praising her cooking.

"Man, you've got a lot of nerve putting Miss Larva down," said Jeff McCormick. "Especially after she made you that incredible birthday cake. Just because you're too stupid to buy your lunch, don't try to ruin it for the rest of us."

"You ought to have your head examined," said Eric Plummer when Fitz approached him. "Miss Larva's food is the best we've ever had in this cafeteria. Would you rather have that terrible cook we had last year come back?"

In desperation Fitz decided to talk to Lexi about it. He hurried outside and spotted her on the playground.

"Hey, Lexi," he said, running up to her. "I need to talk to you about Miss Buggy."

"Hello, Fitz," said a familiar sickly sweet voice. Too late Fitz noticed that Sarah was with Lexi. He groaned in dismay, but Sarah didn't notice. She was fluttering her eyelashes at him. 'Why do you call her Miss Buggy, Fitz? That's not a very nice name," she said with a flirtatious pout.

Fitz clenched his fists at his sides and glanced at Lexi in desperation. She was gazing at him thoughtfully, but she didn't say anything. Fitz turned back to Sarah, feeling annoyed that Lexi obviously wasn't going to help him out. "I call her that because Miss Buggy is part fly," he said in his nastiest voice. He held his arms out like wings and made a buzzing sound.

Sarah wrinkled her nose. "Oh, *gross*! Don't say things like that."

"Well, she is," Fitz insisted. "Just get her to take off her sunglasses and look at her eyes. They've got all these little bitty eyes inside them, and they can look all different directions at once. I'll bet she eats slimy rotten stuff out of the garbage can." He paused. "I saw some rotten wormy tomatoes out in the dumpster this morning—maybe

47

she'll make sandwiches out of it and serve it for lunch!"

Sarah turned green and her mouth started to quiver.

"It's true," Fitz insisted, backing away from her. "I hope you like tomato mush, Sarah. But watch out for the worms—they can be crunchy."

Just then Sarah grabbed her stomach and opened her mouth. Then she heaved and threw up all over her shoes.

Lexi shot Fitz a dirty look. "What did you have to do that for?" she hissed as she hurried to help her friend. "We're going to have enough trouble getting people to believe us about Miss Buggy as it is!" She put her arm around Sarah's shoulders and led her off in the direction of the girls' bathroom.

Fitz shoved his hands into his pockets and wandered away in the opposite direction. He was glad that somebody finally believed him, even if it was only Lexi. But now he wished he hadn't goofed around and made Sarah throw up—maybe he could have gotten Lexi alone and talked to her about what to do.

*

By the second week of school Fitz and Lexi were the only ones still bringing their lunch. In fact, most of the other kids were even complaining about having to stay home on weekends and eat their parents' cooking—despite the fact that Miss Larva's menus had gotten a little strange. Although she usually served normal things like spaghetti or hot dogs, she had started occasionally fixing more bizarre meals as well. One day she served eggplant-and-zucchini casserole with a side dish of deep-fried frogs' legs. Another time she presented the students with a deep-dish sardine pizza with pineapple chunks. Both times Fitz had been disgusted by the sight of the food, but had secretly thought it smelled pretty good.

That wasn't the only thing that was different around school these days, though. Fitz had noticed that the teachers were getting nicer and nicer—even the ones who were really strict or mean. All of a sudden none of them were giving homework anymore. Tests were unbelievably easy. For the first time in his life Fitz was getting A's and B's.

But perhaps the strangest change of all was in everyone's appetites. They were getting bigger and bigger with every passing day. Especially Brian's.

"Look at all the food on your plate," Fitz said one day when Brian came to the table with four pieces of fried chicken, two helpings of mashed potatoes and gravy, and five warm buttered rolls. "You can't possibly eat all that."

Brian stuffed a roll into his mouth. 'Uh course ah can," he said.

Fitz nibbled on a bologna sandwich and watched Brian devour everything on his plate and go back for a second helping. This time Brian had six rolls and five pieces of chicken, and they were sitting on top of an entire plateful of mashed potatoes and gravy.

It almost made Fitz sick to his stomach to see all that food. But Brian ate every bite. He even sopped up the last of the gravy with a roll. Then he looked sadly at his empty plate.

"How can you eat so much?" Fitz asked as he followed Brian to the tray return.

"I keep telling you, dude, it's Miss Larva's cooking," Brian said with a burp. "It's great!"

Fitz nodded, but he didn't say anything. At least the food had looked pretty normal lately. There had been nothing to remind him of beetles or maggots.

"You don't know what you're missing," Brian went on.

"That's right," said Sarah. She and Lexi had just come up behind them. "It shows how stupid you are." Sarah was eating a gigantic brownie. It was that day's dessert, and it looked delicious. It looked moist and chewy, and it was packed with nuts. Fitz could hardly take his eyes off it. He heard his stomach grumble.

"What about Lexi?" asked Fitz, tearing his eyes away from the brownie with difficulty. "I haven't seen her eat any of Miss Larva's food either."

"Lexi's different," said Sarah with a shrug, glancing at her friend. "She has to bring her lunch because of her allergies. But you don't. And you bad-mouth Miss Larva and call her names when you don't even know how great her food is. Just looking at you makes me want to throw up again!" With that Sarah spun around and pranced away.

"Sarah's right. You're just being stubborn," said Brian. "I don't know what the big deal is. You've got to be a moron to want

51

your puny little sandwiches instead of Miss Larva's great food."

Fitz threw up his arms in frustration. Why was he the only kid in school who didn't trust Miss Larva? Maybe he really was over-reacting. Just because she had eyes like a fly didn't mean she was out to poison the whole school or anything. Besides, he was really getting curious about her famous cooking. That brownie sure had looked delicious—not to mention the fried chicken and mashed potatoes. Maybe he should try buying his lunch, just once. Just to find out what the big deal was. How much harm could it do?

"Okay, okay!" said Fitz, almost before he knew what he was saying. "I'll do it tomorrow. I'll buy my lunch."

Chapter
8

Fitz headed for school earlier than usual the next morning. He had lunch money in his pocket instead of a sandwich in his backpack. He wasn't going to go back on his promise to Brian.

But he wasn't going to eat Miss Larva's cooking without finding out a few things, either.

When he got to school, the playground was empty. He slipped in the front door and looked around. The halls were deserted. He could see teachers in their classrooms, preparing for the day. Luckily none of them noticed him as he tiptoed down the hall.

Fitz's heart fluttered in his chest as he stopped in front of the double doors to the

53

cafeteria. *What if she catches me?* he wondered nervously. *She might grind me up and turn me into meatloaf!*

The idea made him shudder. Taking a deep breath, he pushed open the door and slipped inside the deserted lunchroom. Silently he moved among the empty tables toward the kitchen door. As he got closer, he heard singing coming from inside the kitchen.

"Itsy bitsy spider, climbed up the waterspout."

Fitz's eyes widened. It was Miss Larva. She was singing to herself.

He swallowed hard and eased the door open a couple of inches, being careful not to make a sound. By closing one eye and looking through the crack with the other, he could see the cook.

She had her back to him, and her chef's hat was perched on her head as usual. She was stirring something in a gigantic pan that covered the entire top of the stove.

Lunch! he thought, and gulped.

"Come in, Fitzgerald!" Miss Larva said suddenly in a commanding voice, without turning. "It's impolite to spy."

Fitz's other eye flew open. His heart

started to pound, and his mouth went dry.

Her back is to me. How could she know I'm here? he thought frantically.

Miss Larva put her spoon down and slowly turned around. Staring straight at him, she boomed, "I said come in, Fitzgerald. *Now!*"

Opening the door wide, he went inside on shaking legs.

Chapter
9

Fitz wondered if Miss Larva could see how hard he was trembling.

She raised an eyebrow and studied him for a long time. Then she took off her sunglasses and studied him even harder.

To his alarm Fitz could see that the dark parts of her eyes had grown larger since the first time he'd seen them. The whites were now nothing more than a thin rim around the huge pupils.

"Why *were* you spying on me?" she demanded.

Fitz could hear a faint buzzing in the room. He trembled harder and tried to speak.

"I . . . I was . . . I mean . . ."

"*Fitzgerald*, answer my question!"

"I . . . I was just wondering what was for lunch," he said weakly.

A slow smile spread across Miss Larva's face. Her black eyes brightened. "Oh, I see! So you're enjoying my lunches, are you?" She sounded pleased.

The cook stepped aside and waved her hand toward the huge flat pan she had been stirring. It was the largest pan Fitz had ever seen.

He moved cautiously forward to take a closer look. In the pan was a thin layer of reddish sauce with lots of lumpy things swimming around in it.

He gasped and shrank back. "Those are *caterpillars!*" he cried in shock.

He couldn't take his eyes off the slimy writhing mass of caterpillars that filled the pan. Some of their thick pulsating bodies were green. Some were purple. Others were yellow or black-and-white-striped. Red gooey stuff clung to the fuzz on their bodies. He watched in horror as they crawled and squirmed over and around and under each other in the liquid. His stomach started doing flip-flops.

Miss Larva threw back her head and

laughed heartily. She reached into the pan and picked up a large purple caterpillar with two fingers. Holding its dripping body high, she danced toward Fitz and stuck the squirming creature in front of his nose.

Fitz flinched and tried to move away, but the cook grabbed his arm with her free hand and held him tightly.

"Many insects go through four different stages to become adults," she said cheerfully. "The egg stage is the first one. The larva or caterpillar stage comes next. This is a larva—stage two."

Larva? thought Fitz. *That's Miss Buggy's name!*

Fitz stared in horror at the wriggling purple caterpillar. It was the ugliest thing he had ever seen.

A second later the cook whisked the larva away from his face and dropped it back into the pan.

Fitz curled his lip and wrinkled his nose in disgust as he watched it burrow into the moving mass of caterpillars.

While he was staring into the pan, Miss Larva produced a large jar of blood-red sauce. She opened the jar and began pouring the sauce over the larva. Next she topped that with large slices of cheese. With each addition Fitz's mouth dropped open wider.

"Lasagna!" she announced cheerfully. Opening the oven door, she took the big pan off the stove and popped it inside. "Does that answer your question, Fitzgerald? We're having lasagna for lunch. My special recipe."

Fitz whirled around and crashed through the kitchen door. He was panting loudly as he streaked through the deserted lunchroom, knocking over chairs and bumping into tables.

Finally he reached the hallway. He ran all the way to the main lobby, where he stopped and leaned against the wall. Perspiration was running down his face. Everything was silent except for the sound of his ragged breathing.

A second later the front doors burst open with a bang, and kids started pouring into the school, chattering and laughing. Fitz watched them as they headed for their lockers.

He was the only one who really knew what they were going to have for lunch.

And no one would believe him if he told them.

Chapter
10

As soon as he caught his breath, Fitz hurried outside to the playground. He searched frantically until he spotted Brian standing by the monkey bars.

"Brian!" he called, racing toward him.

Brian looked around and grinned. "What's the big rush? Your shoes on fire?"

"Listen, Brian. This is important," Fitz said as he skidded to a stop. "You're not going to believe this, but it's true. I swear it is."

"What are you talking about?" asked Brian.

"Miss Buggy, er, Miss Larva is cooking caterpillars for lunch," said Fitz. "I saw it with my own eyes."

Brian's expression changed—first to bewilderment, then to annoyance. He studied Fitz, frowning. "You're a nut, Traflon. Did you know that? A real nut."

Fitz grabbed Brian's arm. "No, I'm not," he pleaded desperately. "Honest, Brian, I saw her do it. They were in this big pan, and they were wiggling around and everything. First she poured tomato sauce over them. Then she put cheese on top of that and put the pan in the oven. And then do you know what she said?"

Brian rolled his eyes and shook his head.

"She said, 'We're having lasagna for lunch.' That's what she said. I swear it," Fitz said. "You've got to believe me, Brian."

Brian shook his head again. "Hey, guys," he yelled to Jeff, Eric, and some other boys who were hanging out near the basketball court. "Fitz says Miss Larva's cooking lasagna with caterpillars in it for our lunch. Can you believe that?"

The boys went into fits of laughter as Fitz stared at Brian in disbelief. He couldn't believe his best friend was making fun of him in front of everyone. And what was worse, Brian obviously didn't believe a word Fitz had said.

"Look, Traflon," Brian said angrily, turning back to Fitz. "Nobody bad-mouths Miss Larva and gets away with it. Not even you. Now knock it off."

"But . . . but, Brian . . ." sputtered Fitz.

Brian grabbed Fitz by the front of his shirt. "You heard me," he said between clenched teeth. "Now *bug off*!"

Fitz's heart was in his throat as he turned and scuffed away. He couldn't believe the way Brian was acting. If his best friend didn't even believe him, who would?

"Hi, Fitz," said a voice behind him. It was Lexi.

"Hi," said Fitz dejectedly.

"What's wrong?" asked Lexi.

Fitz stared at her for a moment. Lexi had seen Miss Larva's eyes. Maybe she'd believe him. "Miss Buggy is making lasagna for lunch, except it isn't really lasagna," he told her.

"What do you mean?" asked Lexi. "How can it be lasagna if it isn't lasagna?"

"It's got caterpillars in it," said Fitz. "They're covered with tomato sauce and mozzarella cheese. I was in the kitchen—I saw her making it.'

Lexi gasped. "Gross! But why do you

think she would put caterpillars in the lasagna?"

Fitz took a deep breath. Lexi believed him! Just knowing that made him feel a little better. He shrugged. "I don't know. All I know is they were big and fat and green and yellow and black-and-white-striped."

"Yuck!" said Lexi. "I never thought I'd be glad I've got allergies. Are you going to buy your lunch today like you said you would?"

"I don't know," said Fitz. "I didn't bring my lunch, so I guess I don't have much of a choice."

"Well, I don't think you should do it," said Lexi. "We don't know what Miss Buggy is up to."

Fitz smiled in spite of his fear. For once a girl was making sense. "I don't know what I'm going to do," he said. "I think I should try buying lunch to see if it looks suspicious or anything. But I'm not going to eat anything that looks like a caterpillar, that's for sure."

"Fitz," Lexi said softly, "do Miss Buggy's eyes really look like fly's eyes, or did we just imagine it?"

Fitz shook his head. "We didn't imagine it."

Lexi gulped. "I didn't think so. She scares me, Fitz."

"Me, too," he said before he could stop himself. He was afraid Lexi would make fun of him for admitting it, but she didn't.

"Just be careful, okay?" was all she said.

Fitz nodded. His shoulders sagged as he trudged away. Finding out that Lexi believed him had made him feel better for a minute—but only for a minute. Just because she believed him didn't mean anybody else would. And it didn't mean they'd be able to stop Miss Larva from—well, from whatever strange plan she was hatching.

Fitz didn't hear anything his teachers said for the rest of the morning. All he could think about was that pan of lasagna he'd seen bubbling and writhing as Miss Larva put it into the oven. He kept reaching into his jeans pocket to jingle his lunch money in his hand. What was he going to do?

I'll skip lunch, he thought, remembering those wiggling larvae.

He was trudging down the hall after the lunch bell rang when Brian grabbed him from behind.

"Come on, Fitz. You're buying your lunch today, remember?"

Fitz scowled at him. "I'm not hungry, okay?"

"That'll be the day," Brian scoffed. "You're always hungry. Now let's go eat some caterpillars!" He threw back his head and laughed as if that were the funniest thing anybody had ever said.

Then he grabbed Fitz's arm and dragged him through the lunchroom doors. Fitz started to protest, but then he decided to relax and go along with Brian, at least for the moment. He figured he should at least see what Miss Larva was serving that day. If it was meatloaf or pizza or something, that would prove that Fitz had imagined the whole thing, or that the cook had been teasing him. But if it was lasagna . . .

He gritted his teeth and stood on his toes as he tried to see the steam table around the long line of kids. His stomach was churning.

Let it be hamburgers today, he prayed silently, *or tacos, or meatball sandwiches—anything but lasagna.*

Just then the line shifted and he could see the steam table clearly. And he could see what was on it.

It was a big pan filled with steaming, bubbling lasagna.

Chapter
11

Miss Larva was cutting the gigantic pan of lasagna into squares and dishing it up onto plates. Kids pushed and shoved in the line, trying to make it move faster.

All except Fitz. More than anything, he wanted to break out of the line and run away. But for some reason he suddenly found himself unable to move. He was almost paralyzed by the delicious aroma drifting toward him from the steam table, and it kept drawing him closer and closer. The lasagna smelled better to him than anything he had ever smelled in his life. He didn't want to eat it, but he wasn't sure he'd be able to resist that incredible smell. His only hope was that Miss Larva would run out before he got there.

She didn't.

"Here you are, Fitzgerald," she said, when Fitz got to the steam table. "Enjoy!" She gave him a big smile.

He looked down at the plate of food on his tray. The piece of lasagna was at least six inches high, and so big that it covered the entire plate and dripped off the edges onto the tray. Holding the tray away from him as far as his arms would reach, Fitz headed for the table. Brian was already there. He was gobbling down his lasagna and grinning at Fitz.

"Hey, I thought we were having bugs for lunch," Brian said.

Fitz didn't answer. He was studying his piece of lasagna carefully. He picked up his fork and poked at it. He could see that it had noodles and meat in it. And tomato sauce and cheese. Just like regular lasagna. He couldn't see any signs of larvae. Nothing green, or purple, or yellow, or black-and-white-striped. Nothing slimy. Nothing pulsating or wiggling. Nothing alive.

He frowned. *How could I have imagined what happened in the kitchen?* he wondered. *She put caterpillars in this! I saw it!*

Fitz looked around the crowded cafeteria. Everyone was gulping down the lasagna as fast as they could, hardly bothering to chew. A few kids were already going back for a second helping.

"What are you waiting for?" asked Brian. "Go ahead. Take a bite. It's fantastic!"

Fitz looked around again. He was the only person in the whole room who wasn't eating lasagna, except for Lexi, who was nibbling salad out of a plastic container.

The lasagna smelled so good that he was having trouble thinking straight. He poked at it with the end of his fork, then scooped up a tiny piece. He touched it with the tip of his tongue. It was unlike anything he'd ever tasted—he couldn't have even imagined food that good. He closed his eyes and savored it.

Then, taking a deep breath, he put a forkful into his mouth. He started chewing furiously. He could feel his face glowing with pleasure.

He took another bite. And another. He shoveled heaps of lasagna into his mouth.

Just then, out of the corner of his eye, he noticed Miss Larva. She was still behind the steam table dishing up lasagna. But she was staring straight at him. He stared back, still chewing.

Her lips slowly curled into a sneer.

Chapter
12

At first Fitz was sure the lasagna was going to make him sick. All afternoon he was on alert for any strange noises coming from his stomach. Or the slightest sign of nausea. Or even the tiniest bit of queasiness.

But nothing happened. He felt perfectly fine. In fact, by the time school let out for the day, he was hungry again. All he could think about was how great it would be to eat some more of Miss Larva's delicious lasagna.

He was positive he had seen caterpillars in the lasagna. Had she been teasing him? Had she thrown away the pan full of cater-pillars and substituted regular lasagna after he'd left the kitchen? She must have. But why?

"So what's it going to be tomorrow? Cafeteria food or a soggy sandwich from home?" asked Brian with a grin as they walked home after school.

"I guess I'll give the cafeteria a second try," Fitz mumbled, still thinking about how good that lasagna had tasted.

"I told you so!" Brian said triumphantly. "Miss Larva has to be the best cook in the world. Doesn't she? Come on, say it."

"She's pretty good," said Fitz, frowning.

But Brian wouldn't let it go. "Come on, Traflon. Say it! Miss Larva's the best cook in the world."

"I *said* she's pretty good," Fitz grumbled. "That's as much as I'm going to say right now."

When he went to bed that night, Fitz dreamed about Miss Larva's lasagna. He saw everything just the way it had been that morning in the cafeteria. He saw the larvae squirming and crawling in the red sauce. He saw the cook's round, pudgy face grinning at him as she held up a fat, wiggling larva dripping with sauce and melted cheese— and shoved it into his mouth.

71

He awoke in a sweat. *It was just a dream*, he told himself. But he had a hard time falling back to sleep.

By the time he was dressed for school, the memory of the dream had faded. All Fitz could think about was how good that lasagna had tasted the day before. The cornflakes he choked down for breakfast tasted like sawdust—all he wanted was some more of Miss Larva's wonderful cooking. He decided to buy his lunch again that day. After all, he'd eaten the lasagna yesterday and nothing bad had happened.

When lunchtime came, Fitz raced Brian to the lunch line, beating him by a fraction of an inch.

"Can you see what we're having?" Brian asked from behind him. "It smells like garlic."

Fitz craned his neck to see the steam tables. His mouth was watering like crazy. "Spaghetti and meatballs! My absolute favorite!" he exclaimed with a grin.

"Awesome," Brian cried. The boys exchanged high fives.

Fitz licked his lips as he watched Miss Larva load his plate with spaghetti. She plopped two gigantic meatballs on top and drowned the whole thing with extra sauce. Then she gave him a massive hunk of garlic bread.

"Could I have another meatball?" Fitz asked.

Miss Larva smiled and put another meatball on his plate. "Of course," she said. "I like to see a boy with a healthy appetite."

Fitz's appetite was humongous. As soon as he sat down he started shoveling the food into his mouth. He barely noticed the sauce slopping onto his shirt or the long strands of spaghetti dangling down his chin.

"That was even better than the lasagna," he said to Brian as he picked up the plate and licked off the last speck of sauce. "Come on, let's get some more."

This time Fitz started gorging himself before he even got back to the table. He shoved a meatball into his mouth with his fingers and raced across the lunchroom.

Five minutes later he was back for a third helping. By this time he had decided that eating with a fork was just slowing him down. Grabbing a handful of spaghetti, he stuffed it into his mouth and then licked the sauce off his fingers.

Across the table Brian was eating with his

hands, too. He looked up at Fitz and grinned. "Hey, man," Brian said, "you've got so much red stuff around your mouth that you look like a girl." Then in a loud voice he sang, "Fitz is wearing lipstick! Fitz is wearing lipstick!"

Just as Fitz swallowed the food in his mouth and opened it to respond, Brian reached across the table and grabbed a handful of spaghetti off Fitz's plate and stuffed it into his own mouth.

"Hey, what do you think you're doing?" demanded Fitz. Then he grabbed a handful of spaghetti off Brian's plate and ate it.

"Food fight! Food fight!" someone yelled. Suddenly kids all over the lunchroom were jumping up from their tables and racing around grabbing other kids' food. Some of them ate it. Some threw it in other kids' hair or smeared it onto other kids' faces and shirts.

Someone threw a meatball that hit Fitz in the side of the head. He picked it up off the floor and shoved it into his mouth.

The cafeteria was in chaos. Spaghetti and garlic bread were flying everywhere. Meatballs were whizzing in every direction.

Suddenly Fitz froze in the act of flinging a

handful of spaghetti at Margie Maxwell. "Look, Brian!" he gasped. "Look at the teachers!" He watched in shock as Mrs Dewberry drew back her arm and fired a meatball right at the principal's forehead.

Suddenly Fitz noticed Miss Larva and a chill ran down his spine.

She was standing behind the steam table again, watching it all with a huge smile on her face.

Chapter
13

The next morning Fitz was walking along a block from school, wondering what Miss Larva would fix for lunch that day.

"Wait up, Fitz," he heard Brian call. "I've gotta show you something. Something important." He looked scared.

"What's the matter?" asked Fitz.

Brian didn't answer. Instead he ducked behind a tree and unbuttoned his shirt. He glanced around to make sure no one was watching, then pointed to a lump the size of an egg sticking out from his chest. His finger was trembling.

Fitz stared at the lump. "Whoa! Where did that thing come from?"

Brian shrugged. "I don't know. It was

there when I woke up this morning."

"Does it hurt?" Fitz asked, leaning a little closer and squinting at the lump. It was pink and its surface was bumpy.

"No, it just feels funny," Brian said nervously. "I wish I knew what it was."

"Did something hit you?" asked Fitz, remembering when he'd gotten hit in the head with a baseball the summer before. He'd had a lump on his head at least as big as Brian's.

"No," said Brian. "Besides, it isn't black-and-blue or anything."

"What did your parents say when you showed it to them?" asked Fitz.

"Get real. I didn't show it to my parents," said Brian, looking even more worried. "I don't want them to know about it until I know how I got it."

"Maybe it's something you ate," said Fitz. He laughed. Then the memory of the writhing, pulsating larvae in the lasagna pan flashed into his mind and choked off the laugh.

"Feel it," ordered Brian. "It feels weird."

Fitz hesitated and then reached out a finger. The skin was stretched tightly over the lump and it was warm. That was all. He didn't notice anything strange about it. It felt like a plain old ordinary lump. He started to pull his hand away and stopped. Had it moved?

Fitz put his whole hand over the lump. It moved again! It slowly pulsated and pushed the skin out in first one place and then another.

Fitz gasped and jumped back.

Looking at Brian in horror, he whispered, "It's *alive!*"

Chapter
14

Neither boy spoke the rest of the way to school. As soon as they got into the building, Fitz motioned for Brian to follow him into the boys' bathroom. There was no one else in there, so Fitz slipped off his shirt.

"Do I have any lumps?" he asked fearfully.

"I don't see any," Brian said with a shrug. "But why would you have one?"

"I don't know. But I don't know why you do, either," said Fitz. "You'll have to admit that things have been pretty weird around school ever since Miss Buggy got here. Maybe it has something to do with her."

"Aw, come on," said Brian. "Don't start that stuff again. I've got enough real problems without worrying about your imaginary bug-monsters."

Fitz stepped in front of the mirror and examined himself closely. There were no signs of any lumps on his chest. He turned, checking his side and back. Then he turned the other side toward the mirror.

"So far, so good," he whispered. He wasn't sure why he felt so sure that Brian's lump had something to do with Miss Larva—but he did.

He was still thinking about Brian's mysterious lump in class a little while later when he glanced at Sarah in the seat in front of his. He blinked and looked again, then caught his breath in terror. There was a lump sticking out on the back of her neck!

Fitz squinted and looked closer. The lump was just below Sarah's short, curly blond hair. He stared at it. If it was the same as Brian's, it would move. He stared at it through narrowed eyes, concentrating so hard that everything else in the room was blurred out of his vision. The lump was the only thing he could see.

"Fitzgerald Traflon, what is the capital of Idaho?"

Mrs Dewberry's words startled him so

much that he almost jumped out of his seat. But he still couldn't take his eyes off the lump on Sarah's neck.

"The capital of . . . I think the capital, uh . . ." he stammered. His mind refused to think about Idaho—or any other state, for that matter. All he could think about was that lump.

Suddenly Sarah's lump shivered ever so slightly. Then it gave a definite wiggle.

Fitz's mouth dropped open and his eyes went wide with fright.

"Fitzgerald, are you daydreaming instead of paying attention to the lesson?" Mrs Dewberry demanded.

"Yes, ma'am . . . I mean, no, ma'am," said Fitz. He finally managed to pull his eyes away from the pulsating lump to look at the teacher. "I'm sorry, Mrs Dewberry."

She shook her head, then turned away and called on someone else. She didn't even yell at him. That was strange. But then again, Fitz had grown accustomed to strange behavior from his teachers over the past couple of weeks.

When he was sure Mrs Dewberry wasn't looking at him anymore, Fitz leaned forward and tapped Sarah on the shoulder.

"Did you know you have a lump on your neck?" he whispered.

Sarah whirled around and gave him an angry look. "So what?" she hissed. "Shut up and mind your own beeswax if you know what's good for you!"

Chapter
15

Lunch that day turned out to be liver and onions. Normally Fitz refused to be in the same room with liver and onions. Even the smell made him gag.

But today the smell made his mouth water. When he stepped up to the steam table to be served, he couldn't help thinking how delicious the dark, slimy slabs of meat looked. And he noticed with delight how the rings of onion sitting on top of the meat looked appetizingly like pale, limp worms. He licked his lips in anticipation.

"Yum!" he whispered to himself. He grabbed a tray and tapped his foot impatiently, wishing that the line would move faster.

When he had finally been served, he gobbled down the liver and onions eagerly, loving every bite. The meat was as tough as the soles of his shoes. Cutting it with his knife and fork only slowed him down. He scooped up the onions and ate them with his fingers. Then he picked up the whole piece of meat and crammed it into his mouth.

He had hardly finished chewing the first helping before he went back for seconds. And thirds.

On his fourth trip to the steam table he grinned at Miss Larva. "This is great. What'd you put in it? Road kill?"

The cook looked up. She peered at him through her dark sunglasses. He imagined he could make out all the tiny irises in her eyes behind the glasses. They all seemed to be focusing on him.

"Were you spying on me again?" she demanded angrily.

"No way!" Fitz protested. "I was just making a joke. Honest."

Suddenly someone jerked him roughly from behind. Fitz spun around and came face-to-face with his best friend. Brian's face was blazing with anger.

"What's the big idea?" he screamed. "You're making Miss Larva mad! I don't like that! Got it?"

Fitz's mouth dropped open in amazement. He couldn't believe what was coming out of his best friend's mouth. Brian had never yelled at him that way before.

"Brian, no kidding. I was just making a joke," Fitz insisted.

Brian shoved him against the wall. Putting his face close to Fitz's, he growled, "You dirtbag. Make a joke like that about Miss Larva again, and I'll beat you to a pulp."

Suddenly other angry kids were swarming around Fitz and Brian.

"Leave Miss Larva alone, you big creep," shouted Sarah.

"Yeah, you better watch what you say, you loser," added Jeff McCormick.

He and Brian were advancing toward Fitz from one side. Jimmy Forsyth was leading an angry group from the other direction.

Fitz gulped and took a step backward. He could see the lump on Brian's chest sticking out from beneath the collar of his shirt.

It had grown! It was at least double the size it had been that morning.

And what was that bulge under Jeff's

shirt? Fitz could hardly believe his eyes. It was a lump—just like the ones Brian and Sarah had.

Then Fitz noticed something else. As his angry classmates advanced on him, threatening looks on their faces, all three of the lumps were pulsating faster and faster. *As if they were excited!*

Chapter
16

Fitz raced down the hall. His heart was pounding even faster than his feet. Ducking into an empty classroom, he could hear the mob of kids coming after him. He crouched down in a corner and held his breath as the angry shouts came closer and closer.

Suddenly the door opened and Brian's head popped into the room.

Fitz froze, afraid to move, as Brian made a quick survey of the room. Luckily he didn't notice Fitz huddled in the dark corner.

"He's not in here," Brian called out. His head disappeared again.

Fitz breathed a sigh of relief as he heard the crowd moving on down the hall.

"What's the matter with everybody?" he

whispered to himself. "They've all gone berserk!"

Fitz hid out in the empty classroom until the bell rang ending lunch period. He knew he had to go back to his own classroom and face Brian, Sarah, and the others who had turned on him. He was terrified. What if they jumped him again?

Mrs Dewberry will be there. She won't let them try anything, he thought.

Cautiously he stepped out into the hall. He looked first one way and then the other. Two kids hurried by on their way to their classes. They didn't pay any attention to him.

Tiptoeing along, Fitz suddenly stopped short when he turned the corner and saw Brian leaning against the wall outside their room.

Fitz's heart thumped against his chest. His palms were sweaty. He looked around for a place to hide. But before he could move, Brian spotted him.

A smile spread over Brian's face. "Hey, Fitz. Where have you been? I've been looking all over for you," he called out cheerfully.

Fitz swallowed hard. What was going

on now? "Just around," he mumbled uncertainly.

"Man, I don't know what happened to me in the cafeteria," said Brian. He shook his head and frowned as if he were still trying to figure it out. "I didn't want to say those things, but I couldn't help it," he went on. "It was like somebody else was inside my head, talking and acting—and *thinking* for me. Anyway, I just want you to know I'm sorry."

Fitz stared at Brian in horror. The things Brian was saying were supposed to make him feel better.

Instead, they were making him feel worse—a *lot* worse!

Chapter
17

Fitz couldn't understand it. How could somebody—or some*thing*—make Brian say things and do things he didn't want to say or do?

"Hi, Fitz," Sarah said in her usual flirtatious voice as he slid into his seat. She turned around, grinning and batting her eyelashes at him.

Fitz looked at her in surprise. Then he looked around the classroom. All the kids who had made up the angry mob a few minutes ago were now sitting quietly in their seats. No one seemed the least bit angry anymore. The situation was getting crazier by the moment.

"Okay, people. Everybody get into your

seat! And *shut up!*" screamed Mrs Dewberry.

Fitz glanced up in amazement. Even before all the teachers had started acting so nice, Mrs Dewberry had always been mild-mannered and cheerful. But now there was a wild look in her eyes. Her face was bright red, and her straight brown hair was sticking out every which way, making her look as though she had stuck her finger into a light socket. She was pacing back and forth in front of the class with a nasty look on her face.

"Put away your books," she ordered. "We're going to have a test. *Right now!*"

Meekly Fitz obeyed. So did everybody else. The room was so quiet you could practically hear the dust settle.

Fitz kept his head down and peeked up at Mrs Dewberry out of the corner of his eye. She was stomping up and down the rows, slapping papers down on the desks.

He jumped when he got his, afraid even to look up at his teacher.

The test was horrible. Fitz read over the first question:

If you have seven bananas and you take away nine eggs, how many frogs do you have left?

He read it again, then shook his head in

frustration. It didn't even make sense!

Across the room Brian raised his hand. "Excuse me, Mrs Dewberry, but I don't understand the first problem," he said.

The teacher whirled away from the blackboard and glared at Brian. "How dare you open your mouth during a test!" she cried.

"But . . . but . . . I was just asking a question," he protested.

"That's enough smart mouth out of you, young man," the teacher said angrily. "No one talks during a test in *my* class and gets away with it. Go to the principal's office this instant!"

Fitz watched his best friend get slowly to his feet and scuff out the door, a look of disbelief on his face.

Fitz struggled over the problems, doing the best he could. None of them made any more sense than the first one. But he didn't dare raise his hand after what had happened to Brian. Instead, he just guessed at the answers.

The second part of the test looked like algebra. He frowned and scratched his head in confusion. They hadn't even studied that stuff yet. How could Mrs Dewberry put something on the test that they hadn't studied? But he kept his mouth shut.

Mrs Dewberry gave them only ten minutes to finish the test. When she collected the tests, she announced, "Your homework for tonight is to read pages nineteen through eighty-five in your textbook and do all the problems."

Fitz cringed. *Pages nineteen through eighty-five! That's almost half the book!*

He ducked down behind Sarah and studied his teacher closely. Mrs Dewberry was sitting at her desk, grading the test papers. What was happening to her?

"Oh, no," he whispered to himself.

He had just spotted the thing he had dreaded finding.

A lump on the teacher's shoulder was pushing out the fabric of her dress. A big lump that moved, even when she didn't.

Lexi caught up with Fitz as he was leaving the building after school.

"I couldn't believe what happened in the cafeteria today," she said. "It was freaky, all those kids picking on you like that."

"Tell me about it," grumbled Fitz.

Lexi was silent for a moment as they walked. Then she said, "Fitz, can I ask you something kind of personal?"

He looked at her. "Yeah, I guess."

"Do you have any . . ." She paused and gulped, looking a little embarrassed, but scared at the same time. "Um, do you have any funny bumps on your body?"

Startled, he looked at her closely. "No," he answered slowly. "Why?"

"Sarah does," Lexi said quietly. "And . . . and I was just wondering if anyone else did. Because I was also wondering if Sarah's lump had anything to do with her eating Miss Buggy's cooking. But if you don't have any, then that must not be the reason."

"Why don't you tell her to show it to her parents?" said Fitz.

"I did," said Lexi. "But she went ballistic on me." She shook her head. "She's never yelled at me like that before. It was like she was—I don't know—*possessed* or something. It was weird. But anyway, I guess I don't have to worry. You've been buying your lunch, so if you don't have any lumps, I guess there must be some other explanation."

"I guess so," said Fitz. He watched as Lexi turned the corner toward her house and waved cheerfully. He wasn't sure why he hadn't told her about Brian's lump. Maybe he should have, he thought. Maybe she could have helped him figure the whole thing out. It just felt strange to confide in a girl that way. He shook his head, feeling almost as confused about Lexi as about Miss Larva.

When Fitz reached home, he went straight

to his room. He undressed quickly and examined himself all over for lumps. He stood in front of the mirror, inspecting every inch of his body. Then he poked and prodded himself from head to toe, searching for any mysterious growths under his skin.

He breathed a deep sigh of relief. Nothing.

"Wow. Am I ever lucky," he mumbled to himself. He paused and thought for a moment. "So far, at least."

As he was getting dressed again, Fitz heard the phone ringing out in the hall. A moment later his mother called him. "Fitz, it's for you. It's Brian."

Fitz raced to the phone. "Hi, Brian, what's up?"

"Can you come over?" asked Brian. "Right now? I need to talk to you." His voice was low and shaky.

"What's the matter?" Fitz was almost afraid to ask.

"I can't talk about it over the phone," Brian said. "Just get over here *fast*. Okay?"

"Sure," said Fitz. "I'll be there in a minute."

He grabbed his jacket and ran the three blocks to Brian's house. The front door flew open as soon as Fitz turned up the sidewalk, and Brian motioned for him to come in.

"What's the big emergency?" Fitz asked as Brian closed his bedroom door behind them.

Brian's hands were shaking as he peeled off his shirt. "Look," he said, turning his back to Fitz.

Fitz's eyes opened wide with alarm. "Oh, no. Another lump!" he cried. "When did you find it?"

"Right before I called you. My back felt funny, so I took off my shirt to look. What am I going to do, Fitz?"

"I dunno," said Fitz. He reached out and poked the second lump. It was a lot smaller than the one on Brian's chest. But it was warm. And it was moving slightly under his skin.

"It's awful," said Brian. "And the lumps aren't the only weird thing that's happening to me these days. Sometimes things come over me that I can't fight off. Like today in the cafeteria—I knew you were making a joke. But it was as if there was another person inside me. Controlling me. Making me say things I didn't want to say. And do things I didn't want to do."

"What do you mean?" asked Fitz.

"It's really bizarre. Sometimes I think I can hear voices," said Brian. He paused and shook his head. "No . . . not voices exactly. It's more like someone else's *thoughts* are in my *head*. Fitz, you've got to help me!" There was fear in his eyes. "I don't know what to do."

Fitz swallowed hard. "I think you'd better tell your parents," he said.

"No," Brian insisted. "I can't. What if they take me to the doctor and he finds out I've got something awful? Something— terminal?"

"Brian, listen to me," said Fitz, grabbing Brian by the shoulders. "I saw a lump on the back of Sarah's neck this morning."

Brian eyed him nervously. "So? What's that supposed to mean?"

"It means you're not the only one. I also saw a lump on Mrs Dewberry's shoulder when she was giving us that awful test," said Fitz. "Don't you get it? I think it may all be connected to Miss Buggy in some way. You've got to go to the doctor. We can't figure out what to do about it until we know what it is!"

Suddenly Brian's face changed. He looked

furious. *"Didn't you hear me?* I said forget it! And for the last time, it's Miss *Larva*. Now get off my back, Traflon."

Fitz held up his hands in surrender as he backed away from his angry friend. He realized that whatever strange mood had come over his friend earlier had returned. "Okay, okay. I was only trying to help."

Brian glared at him and balled his hands into fists. Fitz left without another word.

When Fitz got home a little while later, he was more scared than ever. Something terrible was going on. And it was getting worse all the time.

He went to his room and closed the door. Standing in front of the mirror, he took off his shirt. He had to check again, even though it had been less than an hour since he had last looked for lumps. He had to know if his luck was still holding out.

Fitz squinted first at his chest and stomach, running his fingers over them carefully. Then his arms, turning them so that he could see all the way around each one.

And then his eyes bugged out in horror.

He saw it.

A tiny lump, growing on his left side.

Chapter
19

Fitz couldn't sleep at all that night. All he could do was stare at the ceiling and worry about the horrible thing growing on his body. Each time he turned onto his left side, he could feel the lump throb. It felt as if the lump were demanding more space.

By morning the lump had grown to the size of a Ping-Pong ball and felt warm. For the millionth time since he'd found it, Fitz cupped his hand over it and felt it moving.

Fitz threw on his clothes and left for school without eating breakfast or saying good morning to his parents. There was something he had to know—and only one person could give him the information he needed.

He ran all the way to school. He barely slowed down as he burst through the wide front doors and sprinted down the hall to the cafeteria. This time he didn't sneak in on tiptoe. He pushed open the door to the kitchen and boldly strode inside.

"Miss Larva, I have a question about insects," he said loudly.

The cook was mixing something in a large bowl. At the sound of his voice she turned around and smiled. "Certainly, Fitzgerald," she said in a lilting voice. "I'm always glad to help a child who's *hungry* for knowledge. Hee hee. What is your question?"

Fitz hesitated an instant. Now that the moment had come, he was almost afraid to ask. But at the same time, he had to know the answer.

"When I came in here before, you said that all insects go through four stages to become an adult, and that being a larva was stage two. My question is—what is stage three?"

Miss Larva put down her spoon and looked at him thoughtfully. "Stage three is when the larva makes a pupa or a cocoon. A cocoon is a sort of nest where the insect can burrow in and be warm and well fed

101

and where it can grow. Then, when it's finished growing to its adult size, it will go into stage four."

"What's stage four?" asked Fitz.

"That's the best stage of all," said Miss Larva. "That's when it bursts out of its cocoon and becomes the beautiful creature it was meant to be."

She let out a sigh of ecstasy and rolled her eyes toward the ceiling. "The whole process is known as metamorphosis! Isn't it wonderful?"

"But what happens to the cocoon?" Fitz asked, his voice barely louder than a whisper.

"The cocoon?" asked Miss Larva in surprise. Then a nasty smile spread across her face. "When the insect hatches, it no longer has any use for it. So the cocoon withers up and dies."

Fitz stared at her in terror.

Now he knew the awful truth.

He finally understood what was happening to him and his friends.

Chapter
20

Fitz ran out of the building like a bullet shot from a gun. He had to find Brian and tell him what he'd learned.

Kids were just starting to arrive at school. Some were walking. Others were pouring off the buses parked at the curb. Sarah waved at him from across the playground. He ignored her and kept looking for Brian. It took him another minute or two to locate his best friend by the bike rack.

"Brian! I've got to talk to you!" Fitz yelled, racing toward him. Pulling Brian over to a deserted corner of the playground, he whispered hoarsely, "I just talked to Miss Buggy, and I've got it all figured out. Oh, man, you're not going to believe this!"

"What are you talking about?" asked Brian.

"She put larvae into our food and turned all of us into living, breathing, walking-around *cocoons*!" Fitz cried. "That's what her big experiment is!"

"What are you talking about, dude?" Brian said, looking confused. "You talked to Miss Larva? And what do you mean by cocoons?"

Fitz took a deep breath. He had to convince Brian that what he was saying was true. "You know those lumps of yours? You know how Sarah and Jeff and Mrs Dewberry have them, too? Well, now I've got one."

Brian's eyes widened. "No kidding?"

"No kidding," Fitz said solemnly.

"But what does that have to do with Miss Larva?"

"Well, you know how the lumps are kind of warm?" Fitz said. "And you know how they move around—like there's something *alive* inside of them?"

Brian nodded.

"Think about it," Fitz said urgently. "Miss Buggy is always talking about bugs, right? Well, she told me that one of the stages in a bug's life is burrowing into a cocoon—you know, a warm, cozy place where it can grow. And the next stage is *bursting out* of it."

Brian's mouth dropped open. "You mean, we've got bugs growing inside our bodies? That's what those lumps are? *We're* cocoons?"

Fitz nodded. "I wasn't imagining things the day I saw caterpillars in the lasagna."

"I should have believed you," said Brian, shaking his head. "You're my best friend. I really should have believed you. But do you know how bizarre that story sounded?"

"Yeah, I know. It seemed pretty bizarre to me, too, and I was there," said Fitz. "But anyway, we've got bigger problems now. Miss Buggy also told me that after the bugs burst out of the cocoon, the cocoon withers up and dies."

"You mean—you mean that's what's going to happen to us?" Brian asked, his face paling. "All of us?"

Fitz just nodded. Neither of them said anything for a moment.

Then Brian shook his head. "Hey, man, I'm sorry about jumping on you last night. If only I'd known . . ."

"Forget it," said Fitz. "Just try to hold off

whatever's making you act that way until we can figure out what to do."

"I'll try," said Brian. "You know, this must have been what Miss Larva meant that day she showed us her experiments and told us we were going to be part of her biggest one."

"Yeah," said Fitz. "Who knew we'd be the ones she was experimenting on? Anyway, I don't think we have much time. The lumps are growing fast. It's up to you and me to figure out a way to destroy whatever's in them before it destroys us."

Brian's eyes narrowed menacingly. Then his face twisted, as if he were fighting something. "No, I . . . I . . . leave me out of this, you stupid creep," he suddenly spat out. "You make me what to puke!"

He whirled around and stomped away.

Fitz watched him go. Fear clogged his throat and choked off his breath. It had happened again. Whatever the terrible things were that were growing inside them, they were in control of Brian again.

Slowly, Fitz realized that it was all going to be up to him. He had been the last one to eat the cafeteria food, so the things hadn't had as much time to grow inside him—they weren't powerful enough to take him over yet. But they would be soon. And then Fitz wouldn't be able to help Brian or himself or anybody. He didn't know how much time he had.

He had to do something fast. But what?

Chapter
21

Fitz vowed that he wasn't going to eat Miss Larva's cooking anymore. Before leaving for school on Monday he made himself a triple-decker ham-and-cheese sandwich with mustard and onions—one of his favorites. But when lunchtime came, the aroma that filled the cafeteria was so appetizing that he tossed the sandwich into the trash can and borrowed money from Brian to pay for lunch.

He gobbled up everything Miss Larva served as if it were going out of style. He loved the cooked carrots and broccoli and the boiled cabbage. He devoured the bird's-nest soup, goat cheese, and pickled pig's feet.

"Save room for dessert," she said sweetly as he came back for a sixth serving. "I fixed fried-brains pudding. It's my specialty. It will be out of the oven shortly."

Yum! thought Fitz, licking his lips hungrily. *Fried-brains pudding!* He had never tried it, but it sounded delicious.

He waited impatiently for Miss Larva to bring the pudding out of the kitchen. He drummed his fingertips on the table. He was so ravenously hungry that he was tempted to go back for another helping of pickled pig's feet just to tide him over.

"What are you doing in there?" he shouted impatiently. "Bring on the fried-brains pudding! Bring on the fried-brains pudding!"

Brian joined the chant. "Bring on the fried-brains pudding! Bring on the fried-brains pudding!"

Pretty soon the entire cafeteria was chanting and banging their spoons on the tables.

Finally the kitchen door swung open and Miss Larva marched out, carrying an enormous pan filled with what looked like pale-gray scrambled eggs. A strange but fascinating smell filled the air.

"Here it is, everyone," sang Miss Larva.

"What you've all been waiting for. My fried-brains pudding."

Fitz pushed and shoved his way to the front of the line. His mouth watered as he carried the bowl of slimy, runny pudding back to his table.

When he finally tasted it, he almost couldn't believe how good it was. He held the first bite in his mouth for a long time, savoring the sickly sweet taste.

Miss Buggy's cooking is terrific! She's the best cook in the world! More! More! he thought.

Then suddenly he realized those weren't his thoughts at all.

They were the thoughts of something inside him!

Chapter
22

Voices woke Fitz in the middle of the night.

He couldn't make out what they were saying. But they were voices all right, and they were right there in his room. Little prickles of fear ran across his scalp and down his spine.

He peered into the darkness. Nothing moved.

I can't be hearing voices, he told himself.

Then he heard them again. Soft, whispery voices.

He strained, listening as hard as he could. Suddenly he realized that the voices weren't in his room at all.

They were in his head.

"Fitzgerald Traflon the Third," came a

dry, rustling whisper. It was like the sound of leaves scuttling across a sidewalk. "We can make you do anything we want you to do. *You are ours*."

Fitz put his hands over his ears, trying to stop the voices.

"*You are ours! You are ours!*" The voices swirled in his mind, over and over again, until he thought he was going crazy.

Fitz shook his head violently from side to side. "Who are you? What do you want?" he shrieked into the darkness.

The next thing he knew, his bedroom door flew open and light spilled in from the hallway.

"Fitz, are you okay?" his father shouted as he burst into the room.

His mother ran to his bed and put her arms around him. "What's wrong, sweetheart?"

Fitz snuggled into his mother's arms. The rustling whispers were gone—for now. "I-I thought I heard something. Voices," he said.

"Voices, sweetheart?" asked his mother as she stroked his hair. "You must have been dreaming."

"That's right, son," said his father, pulling

the door open even farther so that the room was light. "There's no one in here but you. See? No ghosts. No goblins." He pulled back the curtains and opened the closet door, showing Fitz that nothing was there.

Fitz wanted desperately to tell his parents the truth. He wanted to show them the lump growing on his side. He longed to explain to them about the voices in his head that could control him and make him do things he didn't want to do.

He tried to force the words out, but he couldn't.

"Now you forget all about your nightmare and go back to sleep," said his father. "Your mother and I are right across the hall if you need us."

"That's right, sweetie," said his mother, standing up to leave.

Fitz didn't want them to leave. He didn't want to be alone again—with the voices. He tried to call out as his parents headed for the door. His lips moved, but no sound came out.

He watched the door close behind them, feeling lonelier than he had ever felt in his life.

Chapter
23

By morning the voices had stopped, but a second lump had appeared on Fitz's leg. And the lump on his side had grown even larger.

Fitz knew that time was running out.

I have to find a way to destroy the larvae, he thought as he rubbed the new lump on his leg. *Before they destroy us.*

He kept an eye out for Brian all the way to school. Maybe the two of them could put their brains together and come up with a plan. It was definitely worth a try. He had to do something—and do it fast.

But even after he got to school, he couldn't find Brian anywhere. Fitz had almost given up when he spotted Brian walking toward him across the baseball diamond.

"Hey, Brian! Over here! I've got to talk to you," Fitz shouted.

Brian waved and trotted toward him.

But as Brian got closer, a strange sensation came over Fitz. He suddenly felt boiling mad. His breath was coming out in snorts. His fists were doubling up into hard, round balls.

He was nose-busting mad! By the time Brian reached him, he was ready to explode.

Fitz watched as his own fist shot out and smashed Brian in the face.

Brian reeled back, a look of total surprise on his face. "What the—"

Before he could say another word, Fitz punched him again. He tried not to, but he couldn't seem to stop himself. His arms were flailing like a windmill in a hurricane, and there wasn't a thing he could do about it. The more he punched Brian, the more he wanted to punch him again.

Brian's nose was bleeding by this time, and blood dripped from a cut on his lip.

Fitz socked him in the nose once more and watched with satisfaction as Brian went down, sprawling in the dirt. "Serves you right, you jerk," he said with a sneer.

Other kids were rushing over from all directions to watch the fight. Some of them started cheering for Brian. Others yelled for Fitz.

"Hit him, Fitz!" yelled Jimmy Forsyth. "Smash him good!"

"Go get him, Brian!" shouted Eric Plummer. "Beat him up!"

A mean look came into Brian's eyes. He jumped to his feet and started fighting back.

"Hit him, Fitz!" yelled Sarah.

Brian caught Fitz in the mouth with a right. Fitz grabbed Brian around the neck, and the two of them fell to the ground, hitting and kicking and pounding on each other. They rolled over and over in the dirt.

Gradually the blows began to slow down. Fitz was getting tired, and so was Brian.

Finally they stopped.

"Aw, come on, guys, fight some more!" yelled Jeff McCormick eagerly.

Brian got up and wiped a mixture of blood, sweat, and dirt off his face. Then he moved off the dusty baseball field and sat down in the grass behind first base, panting hard. The crowd started to drift away. Fitz, exhausted, dropped down onto the grass next to his friend.

As he sat there, the remnants of his anger faded away. He realized that he wasn't mad at Brian anymore. He never really had been. He had never wanted to fight his best friend.

He glanced over at Brian. "I guess it's my turn to be sorry," he said tentatively.

"Don't be," said Brian. "I understand why you did it."

Fitz looked at his friend sadly. *I'm not the one who picked the fight*, he thought. *I didn't have any more control over it than Brian did when he got mad at me.*

Then the whispers came again, as dry and crisp as the crackling of a fire.

"Fitzgerald Traflon the Third, we told you that you were in our power. Now you know it's true. *Hee hee hee.*"

Chapter 24

"You are in our power," the voices whispered again.

Fear prickled Fitz's scalp, like a hundred spiders dancing in his hair.

The voices had to be the larvae, he decided. They were not only in his body, they had to be in his brain, too. They could make him think things he didn't want to think and do things he didn't want to do, like slugging Brian.

And when they decided to come out, they wouldn't just come bursting out of his side and his leg. The thought of what else might happen made him shiver.

Fitz got slowly to his feet. His body ached and his head throbbed. Dark bruises were starting to appear on his arms and knuckles.

Just then Lexi came over. She looked scared. "What happened? Why were you two fighting like that?"

"Do you remember when you asked me if I had any lumps on my body, and I said no?" asked Fitz.

Lexi nodded.

"Well, I do now," said Fitz. "And so does everyone else, including Mrs Dewberry. I'll bet Mr Gladstone and the other teachers have them, too. Everybody has them but you. You're the only one who has escaped, and do you know why?"

Lexi looked from Fitz to Brian and then back to Fitz. "Because I haven't eaten any cafeteria food," she whispered, her voice so low that the boys could hardly hear her.

Fitz nodded grimly. "I know it sounds crazy, but Miss Buggy is putting larvae in the food, and the larvae are using us as cocoons so they can grow."

"But that's impossible," Lexi insisted, shaking her head. "I mean, I know she's weird, but . . ." Her voice trailed off and her eyes widened. "The experiment! She told us that day in the cafeteria that we'd all be part of her big experiment."

119

"You've got it," said Fitz. "That's why Sarah has been acting so mean toward you lately. And that's why Brian and I were fighting. The larvae are taking control of our bodies and making us do all kinds of strange things."

"And it's getting worse," said Brian in a panicky voice. "It's getting worse *fast*. What are we going to do?"

"That's what I wanted to talk to you about when I slugged you," Fitz said. "I think we should come up with as many ideas as we can to fight this thing. You too, Lexi. We need your help. Let's think during school today. Then after school we can get together again to figure out which ideas are the best."

"I can't do it after school today," Lexi said. "I have my weekly appointment with my allergist."

"I can't make it today either," said Brian. "My mom says I have to come straight home and clean out the garage. I've been putting it off all week—if I don't do it today, she'll kill me."

Fitz gritted his teeth. With things getting so bad, even one day's delay seemed too long. But there was nothing he could do about it. "Okay, how about tomorrow morn-

120

ing?" he suggested. "The three of us could meet here on the playground before school."

"Cool," said Brian. "I'll be here."

"Me, too," Lexi promised.

Fitz had trouble sleeping again that night. He couldn't come up with any ideas for getting rid of the larvae. And every time he snuggled down in his bed and got comfortable, the lumps started throbbing furiously. Then the dry, crackling voices started up again. They were faint and far away. They seemed to be talking to each other inside his head.

Fitz listened hard over the terrified thumping of his heart. He wanted desperately to know what the voices were saying, but they were speaking too softly for him to hear.

He took a couple of deep breaths. That calmed him a little, and his heart seemed to beat a little more quietly. He strained to listen again.

Finally, coming so faintly that he wasn't sure if he really heard them, were two words.

". . . *Fitzgerald* . . ."

". . . soon . . ."

Chapter
25

"I sure hope you've thought of a good plan, because I haven't," Fitz said when he met Brian and Lexi at the playground.

Brian grinned. "Have I ever," he said. He was carrying a small paper bag. He reached in and drew out a bottle. "It's liquid insect poison. I found it in our garage," he said. "One sip of this, and they're *zapped*!"

Lexi gave him a disgusted look. "Are you crazy? One sip of that stuff and *you'll* be zapped. You can't drink poison."

For a second Brian looked angry. Then his expression changed to embarrassment as he realized Lexi was right. "Oh, yeah. I guess I wasn't thinking," he said quietly. "So do you guys have any ideas?"

Lexi shook her head. "I've been thinking about it nonstop, but I can't think of a thing," she admitted.

Fitz was eyeing the bottle of poison. "What do you think would happen if we rubbed some of that stuff on the lumps? Do you suppose it would soak into the skin and kill them that way?"

Brian gave him a skeptical look. "I don't know." He handed the bottle to Fitz. "But it's your idea. Here, you try it."

"I don't know about this," Lexi said uncertainly. "It seems kind of dangerous. You could end up burning off your skin or something."

Fitz shrugged. "We've got to try something." He took the bottle and set it on the ground beside him. Then he unbuttoned his shirt and picked up the bottle again. The lump on his side was the size of a grapefruit half. It was quiet now, as if the larvae inside were asleep.

He hesitated and looked at Brian. "Maybe Lexi's right. Maybe this isn't such a good idea after all," he said.

"Go ahead," urged Brian. "Who knows? It might work."

Fitz took a deep breath and unscrewed

123

the top of the bottle. He sniffed the poison and wrinkled his nose. It smelled awful.

Suddenly a weird and powerful force seemed to take over his vocal cords. He let out a piercing scream that was so loud that Brian and Lexi jumped in surprise. Fitz looked down at the lump on his side. It was pulsating like crazy. The throbbing was getting stronger by the second, pushing and pulling and pounding his insides. Fitz had to lean against a tree to keep himself from falling down.

"I didn't even touch it with that stuff!" Fitz exclaimed as soon as the lump calmed down enough for him to speak. "All I did was open the bottle. But it knew. It knew exactly what I was going to do!"

"Yeah," said Lexi, her voice shaky. "It's as if it could read your mind."

"I wonder what would happen if we tried to cut the lumps out," Brian said.

Fitz shuddered at the thought. "Ouch," he said. "Hey, I know. Maybe we could make tiny little slits in the tops of the lumps and squeeze them like big pimples."

"Oh, ugh," said Lexi, her face turning a little green.

"Hey, yeah," said Brian. He made a loud

popping sound with his mouth. "We could pop them like zits!"

"Gross!" moaned Lexi. "You guys are making me sick. Anyway, don't you think that would hurt pretty bad, too?"

"I guess it would," agreed Fitz. Suddenly he didn't like the idea so well himself. "Maybe we can come up with a better plan if we keep trying."

"All right, but we should hurry," Lexi warned. "We don't know how much time we have before those things explode." She shuddered. "I may not have any myself, but I sure don't want to be around to see everybody else's hatch. That's for sure."

Fitz didn't want to think about that, but he knew Lexi was right. They had to hurry. He glanced toward the school building. "What if we sneak into the school and look around in Miss Buggy's kitchen?" he suggested.

"What good would that do?" asked Lexi. "I don't want to go near that place."

"Why not? Maybe we'll find some kind of clue. Miss Buggy won't be expecting us to go into the cafeteria. Maybe she left some notes on her experiments lying around."

"Great idea, man!" said Brian. "They

might even tell how to kill the larvae."

"Yeah," said Fitz. He closed his eyes and imagined his skin tearing open and giant insects bursting out of his side and his leg and crawling out his mouth. He could almost feel the searing pain and smell the awful stench. "Before they kill us," he murmured.

"Well, all right. But how are we going to get in?" asked Lexi. "They keep the school locked up on the weekend."

Fitz scratched his head and thought for a minute. "Let's go around back," he suggested. "There's a door leading straight into the kitchen. It's where delivery trucks bring in the food for the cafeteria. Maybe we can get in there somehow."

The trio hurried around the school. The door at the back was closed. But to their surprise it unlatched with a click when Fitz turned the knob. He pushed the door slightly ajar.

"If my parents could see me now," Lexi commented. "Breaking and entering."

Fitz ignored her. He was nervous enough already without any help from Lexi. "Ready?" he whispered.

Brian looked anxiously at the door for a

second and then nodded. "I'm with you, dude."

"I'm not sure I like this," said Lexi. Her voice was trembling again.

"You could stay out here and be our lookout, Lexi," Fitz offered.

"Gladly," she said, looking relieved.

Fitz pushed the door all the way open and the two boys slipped inside. They tiptoed cautiously into the silent kitchen and stood in the middle of the room, looking around. Everything seemed to be in perfect order, scrubbed and shined.

Where would Miss Buggy keep the notes on her experiments? Fitz wondered. He glanced first toward the cabinets and then toward the drawers.

Suddenly Fitz heard a loud click behind him. He exchanged panicky glances with Brian. They whirled around together and gasped.

They were face-to-face with Miss Larva.

She was blocking the door, her hand on the lock. She had taken off her dark glasses, and her sinister insect eyes had grown even larger. They were bulging out hideously, covering more than half her face. Every facet of every eye was staring straight at the boys.

"Brian Collins and Fitzgerald Traflon the Third," she rasped, "my friends told me you might try something like this. I've been waiting for you in the storage room." She threw back her head and cackled wildly. "I have you in my power now. *You'll never escape!*"

128

Chapter
26

Suddenly Fitz heard a sound coming from the other side of the door.

"Fitz! Brian! Are you in there?" It was Lexi, and she sounded scared.

"Run, Lexi!" Fitz cried. "Go for help! Miss Buggy's got us trapped!"

Like a flash of lightning, the cook whirled and threw open the door, grabbing the startled girl and dragging her inside.

"Let her go!" screamed Fitz. "She's not a cocoon! She never eats in the cafeteria. She has too many allergies."

"Don't hurt her," Brian added. "It's us you want."

Suddenly Miss Larva's expression changed. The evil look faded away. A smile spread slowly across her face. She loosened her grip on Lexi, who stumbled across the room and collapsed against the counter beside the boys.

"What's she going to do?" Lexi whispered. Tears brimmed in her eyes.

Miss Larva turned and locked the door. Then she held up the keys for the kids to see before she dropped them into her apron pocket.

"Are you children hungry?" she asked sweetly. "I'm famished. Why don't I just whip up a little something for us to eat?"

Food! thought Fitz. *That's the worst thing she could do!*

But he realized it was part of her plan. She knew that neither he nor Brian would be able to resist her cooking. And the more she fed them, the faster the larvae would grow—until they finally grew large enough to burst out of their cocoons. She really did have them in her power.

"Come on, guys," Fitz whispered to his friends. "Let's make a break for it." He was desperate. He was ready to try anything.

He skidded across the kitchen to the swinging double doors leading into the lunchroom. Brian and Lexi were right

130

behind him. All three shoved as hard as they could with their shoulders.

The doors didn't budge. They were locked tight.

Fitz turned around, panting, and leaned against them. He looked around frantically for another way out.

There wasn't any.

"Ladybug, Ladybug, fly away home," sang Miss Larva as she busily pressed ground meat into hamburger patties and sliced potatoes into french fries. She worked like a whirlwind, and soon the smell of grilling hamburgers filled the room.

Fitz watched in horror as she cooked. His mouth watered from the heavenly smell. He could feel himself weakening. Suddenly, escaping just didn't seem as important anymore. The most important thing he could think of was sinking his teeth into one of those delicious, juicy burgers. He could almost taste it already. The room was starting to spin.

No! I can't eat anything, Fitz told himself. *I can't!*

"But you'll love it," said a voice inside him.

"Just one tiny bite," said another voice.

I'm so hungry. Just one bite, then I'll try to find a way out of here again, he told himself.

NO! That's not me thinking that! Fitz shouted to himself.

Miss Larva glanced at Fitz and smiled. 'I've got to feed my little pets, now, don't I?" she asked with a sinister cackle.

Beside him, Lexi started to cry.

I have to keep a clear head, Fitz warned himself. He fought to push away the voices that were rising inside him.

Then he noticed Brian standing beside the stove, gazing down at the french fries bubbling in the grease. He was licking his lips hungrily.

Fitz closed his eyes to shut out the sight of the food. He had to get hold of himself before it was too late.

Maybe the three of us can overpower her and get the key, he thought. *All I have to do is get Brian's attention away from the french fries.*

"Psst. Brian," he called softly.

At the same instant, Miss Larva whipped three plates out of the cupboard. In the blink of an eye she loaded four hamburgers and a gigantic helping of french fries on each one. Then she passed the plates under their noses.

"Lunch is ready, children," she cooed sweetly.

Fitz and Brian followed her like a pair of zombies. It was as if the delicious aroma was pulling them across the floor.

Only Lexi didn't follow Miss Larva. Fitz was vaguely aware that she was still cringing by the counter, but he was powerless to do anything but trail after the cook.

Before the plates could even touch the counter, Fitz had grabbed one of the burgers and stuffed it into his mouth.

"Mmm, delicious. How about some ketchup?" he asked around a gigantic bite.

"Yeah. And some mustard, too," Brian added between bites. French fries stuck out of his mouth every which way.

Miss Larva had been about to open a cupboard. Her hand stopped in midair, and she glared at Brian.

"You *know* I don't allow mustard in my lunchroom!" she bellowed.

"But that's stupid," said Fitz, his mouth full. "Why not?"

Miss Larva glared at Fitz. Each one of the hundreds of tiny eyes within her pupils held a fiery glitter.

Fitz's heart beat furiously as he watched

her. She was trembling all over, and a faint buzzing sound came from her direction.

"Don't you ever mention the word 'mustard' again in my presence," she warned in a slow, measured voice. "Not *ever!*"

Turning back to the cupboard, she opened it just far enough to stick her hand inside. She pulled out a red plastic squeeze bottle of ketchup and thrust it toward the boys. Then she slammed the cupboard shut again.

In the instant that the cupboard door was ajar, Fitz saw the shelf filled with ketchup bottles.

But at the same time, he spotted dozens of yellow plastic squeeze bottles on another shelf.

His eyes flew open. *Mustard!*

Why hadn't he thought of it before? Was *that* what they had been looking for all along? Plain old *mustard*? He felt his excitement growing.

That had to be the answer! he thought. Mustard was poisonous to the larvae! Why else would she forbid them to use it in the cafeteria and keep it hidden away?

Fitz made a flying leap, barreling into the cook and ramming his head into her stomach. Miss Larva sucked in her breath in surprise and sat down hard on the floor.

Fitz turned, ran across the room, and scrambled up onto the counter. He opened the cupboard door and grabbed a bottle of mustard.

"Don't touch that, you little *brat!*" screamed Miss Larva. She had clambered to her feet and was lunging for him.

Skittering across the counter out of her reach, Fitz plunged the yellow plastic bottle into his mouth and tried to squeeze.

But suddenly he felt weak. He tried to squeeze the mustard into his throat, but he couldn't.

"You are in our power," came the crackling voices from inside him. They sounded louder than ever before.

Then Miss Larva's hideous laughter drowned out the voices in Fitz's head.

"You think you're so clever, don't you?" she demanded. "Well, you aren't. Drop that mustard bottle this instant if you care about your little friend. I know all about her allergies. Especially her allergy to hamburger meat!"

To Fitz's horror the cook had Lexi in her grasp and was shoving a gigantic hamburger into her mouth. Lexi was gagging. Her eyes were open wide with terror.

Fitz knew he had no choice. There was only one way to save Lexi. And Brian. And himself.

Grasping the mustard bottle in both hands, he squeezed with all the strength he had left. It was the hardest thing he'd ever done—harder than running the cross-country course and then doing five hundred sit-ups. He squeezed even harder, gasping at the effort. The voices were chattering away rapidly inside his head.

Then he heard a gushing sound and felt the thick spicy mustard rushing down his throat.

Chapter
27

"Here! Drink this!" yelled Fitz. He pitched the mustard container to Brian.

Grabbing a second bottle, he pointed it toward Miss Larva. She was struggling to hold on to Lexi and cram the hamburger into the frightened girl's mouth.

"Let her go!" he cried.

His hands were trembling. He was holding the mustard bottle straight toward her, but the cook was not going to give in easily.

Pitching the hamburger onto the floor, she ducked behind Lexi, using the girl for a shield.

"You'll never outsmart me," she croaked, backing slowly toward the door and dragging Lexi along with her.

Fitz tried to steady himself and aim the bottle so that the mustard would strike Miss Larva.

A humming filled the air. It sounded as if an angry swarm of hornets were swirling through the room. Fitz looked around. If there were hornets in there, they were invisible.

Suddenly he could feel a rumbling deep inside his body. He shuddered uncontrollably as a giant wave of nausea rolled over him. His stomach was pitching and heaving.

The lumps on his side and leg were changing, too. They throbbed wildly. It was as if they were fighting against a force that was trying to suck them into his body.

The nausea was getting worse by the second. Fitz had never felt so sick in his life. He had a puckery feeling in the back of his mouth. He tried to swallow it away, but a putrid mass of vomit was rising in his throat, gagging him. And the sound of hornets was getting louder.

He raced for the sink, but he didn't make it. Opening his mouth as wide as he could, he started to retch. It felt as if his guts were pouring out. His breath was nearly choked off as slimy, foul-smelling larvae gushed out of his mouth and onto the floor.

There were purple larvae, green larvae, and black-and-yellow-and-white-striped larvae—just like the ones Fitz had seen in Miss Larva's lasagna pan. Only they were five times the size, and they were squirming and flopping around on the floor like fish out of water.

Beside Fitz, Brian was throwing up larvae, too.

Fitz held his nose. A terrible stench filled the room as the flopping larvae gradually stopped moving and died one by one.

The two boys clung together on wobbly legs. They panted with exhaustion.

From across the room Lexi let out a scream and bolted toward them. "Look out!" she cried. "She's behind you!"

Fitz whirled around. His mouth dropped open. He gasped and stared at a huge insect that was sitting on a counter across the room. It was nearly three feet long. Fitz had never seen anything like it before. It had the head of a horsefly and the body of a cockroach!

"Oh, my gosh!" he cried, pointing to the giant insect. "Look at that thing!"

Brian was as pale as a ghost. "It's Miss

Buggy," he whispered.

Suddenly it was all perfectly clear to Fitz. "She's one of her own experiments! She turned herself into a mutant bug! And now she's—"

He stopped in midsentence. Out of the corner of his eye, he saw the huge insect moving slowly toward them. On its fly-type head were long cockroachlike antennae. The giant feelers waved crazily in the air as the bug advanced on the boys. The humming sound was coming from it, only now the sound was as loud as a jet airplane on takeoff.

"Watch it! She's coming after us!" Brian said in a trembling voice. "What'll we do? We can't get away! She's between us and the door!"

Miss Larva crept closer.

Fitz backed slowly away, bumping to a stop against the stove. He was staring into a mutant face that looked partly human and partly insect.

Suddenly the horrible bug reared up onto its back legs and waved its front legs menacingly at him. Its mouth opened wide, exposing razor-sharp pinchers.

"Look out!" screamed Brian. "She's going to jump us!"

Fitz looked around desperately for the plastic mustard bottle. He had dropped it when the terrible nausea overcame him. Where was it!

Then he saw it. It was on the other side of the kitchen. He would have to run past Miss Larva to get it. Taking a deep breath, he darted through the foul mass of dead larvae until he spotted it, floating in the slime. He almost lost his balance, slipping and sliding across the floor.

Miss Buggy turned towards Fitz, crouching to spring.

Fitz saw her jump into the air.

He stretched as far as he could, and his hand closed around the mustard bottle. But just as he started to pick it up, it slipped away.

He grabbed for it again. This time he was able to grasp it. Whirling toward Miss Larva, he pointed it and squeezed with all his strength.

A golden stream of mustard arced across the room like a missile and hit the giant insect squarely in the mouth.

A human scream pierced the air when the mustard found its mark. Splashes of yellow filled the room like golden rain.

Fitz stared openmouthed at the huge bug as it crashed to the floor.

"Look!" cried Brian. "Look at her kick."

The bug had landed on its back. Mustard dripped from the side of its mouth. Its legs flailed for a few seconds as what was left of Miss Larva squirmed and squirmed, struggling desperately to turn onto her stomach and get back on her feet.

They watched in silence as her legs waved more and more slowly and gradually grew still. The hundreds of tiny eyes in her pupils turned milky and dull.

"She's dead," whispered Fitz. The three of them collapsed against each other in relief.

"We did it," Brian said in a weak voice. "We found the one thing that was poison to larvae."

Fitz nodded. "Yeah, and you'll have to admit that Miss Buggy was pretty smart. She made her food so good that we all stopped eating at fast-food places. We hated our parents' cooking, too. There wasn't much of a chance that any of us would eat mustard and find out her secret—*that mustard was poison to larvae!*"

Suddenly he looked at Lexi. "Are you okay?" he asked her in alarm. "I mean, your allergies!"

"I'm fine," Lexi said proudly. "It was hard, but I didn't swallow anything."

"Wow," said Fitz in genuine admiration.

They set to work cleaning up the kitchen. They scooped up the dead larvae in the cook's lasagna pan and poured them down the garbage disposal. When the floor was mopped clean, they dragged Miss Larva outside and heaved her into the dumpster.

"I guess that's about all we can do here," said Fitz as they headed back to the kitchen. "Let's pass out the poison to everybody else."

"Can we start with Sarah?" asked Lexi. "She's my best friend, and I'd really like to save her first."

Fitz grinned slyly at Lexi. "Let me do it. I'm good at making her puke."

Laughing, they loaded themselves down with the yellow plastic mustard bottles Miss Larva had hidden away so carefully and hurried off to find their teachers and friends.

Fitz looked at Lexi as she trotted along

beside him. She had been awfully brave when Miss Larva had her in her clutches. He was actually starting to like her in spite of the fact that she was a girl.

In fact, he thought, and smiled to himself, *I'm starting to like her a lot!*

About the Author

Betsy Haynes has written over fifty books for children, including *The Great Mom Swap,* the bestselling The Fabulous Five series, and the Taffy Sinclair books. *Taffy Goes to Hollywood* received the Phantom's Choice Award for Best Juvenile Series Book of 1990.

When she isn't writing, Betsy loves to travel, and she and her husband, Jim, spend as much time as possible aboard their boat, *Nut & Honey*. Betsy and her husband live on Marco Island, Florida, and have two grown children, two dogs, and a black cat with extra toes.

TO SCARE YOU OUT OF THIS WORLD!

BONECHILLERS

Welcome to Alien Inn

When Matt and his family are
stranded during a blizzard they
take shelter in a roadside inn.
The innkeeper keeps staring
at Matt, and the other guests
ask him really weird questions.
What's more they cook up the
strangest breakfasts and their
language is out of this world.

Matt sets out to find the truth,
before it's too late, before his
whole family is...

EXTERMINATED.

TO SCARE THE STUFFING OUT OF YOU!

BONECHILLERS

GOBBLE-DE-SPOOK

Kyle and Annie love
Gobble-de-gook like he's
a real pet. They certainly
don't want to eat *him*
for Thanksgiving dinner.
But then they find another
turkey, and what a turkey
he turns out to be.

Frankenturkey is big.
Frankenturkey is bad.
Frankenturkey is mad...
If Kyle and Annie don't
watch out he'll eat *them*
for his Thanksgiving dinner!

STIRRING UP BIG TROUBLE!

BONECHILLERS

STRANGE BREW

Tori's bored stiff. She's totally
sick of school. Her little brother
is a pain and even her best friend
is driving her crazy. Tori would
do anything to have some fun.

Then she finds a mysterious
notebook. Each time she opens
it, a new spell appears. And
each time Tori tries a spell,
things happen – silly things,
gross things, hilarious things.
Now Tori is really having fun –
until the spells start to turn
dangerous. Until they start to
turn... GRUESOME.

BONECHILLERS

Teacher Creature

There's something odd about the new teacher who turns up at school after the big storm. He looks as if he's crawled straight out of the swamp. He has a wide mouth, slightly bulging eyes, a soft, pulsing neck, a row of warts across his forehead and he hisses when he speaks. And when Joey and Nate find him reading a children's cookery book, they freak – the book gives recipes for cooking CHILDREN!

THERE'S A TERRIBLE TURKEY AT LARGE!

BONECHILLERS

THE RETURN OF GOBBLE-DE-SPOOK

He's big,
he's bad and...
HE'S BACK.

Kyle and Annie
cannot believe
it. They thought
he was dead.
They thought
they were safe.
But Frankenturkey
has returned...
and this time he's
really out for vengeance!

THERE'S A NASTY COLD GOING ROUND...

BONECHILLERS

SLIME TIME

When Jeremy Wilson sneezes in
the school canteen, little does
he realize that his snot will
take over the whole town. The
droplets trickle across the floor
and stick together. Every time he
sneezes the green glob grows
bigger... and bigger... and bigger.
If Jeremy doesn't work out how
to stop it, the whole town will
drown in a tidal wave of slime!

Order Form

To order books direct from the publishers, just make a list of the titles you want and send it with your name and address to:

Dept 6,
HarperCollins Publishers Ltd,
Westerhill Road,
Bishopbriggs,
Glasgow G64 2QT

Please enclose a cheque or postal order to the value of the cover price, plus:

UK and BFPO: Add £1 for the first book, and 25p per copy for each additional book ordered.

Overseas and Eire: Add £2.95 service charge. Books will be sent by surface mail, but quotes for airmail despatch will be given on request.

A 24-hour telephone ordering service is available to Visa and Access card holders on 0141-772 2281.